Chapter One

The Book of Durand

I learnt about justice at an early age. The trouble was, in my family, justice walked hand in hand with punishment. Repentance wasn't enough, despite the fact that my father was a reverend and preached exactly that.

My parents believed that people were good because they feared the consequences of sin, be that a swift slap or the fires of hell. But for all their disapproval and spite, do you know what the main lesson that they taught me was? Not to do what was right but, if I was going to wrong someone, to make sure I was stronger than they were.

I know I disgust you. It's understandable; I did some terrible things to you when we were children. But at least hear me out before you pass judgement.

I guess you will try and paint me as some flimsy caricature of a bully. Such stereotypes are convenient, I suppose.

But I don't think anybody makes a conscious decision to act that way; not at first, anyway.

The first time I was accused of being a bully was an accident. Perhaps you don't believe that, but it really makes no odds to me. A child shouldn't have to defend their own parent. But that became my life. At first, the comments were spat as he passed me in the halls or hidden behind the facade of a cough. Then, as others began to notice the tension between us, the air became electrified. They were waiting for me to snap. And I did. I grabbed him by his school tie and smashed his face against my knee, once, twice, three times. The soggy crunch of his nose breaking brought me back to my senses. He was curled on the floor, his knees to his chest.

Maybe 'accident' is the wrong word, but it certainly wasn't planned. I just wanted to be left alone.

His name? That doesn't matter. He's of no consequence to my story except as a catalyst.

As I stepped towards the crowd surrounding us, they took a step back. If it had stayed like that, if I'd continued to repel them, perhaps I'd have taken a different path. But that wasn't how it happened. Instead, they were like iron filings caught in my magnetic field. They were drawn to me. That kind of power is addictive, especially for somebody who has never had any.

Do you know the strangest thing about it? Not one of the boys watching questioned my actions. Not one of them intervened. To my peers, I had proven myself the victor, and that meant I was right and he was wrong. That day I learnt that justice was defined by the powerful.

～

THE BOOK OF DURAND

Feisty Scholar Publications

www.feistyscholar.com

Escaping Sanctuary
The Book of Durand
First Edition 978-1-913619-43-5 (paperback)
978-1-913619-45-9 (eBook)
For news and details of upcoming publications from this author visit:
www.cherjones.co.uk

Seb

Seb stretched out his fingers and watched as the red light of the portal weaved between them. He looked back at his accusers, hoping for...well, he wasn't sure what. Forgiveness, perhaps, although he'd done nothing wrong. Not lately, anyway. Although he still flushed with shame when he thought about that day at the lake, when he'd held Jared under the water. Maybe this was his punishment. He'd crushed somebody else's happiness to protect his own, and now karma was catching up with him.

Empathy then. Some admission that, even if he had been wrongly labelled a criminal, the punishment did not fit the crime.

Durand smiled in return. 'Don't worry. I won't be sending you far. But you'd better hurry up and go through or you'll miss your train.'

Seb had no idea what he meant, but Millicent interrupted before he could ask. 'Please.' She clasped her hands below her chin. 'He's just a child. Can't we think of some more suitable—'

Durand growled at her. 'He knows the law and he still chose to break it. I'm doing my best here, Millicent. If we let this disorder continue then we'll end up like David.' He lowered his voice and straightened his clerical collar. 'Besides, he's no child. He's a grown man who must now face up to the consequences of his actions.'

'But—'

'Enough!' Flecks of Durand's spittle showered Millicent.

It made Seb want to hug her, to thank her for being one of the few to speak up for him. It was strange that he felt sorry for her when it was he who had been given what equated to a death sentence.

'All right,' Durand said. 'I'm not a monster.'

'So, you'll reconsider?' Millicent asked.

'No. The sentence stands. But I will make sure he has company for his journey.' Durand nodded towards the guardian, who opened the door to the Grand Chamber. Another guardian walked in, grasping Isaac by the top of his arm. 'It would be wrong to split up such a winning team.'

Seb was enveloped by a cold sweat. When he'd been arrested, he thought the worst thing that could happen to him was that he would be separated from Isaac. But the realisation that he wasn't going to be, that Isaac would share his fate, was far worse.

'You've got it all wrong,' Seb said. 'He's nothing to me.'

'Oh really?' Durand asked. 'Well, I guess you'd better tell him that.'

'You...' Seb forced the words over his tongue. 'You mean nothing to me.' He looked at Durand. 'Happy? You can let him go.'

'I'm not stupid. Now move yourself, or I'll think up somewhere far worse to send him. Only it will be without you.'

'It's okay,' Isaac said. 'At least we'll be together.'

'Stop with the theatrics, both of you. You brought unrest to our society, incited mutiny. For over four years, I've been trying to bring harmony back to our community, and you two try to undo that because you think the rules shouldn't apply to you. Don't act like it's you who's been wronged.' Durand took a weapon from a nearby guardian and pointed it at Seb.

'Now let's get this over and done with. This isn't the only trial we have today.'

Seb scanned the chamber, weighing up his chances if he were to resist. But Durand had his usual back up. His sons stood poised and ready to pounce. So Seb tried to see what waited through the portal, to decide if he had a better chance on that side.

It was only as he lurched forward onto rough stone, shredding the skin from his knees, that Seb realised he had been shoved through. He caught the briefest glimpse of Durand before the portal snapped shut.

'No. You said you were sending Isaac with me,' he shouted at the empty air.

'What are you doing, boy? Get up before you see the wrong end of a rifle.' A stocky man with a halo of grey hair held his hand out. 'Not that there is a right end with this lot.'

Seb took it and allowed himself to be heaved to his feet. 'Where am I?'

The man pointed to a sign that read *Warszawa*.

'I'm sorry, I don't understand.'

'You can't read, boy? It says Warsaw.'

No, Seb thought, *it doesn't*. Not in English, anyway. Despite being away from the Sanctuary, the translator part of his chip was still working.

'Everyone on board!' A soldier, his domed hat low over his eyes, blew a whistle. 'Now!'

'Get moving,' the man said, guiding Seb by the elbow into a stream of people who pushed at his back.

'This is a train platform?' Seb asked.

'Of course, it is,' the man said. 'We're being deported. Whether we like it or not.'

'I need to go back,' Seb said, determined to return to his entry point.

'Whatever it is you've left, you'll have to live without it.'

If only living without Isaac were that easy, Seb thought. But it was no use anyway; the tide of people continued to propel him forward. He struggled to pass a woman carrying a toddler. A man, probably the child's father, jabbed a suitcase into his ribs. 'The train's that way.'

From the corner of his eye, Seb noticed a flash of red. Perhaps they had sent Isaac through after all. 'Please, I just need to get past. My friend is back there.' The swell of people battered him from every angle as they surged away from the shouting soldiers.

Only the man who had helped him up from the platform remained, tethered by the grasp he held on the back of Seb's shirt. 'I'm sure your friend can look after himself.'

'But he—' Seb's temple exploded with pain and he sank below the current of bodies. Blood clouded his eyes, but still he could make out the soldier standing over him, rifle butt poised to hit him again.

'Please,' he heard the man say. 'My grandson was just looking for his mother. He's a good boy. Don't—'

The world went black before Seb could hear the end of the sentence.

The Book of Durand

I'm the wrong son. That isn't self-pity or paranoia; I've been told as much. I was supposed to be a twin, you see. I absorbed him. On the first scan, there were two heartbeats bleeping in unison. The next he was gone. I like to think I had no choice, that it was him or me.

But to my parents, this was proof I was bad from the start. A convenient narrative that absolved them of any responsibility. Every time I did something to disappoint them (and there were many occasions) they would give me that look, the one that said, *It should have been you. He would have been everything you aren't.*

I don't actually know it was a 'he', of course. A sister is just as likely. But I know in the same way that the prickling of your skin alerts you when you're being watched.

Did I miss him? Quite the opposite. I would have done anything to have erased the memory of him from history.

Don't judge me. You can't understand how it feels to be haunted by somebody who never was. It's worse than a ghost because, though someone who died might be viewed through rose-tinted glasses, at least they were an actual person, faults and all.

My brother was a shadow puppet who my parents could shape into whatever they wanted. Compared to that I would always be lacking. I hated him for it.

I'd never felt the weight of their disappointment as heavily as I did the day of the fight. In the years after that, it threatened to crush me. But until that day I had managed to keep to the background, an irritation to be fed and watered and then ignored.

My father sat at the kitchen table, his hands covering his face. 'What will the congregation say?'

Liquid sloshed over the side of my mother's glass as she thumped it down on the table. 'Is that all you care about? He broke a boy's nose!'

'One of us has to, Serena. Between the two of you, you are going to ruin this family.'

'You're so dramatic.' She took a sip of her drink, never breaking eye contact with him. 'Besides, why are you bringing me into this? It's not my fault he got into a fight.'

My father let out a snort of laughter.

She set her drink back on the table and leant back in the chair, crossing her arms over her chest. 'If you have something to say, don't hold back.'

It was a challenge; we all knew it. Inside, I begged my father not to answer, although I knew he wouldn't be able to resist. They were as bad as one another, their inflated pride not allowing them to back down.

He chose his words carefully. 'I just think that the boy needs more attention. He's alone a lot of the time. It can't be healthy.'

'And that's my fault, is it?'

'I never said—'

'You don't know what it's like to be the wife of a reverend, Victor; the sacrifices I need to make for you and your precious congregation.'

'Are you serious?' His indignation was so complete that it forced him out of his chair. 'You haven't even stepped foot in the church in over a month.'

'That's not fair! How can you expect me to walk in there, head held high, when she's always there!'

'This again! You're delusional.' He fell silent, studying her as he tried to calm his anger. 'Serena, this needs to stop. Maybe it's time you went back to the doctor.' His tone was soft, as though he were trying to calm a skittish cat.

She considered this for so long that I was foolish enough to hope that this time it wouldn't escalate.

Then she threw the wine glass at him. It exploded on the cupboard door just behind his head. Splinters of glass landed on the shoulders of his suit.

His face reddened but he kept his tone light. 'Martin, get upstairs.'

I could tell you how I held the pillow over my head to block out their yells. I could even tell you how a neighbour knocked on the door in the early hours, worried by the crashes and bangs, and how my father's forced laughter floated up to me as he tried to explain it all away. But I'm not sharing all of this for sympathy. You need to know what happened next because it changed everything.

After the neighbour left, the voices below calmed. I thought they'd gone to bed until I heard my mother's sobs.

I padded, barefoot, into the hallway and lingered at the top of the stairs.

'Don't leave. Please, Victor.' Mamma clung to the sleeve of his coat.

He twisted his arm away from her. 'This isn't healthy any more.' His eyes flickered up to the landing where I stood, so that when he said, 'I'm sorry,' it was unclear whether it was to her or me.

She stood staring at the front door long after it closed. When she turned, her brow creased in surprise to see me standing there.

When she finally spoke, her voice was wrung of any emotion. Still, her words stung more than any slap. 'This is your fault, you know.'

Jared

Jared led the group through the portal into the narrow street.

'I don't think I'll ever get used to that,' Aaron said.

Nearby, a woman dropped a basket of fruit, and apples rolled across the ground.

'I thought you said nobody would be around,' Nell said.

Jared shrugged. 'Apparently I was wrong.'

Beth crawled around the floor, picking up the apples and dropping them back into the basket. The woman's eyes flitted towards the end of the narrow street, as though she were thinking about running.

'Don't be afraid,' Beth said. 'It was just a trick. Jared, give me some money.'

'Why?'

'I want to buy some apples.' Beth took the leather purse from him. 'How much for all of them?'

The woman frowned and edged away.

'She can't understand you,' Jared said. 'I suppose I should think about fixing my chip. It would make things much easier.' He massaged the tiny bump where the sabotaged chip sat under his skin.

'What difference would that make?' Aaron asked. Didn't you say it was just a way of tracking you?'

'It wasn't *just* for that. When my grandfather invented it, the chip was supposed to bring the citizens together. It translates as well as tracks. He didn't want language to be a barrier between them.' The mention of Edmond bought a lump to Jared's throat. 'Anyway, I don't want to talk about all that.'

'Well, fear not, because I know something she will

understand.' Beth tipped some coins into her palm and held them out. 'For all of them,' she said, shifting the basket behind her.

The woman inched forward, before swiping the money from Beth's hand. She counted the coins and rewarded Beth with a broad smile.

'You're welcome,' Beth said as the woman rushed away.

Aaron nudged the basket with his foot. 'What are you going to do with all of these?'

'I don't know,' Beth said. 'Eat them. Give them away. That wasn't really the point.'

'You're weird sometimes,' Aaron said.

'I think you'll find all the best people are.' Beth held the basket in the crook of her arm, her auburn hair pooling at her elbow.

Aaron turned in a circle. 'Is this it?'

'Yes. Rome, 18th July, 64 AD,' Jared said.

'Oh.'

'You sound disappointed.'

Aaron stared up at the dank apartment blocks flanking them, each several stories tall. 'It's just—not what I expected.'

'It's going to change a lot after the fire,' Jared said. 'But still, I think there will be plenty for us to see. We have six whole days to look around before we have to worry about work.'

'Have you ever thought about letting one of us go first sometime?' Nell asked. 'We could do all of the boring prep work, and you could just, I don't know, take a holiday.'

'No,' Jared said. 'And why would you want to?'

'Other than to help you? Adventure! How exciting to

discover lost worlds.' Nell's face darkened. 'You can trust me, you know. I wouldn't let you down.'

'I know you wouldn't. It's just...It's not all adventure. Sometimes I learn things I'd rather not.'

'Well, we could help carry some of that burden,' Nell said.

'I'll think about it.'

'Jared, you are a control freak,' Beth said. 'It's one of the things I like best about you. There's no need to worry about the details when you're around.'

Jared headed towards the end of the street.

Beth fell into step beside him. 'So tell me, whose DNA brought us here?'

'Why does it matter?' Jared asked.

'Because one of us must have a distant relative from this era.'

'Which is exactly why I'm not going to tell you.'

'You're no fun.' Beth glanced over her shoulder. 'And what are your thoughts about that?'

Jared followed her line of sight and saw Aaron slip his hand into Nell's. 'I don't think much about it at all. It's none of my business.'

'You know something, Jared? You are terrible at gossip.'

'That's a good thing, right?'

'Sure.' Beth hooked her free arm into his. 'So, where are we going first?'

'The Circus Maximus.'

Beth wrinkled her nose. 'You mean with clowns and such?'

'It's a stadium. We're going to watch a chariot race.'

'That sounds exciting.' She studied his face. 'So why could you not look less enthusiastic?'

'You know why.'

Beth rolled her eyes. 'The Sanctuary. You need to stop with the guilt. You don't owe them anything. Your mother and the rest of them will work it out for themselves.'

'But I made a promise.'

'You made a promise to Aaron, too. He lost everything. Just give him this, and we'll worry about the Sanctuary after.'

'Okay,' Jared said. 'Can I have an apple?'

Beth laughed. 'I think I can probably spare one.'

The Book of Durand

'Fur coat and no panties'; that's what my mother had called her after they first met. It sounded even more ludicrous because we were standing in my father's church when she said it and it was directed towards a member of his congregation.

I crumpled into laughter until I saw the pinched look on her face. The bile in her words was tattooed into the creases around her mouth.

I didn't get what my mother meant at first. Sure, the woman's makeup was a little garish. The slick of colour across her lips looked smudged, like she'd decided it was too bright and had blotted it. That or somebody had kissed it off. And she wore so much jewellery that it clinked when she moved as though she were calling for the attention of the room. But above all, she just looked sort of small, sort of lost.

Although, that's beside the point. The enemy of my friend is my enemy; that's how it works, isn't it? And my mamma hated her. Such strong feelings are contagious.

That hatred began to permeate every area of our lives. For appearance's sake, my parents let the world think they were fine. At first, nobody outside of our family unit knew that my father slept at the church.

When they were forced to meet, they would hiss their words at one another. They sieved them through gritted teeth when they thought I wasn't listening. But I always was. Always am.

One phrase became the common denominator of these conversations: 'Your little whore'.

Soon the rest of the congregation began to talk. How

could they not? My mother practically spat on the ground every time the woman was near, which was often. Every Sunday she appeared, front and centre.

My father denied it. But that was to be expected, my mother would explain over her evening glass of wine, which often became a bottle.

After my father left, she sometimes poured me a glass too. I didn't like the taste, but I would take tiny sips, enjoying the camaraderie. My transition from disappointment to confidant occurred as soon as the alcohol hit her bloodstream. I basked in her attention. If I'm honest, I'd have been happy if my father had never come back.

But my mother had other ideas. 'That whore has met her match. She'll see. As if I'm going to sit back and let her steal my family. No, not steal. Buy. That's what she's doing, Martin. You see that, don't you? Donations to the church, like she's a good Christian woman. She's had her eye on your father from the start.'

Once I interrupted her monologue to reassure her that father had sworn nothing was going on, that she was just another parishioner.

Mamma slapped me. 'I've had enough of your lies, Victor!'

That's not a slip of my tongue. She called me by my father's name.

I think she was as shocked as I was by what she'd done. She'd never hit me before. 'I'm sorry,' she said, caressing my cheekbone.

I could already feel a red welt rising.

She pulled me into her arms. 'You see what she's doing to us?'

Seb

The darkness that had clouded Seb's mind retreated. Still, he lay with his cheek against the rough boards, puzzling over the blurred shapes around him. Gradually their fuzzy edges started to take on angles and sharp lines. An elbow here, a knee there. People lined every side of the...of what, Seb wasn't sure. A carriage for cargo or cattle perhaps. It certainly wasn't equipped for the number of passengers squeezed in, shoulder to shoulder.

'Oh, you're awake then.' The man from the platform crouched against the wall opposite. 'That's lucky, because I only just managed to carry you on. I won't be doing the same getting off the other end.'

Seb pushed himself up and regretted the move instantly. A terrible throb knotted his brain, and he pressed the pads of his thumbs against his eyelids, the pressure behind them making it feel like they were bulging. A memory surfaced through the pain. 'You told that soldier I was your grandson.'

'I did. Not that it did any good. I traded my late wife's pearls for you.'

'Thank you,' Seb said. 'I'll find a way to pay you back.'

'Sure, you will. I'm Uzziel.'

'Seb. Where is he? Your real grandson, I mean.'

'I...I don't know. A better place than this.' Uzziel twisted a gold ring around his little finger. 'What matters is what he did in this life. He fought in the uprising. What happened to him after that, I don't know.'

'I'm sorry.'

Uzziel stared hard at the floor. 'Don't be. He wa— he's a hero.'

Seb saw the same mute despair carved into the face of every one of the people cramped in around him. They released a simultaneous gasp as the carriage rumbled into motion.

'Where are they taking us?' asked a young girl.

Her mother pulled her closer. 'They are taking us to a labour camp. We will meet Tata on the other si—'

A sneer of laughter interrupted her. 'That's a lie and you know it. There's nothing good waiting for us at the other side.'

The girl looked up at her mother, wide-eyed.

It must have made the man feel guilty, because he added, 'I'm sorry, but it's cruel to give her hope.' Then he rested his temple against the planks of the cart, his head rocking with each bump of the tracks beneath.

The woman stroked flat the frizz settling over the girl's ringlets. 'Don't listen. We are going to live in a labour camp for a little while. That's all. The important thing is the three of us will be together.'

The man sniffed but made no further comment. It was enough to start a fluttering panic in Seb's chest. 'Uzziel,' he whispered, although the cramped cart left no space for privacy. 'What year is it?'

'Did that soldier do some damage to that brain of yours? It's 1943.'

Seb thought back to what Durand had said to him at his sentencing. 'Don't worry. I won't be sending you far.' True to his word, he hadn't. When he'd boarded the train, Seb had still been in Poland. But it was now clear that Durand had set him back to the middle of World War Two.

The Book of Durand

The problem with my parents was that they confused the chaos of their relationship for passion. It's how they would explain away the spiteful words and stinging slaps, convincing themselves that outsiders couldn't possibly understand the depth of the feelings they had for one another. This resulted in us moving. A lot. My father wouldn't tolerate the perceived judgement of our neighbours. But the truth was, on the other side of the looking glass, their version of love looked a lot like torture.

In our kitchen there hung a framed map of Europe. It moved with us from place to place. After a few drinks, my mother liked to trace her finger over the city of Eupen, where she was born and raised.

'Do you miss it?' I asked her one day.

'All the time. But I never really felt like I belonged there.'

She'd told me only a little about its history. After the First World War, Eupen had become part of Belgium, but German remained their first language. In the little town of Menton where we lived, a Belgian who spoke German but chose to live in France must have seemed exotic. But I always suspected it made her feel even more lost.

'Did I ever tell you how your father and I met?'

'No.' I always lied no matter how often she asked this, because I knew she wanted to tell me, and I wanted to hear it.

'Well,' she would say, topping up her wine, 'the odds of us meeting were pretty low. I lived in Belgium, about as far from the border with France as you could get.'

'So, how did you meet?'

'Because fate wanted us to. My family were holidaying on the Riviera and he was a waiter at our hotel. One day, he asked me if he could take me to his favourite place. Do you know where that was?' Her eyes sparkled when she asked this. I hated to watch them glaze over, so I always claimed I didn't.

'The Maria Serena Gardens. After he had shown me every corner, he took me by the hands and said to me, 'The most beautiful place in all of France shares its name with the most beautiful girl in the world'.'

'Who was Serena Maria?' I'd ask, playing along.

'She was a saint. And when your father and I welcomed you, he named you for a saint, too. All three of us, a family of saints.'

Even then I thought that was a tough title to live up to. Little did I know how far I would fall short.

Anyway, that time, when it felt like it was the three of us versus the rest of the world, was long gone. We were fractured way before we were forced to leave our latest home, the little French village of Menton.

Since my father no longer lived with us, it was my job to keep my mother safe. He had told me so. During his hurried phone calls, he explained that, until he was home, I was the man of the house. He dangled the possibility of returning like a carrot.

The problem was that I don't think our definitions of 'safe' were quite the same. What he really meant was quiet. It was my job to keep my mother calm and hidden so she wouldn't embarrass him.

But when she said she wanted to go to church that Sunday, who was I to stop her? She put on her best trouser suit and I sat on the bed watching as she applied mascara with a shaking hand.

'You're sure you want to do this?' I asked.

She looked back at me in the reflection of the mirror. 'You're a good boy to worry about me, Martin. Now, go and get changed or we'll be late.'

When I met her in the kitchen, she kissed me on the forehead. I could smell it on her breath, like a strange mix of pears and cleaning fluid. My eyes flickered to the glass on the table.

'Just a little liquid courage,' she said as she picked it up and drained it.

As we made our way through the crowd outside the church, the group of parishioners fell silent. I could feel their eyes tracking us as we headed towards the door.

Although I guided her forward, holding her firmly at the elbow, she kept stopping to pick out familiar faces to greet, flashing them a smile that was a little too bright. 'Oh, Paula, I love that dress. George, how is your mamma? Recovered from her illness, I hope?'

Inside the church, we took a seat at the end of a pew. Mamma sat with her hands folded in her lap as we waited for my father to take his place behind the lectern.

When he entered from his chamber at the back of the church, his eyes widened to see us sitting there.

My mother gave him a little wave.

He didn't return it. Instead, he cleared his throat and pulled his notes from his robe. 'This world can be a lonely place,' he began, 'if we let it be. When we set ourselves up as competition to our fellow man, we turn away from the good they could bring to our lives. 'Dog eat dog', that's the saying that gets bandied about. Man has learnt to love and provide for oneself above all others.'

My mother began to wring her hands. 'This isn't right,' she said to nobody in particular.

Father faltered, but only for a beat. 'You're right,' he said, nodding towards her. 'It isn't. The bible teaches us that love for our brethren is the path to salvation. It is the only way to fulfil the commandments bestowed by the Lord. Matthew 25:40 tells us, 'In as much as ye have done it unto one of the least of these my brethren, ye have—"

'No.' Mamma tried to get to her feet, but I grabbed her hand and yanked her back onto the pew. 'I don't want to hear this one. Tell us about the whore.'

'Jesus.' If the congregation heard my father's blasphemy, they didn't react.

They were too mesmerised by my mother as she scrambled past me and out of the pew.

'Mamma, please sit down,' I begged.

She wasn't listening, though. 'Tell us about the Whore of Babylon.'

'Serena, sit down,' my father hissed.

She cocked her head to one side. 'What's the matter, Victor, can't remember? Don't worry, I know it well.'

I had been too distracted to notice the commotion in the front pew. But now I watched as my mother's nemesis, head ducked, tried to sidle from the row.

My mother took up prime position in front of her, grasping the font for support. 'And the woman was arrayed in purple and scarlet colour, and decked with gold and precious stones and pearls, having a golden cup in her hand full of the abominations and filthiness of her fornication.'

The woman sat back down and looked up into my mother's face.

I couldn't avoid the whispers that came later. They called my mother psychotic, deranged.

But, at that moment, that wasn't how I saw her. With every eye in the room fixed on her, with her face flushed with exhilaration, she looked powerful.

'And upon her forehead was a name written: Mystery, Babylon the Great, the Mother of Prostitutes and Abominations of the Earth.' With that, she scooped water from the font with her cupped hands and covered her enemy and the women flanking her.

The outraged cries of the parishioners bounced around the church. Two men stepped forward and each took one of my mother's arms.

'Take her back to my chamber, please,' my father told them. Then he jabbed a finger in my direction. 'You go with her.'

As I followed, I looked back at my father.

'I'm so very sorry,' he said, offering the woman his handkerchief.

'It's fine.' She snatched it from his hand and wiped streaks of running mascara from her cheeks.

'Please don't take offence.' He stepped back so he could address the whole of his congregation. 'Don't pay her any mind; she's really not well.'

~

Jared

As they entered the Circus Maximus, the crowd was already roaring. Jared waited for the others to edge into the tiered seating before he took his place at the end of the row.

'Wow,' Aaron said, looking up at the towering columns. 'This place is amazing.'

'It's definitely an improvement on the market area,' Jared said.

A driver had already taken to the track. He stood astride a small wooden chariot, grasping the crossbar with one hand. With the other, he waved his whip high in the air, occasionally snapping it towards the crowd and making them gasp and cheer. He was joined by three more charioteers, and together they looped around the track, ramping up the applause before the race began.

'I don't think they'd get much protection if they fell out of one of them,' Jared said.

'I'm more worried about the horses,' Nell said. 'You don't think they're really going to whip them, do you?'

'No,' Beth said, pursing her lips. 'They're probably going to tickle them with it.'

Nell narrowed her eyes, but a gong sounded before she could reply.

'This is it,' Aaron said, shifting to get a better look.

The charioteers made their way to the starting gate. When the gong was struck again, they were off.

Nell was on her feet in seconds. 'Come on! Faster!'

Jared met Beth's eye and they both stifled a laugh. 'Yes,' said Beth, 'we must worry about the poor horses.'

Jared tried to focus, but before the charioteers had even

made their first lap, the onslaught on his senses began to overwhelm him. The screaming people, the smell of manure and sweaty bodies, the thundering of hooves...the bolts of crackling lightning.

Jared jumped up.

'Oh, not you too,' Beth said.

'I saw something. Down on the other side of the stadium. A flash of red electricity.'

'It was probably a firework or something.'

'Not unless I missed the mark on our location by about five hundred years or so,' Jared said.

'I don't know what to say.' Beth edged closer so she could be heard over the cheers. 'Shall we go and look?'

Jared scrutinised the area where he'd seen the flash. The people there continued to clap and cheer. 'It's okay,' Jared said. 'Maybe it was my imagination.'

He sat down and waited for the show to end.

The Book of Durand

It's strange how a person can be invisible yet dominate everything around them. That's what it was like after that day in the church; my mother disappeared into the refuge of her bedroom and didn't come out. Occasionally I would hear her shuffling about, but more often the house was consumed by a heavy silence.

I'd hang around her door, clutching her dinner tray, agonising over whether to knock. Or bring her endless cups of tea as an excuse to check on her. I don't know why I bothered; she barely noticed I was there.

Then one morning, when I came down for breakfast, I found her already in the kitchen.

'There you are,' she said. 'I was about to come and wake you.'

I glanced at the clock. It was 6:15 am and a Saturday. 'Are we going somewhere?'

She continued to spread butter over slices of bread. 'We're going on a picnic.'

I tugged up the roller blind. 'But it's raining.'

She stopped with the knife poised mid-stroke. The light in her eyes flickered and dimmed.

'That doesn't matter,' I said, trying to undo the damage I'd caused. 'We can take our umbrellas. Or we could have a picnic right here.'

'Here?' Her voice was little more than a whisper. She looked at the piles of bread in front of her, far too much for the two of us to eat.

Then her face broke into a grin. 'That's a great idea.

We'll move the furniture out of the way and eat on the rug in the sitting room.' She headed for the fridge.

Although I couldn't see her face, I could picture her disappointment. The fridge was empty; the loaf of bread was the last of the food in the house.

'Don't worry; I'll go to the shop.' I was already heading to the hallway to collect my coat. 'Twenty minutes and we can have our picnic.'

I didn't wait for her to respond. The tension rising from her was making the air crackle, and I needed to get out.

When I got back, a pot of jam wedged into my coat pocket, she had gone. Her bedroom door was closed.

I must admit, I was relieved. At least, at first. But when she didn't emerge again, leaving me alone to spend the day nibbling on bread and jam, I began to worry.

I'll spare you the details. You don't want to hear about the smell of vomit, or the pills scattered on the bedsheet next to her. Or how, when I moved her, a trail of froth escaped her mouth.

All you need to know is that while my mother was taking an overdose, I sat in the room below, eating jam sandwiches.

When I put it like that, maybe I deserve what's coming to me.

Seb

The incessant rattle of wheels over the track drew out time within the cart like the laboured ticking of a clock. Sweat pasted the cotton of Seb's shirt to his skin. His thirst was so consuming that each taste bud stood up tall, neglected and begging. A pounding thud had developed behind his eyes, and Seb imagined his brain, shrivelled like a raisin, bouncing off the inside of his skull. Even as the dim glow from between the planks dulled and the sun set, the heat remained unbearable.

Sleep would be an escape, but whenever he tried to rest, willing dreams of Isaac and his family, the train would go over a bump, jolting his neck and shaking him awake again. He would have liked to ask Uzziel to lean on his shoulder, suggested that they take it in shifts. But his new friend sat with his eyes closed, arms crossed over his chest, his body bouncing in unison with the rhythm of the train car. Jealousy prickled Seb's nerves.

A group of men jostled for a turn at the air aperture in the far corner of the cart. The competition for this prized spot was fierce, the victor snatching a few deep breaths, his face pressed against the mesh, before he was barged out of the way. Seb had no intention of competing for the spot, no matter how good the breeze would feel on his face.

Still, he longed to look outside, to gain some idea of where they were or where they were going. Seb peeled his tongue from the top of his mouth. 'Can you see anything? Is there any clue where they are taking us?' His saliva was thick, glue-like, and his words stuck to his tongue. If they heard him, nobody answered.

Seb watched as the young girl mapped a rivulet of sweat down her dozing mother's arm, before lapping it up. 'Mama,' she said, tugging at the woman's dress.

'Just close your eyes and rest.'

'Mama, please.'

The woman ducked down so the girl could whisper something in her ear. 'Now? Okay,' she said, helping the child to her feet.

The girl swayed as her mother guided her to the corner of the cart, treading with careful steps between unmoving passengers. Seb averted his eyes, embarrassed, as the girl's underwear was tugged down. She let out a sob and her mother glared around the cart, daring anyone to comment or object. Seb swallowed against his gag reflex as the stink filled the air. Then they returned to their places, the girls cheeks glowing, eyes downcast.

'Are we slowing down?' Uzziel asked.

The other passengers chattered with a mixture of expectation and nerves. Seb forced himself to concentrate. Yes, he could feel it. The crunching of the gravel, the humming of the wheels, had all dulled to a slow purr. They were stopping.

'Mama, what's happening?' the girl asked. Her mother quietened her with a gentle 'shh', leaving them all sitting in darkness, listening.

'We *are* stopping,' Uzziel said. 'We must be here.'

'No,' the man said as he peered through the air aperture. 'There's no station outside.' He turned to his group. 'But if we want to try and escape, now might be the time to do it.'

'Escape to where?' Uzziel asked. 'Out there, to the guards with the guns? And even if you do manage to get past them, then what? Should we make our way back to Warsaw just to be deported again?'

The door to the carts opened and two men peered in. The first thing Seb noticed was their khaki green uniforms. The second was the disgust that twisted their features as the smell hit them.

'Up, all of you up,' one of them ordered. 'Put your valuables in the bag.'

The passengers just looked at one another.

'Now!'

They sifted through their belongings, retrieving what few treasures they had remaining. Seb watched the woman unfasten her necklace before dropping it into the sack. She smiled at her daughter. 'Don't worry; when we find Tata, he'll buy me another.'

The soldier stopped in front of Seb.

'I don't have anything to give you.'

He jangled the bag, perhaps thinking Seb's inaction was down to a lack of understanding.

Seb turned out his empty pockets. In return the man delivered a punch to his stomach, squeezing the air from his body. When he'd regained enough breath to allow him to focus, he saw they'd moved onto Uzziel.

'You,' the second man said. 'Take off that ring.'

'It belonged to my wife,' he said. When they stared back stone faced, Uzziel tugged at the gold band encircling his little finger. It didn't budge. 'Just one moment and it's yours.'

But the guard was in no mood to wait and fished something from his pocket. Although Uzziel mouthed the word 'no' over and over, no sound escaped his lips. The only mercy was the speed in which the act was done. Still, the night air was saturated with Uzziel's screams as he fell to his knees, clutching his severed finger.

Laughing, the guards left the car, pulling the door shut behind them. A confused mixture of relieved breath and shocked cries bounced around the wooden planks.

Seb crouched at Uzziel's side but was flapped away. 'Just leave me be.'

The man at the air aperture called for quiet. 'All right, I think they're gone now.' He then dropped to his knees, his body jerking.

Screams filled the carriage, but none loud enough to cover the gunfire. Light flooded through the bullet holes, allowing soft beams of moonlight to illuminate the cowering passengers.

As Seb pulled his knees to his chest, one thought played through his mind. The last thing he had said to Isaac was that he meant nothing to him.

Jared

Jared awoke to screaming. At first, he thought it was from the tavern below. However, he soon realised it was coming from the street.

He had just got up from the bed when somebody knocked at the door of his bedroom.

'Get up. The fire's started already,' Beth called.

Jared padded to the window and leant out. Although he couldn't see anything, there was no denying that the scent of smoke hung in the air.

Beth hammered harder. 'Will you hurry up?'

When he opened the door, she stood with her hand on her hip.

'Have you even been to sleep yet?' Jared asked. Everything from the rose madder tunic to the plait in her hair was the same as when he'd left her.

'Well, hello to you, too. Actually, I joined the party downstairs. My new friends have informed me that the city is on fire.'

'That isn't right,' Jared said.

'The blaze spreading through the city would suggest otherwise. Let's discuss it on the way. We've got work to do.'

'No, Beth, this isn't right. It's not supposed to start until the 25th.'

Beth huffed. 'Have you thought that maybe you got it wrong? You are human, you know.'

'Obviously. And no, I hadn't thought that because I know I'm correct.' He grabbed one of his notebooks and flicked through the pages. 'See. July 25th.' He held the page up in front of her face.

Beth barely glanced at it. 'And the street we arrived in was supposed to be empty. Don't worry about it. Everyone makes mistakes.'

'That's different. We know the path of the odd person can change. But this? No.'

'Well, while you're telling yourself the city isn't on fire, I'm going to start cataloguing what's happened. If we expect anybody to pay to visit this era, we'd better have something to show them. Now get ready.' Beth walked to the end of the corridor and banged on the door there. 'Aaron, time to move.'

Jared pulled on his tunic and followed her out. 'That's Nell's ro— Oh.'

Aaron opened the door. 'Do you have to be so loud?'

Nell appeared in the doorway behind him. 'I was just showing him some memories using the visualiser.' She blushed. 'What's wrong?'

'It looks like our boy genius got his days mixed up.' Beth turned on her heel. 'The fire's started. Let's go.'

Neither Aaron nor Nell moved.

'Do I have to?' Aaron asked.

'You won't see a lot from here,' Jared said.

'I just...' Aaron's voice cracked. 'I don't think I want to.'

Jared felt a pang of guilt. To Aaron, it had been only weeks since his home was obliterated.

'I'm sorry,' Jared said. 'I wasn't thinking.'

'It's all right. I mean, I want to be helpful and play a part...Just not yet.'

Beth patted him on the shoulder. 'Too soon.'

'Yeah. I think I'll spare myself the fiery inferno for now.'

'I'll stay with you,' Nell said. 'If that's okay with you two.'

'The fire doesn't reach this area of the city for days,' Jared said. 'You'll be safe here.'

Beth was already making her way towards the stairs. 'I guess it's just you and me, Jared.'

35

The Book of Durand

After they transferred my mother to the psychiatric ward, I felt myself fading. It was as if the burning bleach smell of the hospital had seeped into my pores and was erasing me from the inside out.

My mother looked right through me. That was a given. She did it to everybody. Even when you stood in front of her, she'd look straight ahead with flat eyes as though she were still focused on the wall behind you.

My father would navigate around me as he stalked in and out of her hospital room, hissing into his phone. Some might have put his mood down to the reaction of a worried husband. I knew better; the whole situation was an inconvenience to him.

The visiting parishioners were no better. They'd talk to my father in hushed tones so that I couldn't hear. Eventually, they talked over my head like I wasn't there at all. I'd linger around the waiting room until somebody remembered me. Then the visitors would salve their guilt by treating me to a vending machine meal of warm coke and candy bars.

I couldn't let that continue, could I? To do so, to let myself disappear from the world, would have been suicide, and I'm the type to go down fighting.

So, fight I did. Nobody was safe. I ridiculed my teachers, unravelling their carefully planned lessons with glee.

I made it clear that anybody who wasn't my friend was my enemy. To be honest, sometimes even friendship didn't shelter them from my rage. My reputation spread like a virus.

Don't shake your head at me. It was a matter of survival. You don't know what you would have done in my position.

Why am I telling you all this? Because it's relevant. If it weren't, I'd be pretty stupid to tell you, of all people, my sins.

My father moved back into the house while my mother was in the hospital. One morning, while we were getting ready for our daily visit, there was a knock at the door.

I hid at the top of the stairs as my father let in my school principal.

'Victor, I'm sorry to bother you at a time like this, but I thought it best to talk to you in person.'

'Not at all,' my father said, directing him towards the kitchen.

I crept to the foot of the stairs so I could hear them better.

'Take a seat. Sorry about the mess; we've been busy...' My father's voice trailed off.

'Please, don't even mention it.' Principal Barnes filled the silence between them with a deep sigh. 'I'm afraid I need to talk to you about Martin's behaviour.'

My father didn't respond, so Barnes continued. 'If the complaints were coming from just one source, I'd think it was boys being boys. But multiple students have accused him of bullying. And the teachers – some of them are refusing to have him in their classes. Even the ones he used to excel in.'

'Excel?' My father sounded unconvinced.

Barnes faltered, as though confused as to why that was the part of the conversation my father had focused on. 'Yes, Martin is very gifted at languages. English and German—'

'German?' My father scoffed. 'He's excelling at a language he's heard his mother speak since he was born. Well, good for him.'

I think he was actually jealous of me at that point, which was stupid as my mother had begged him to learn German. She told him how homesick she was, that she longed to speak her mother tongue amongst her family if nowhere else. Our love for languages was one of the few meaningful things that my mother and I shared. She wanted my father to be part of that, too. He'd refused, of course. Not because she and I could both speak French. It was arrogance. Why should he inconvenience himself?

As always, I'd tried to fill the void. Sometimes I felt I only existed to make her happy. For a while, that was enough. But our conversations over the dinner table had only angered him. He'd called us rude and demanded we speak French, or we shouldn't speak at all.

My father let out a deep breath. 'Look, Mr Barnes, I'm sorry he's causing trouble, but to be honest I'm not surprised. It's been coming for a long time. I mean, just look at the effect he's had on his poor mamma. She couldn't cope with his behaviour any more.'

'Perhaps he needs to feel heard?' Barnes said. 'I know this is a difficult time for you, but if he sees that there are better ways to get attention than his fists—'

Father cut his sentence short. 'And you have children, do you? You know what it's like to raise a child, look after a sick wife and guide a congregation all at once?'

'Forgive me; I've misspoken.'

I could relay the rest of the conversation, the promises of

punishment and change. But what I want you to understand is the realisation I reached at that moment; he'd been laying the guilt over my mother's illness at my feet. That was the first time, but of course not the last, that I was painted as a monster. And it was by my own father.

Chapter Two

The Book of Durand

'**D**id I ever tell you about the time that I nearly lost you?' Mamma hadn't said anything for so long that I jumped and slopped coke down my t-shirt.

'No...no, you didn't.' I sat down next to her, trying to sound casual so as not to scare her back into silence. 'Tell me.'

I was expecting something cliché: she'd lost sight of me in the supermarket, or I'd run off at a fairground. However, what she said was anything but ordinary.

'Some mothers wouldn't have noticed,' she said. 'They'd never have questioned whether the baby in the crib was their own. But where I'm from, we know about these things. I looked down into the face of my beautiful newborn, and I just knew; it was a changeling.'

'A...A what?'

'Your father didn't believe me at first. He thought I was

mad. But I could see it. Your face, your cry, you were not my baby.'

Her use of 'you' began to make me nervous, so I played along. 'How did you persuade him? And how did you get me back?'

'Well, eventually, he saw sense. One day, he stalked in and scooped the baby from the crib.'

'Where did he take it?'

'The river. There was a little bridge, and he dropped it – plop – into the water.'

My throat was dry. 'And then?'

'Oh Martin, the most wonderful thing happened. The following day, when we woke, there you were, in your crib, cooing like nothing had happened. A miracle.'

I patted her hand. 'It all worked out then.'

'Yes...I think so.' Her face darkened. 'Although I sometimes wonder.'

'About what?'

'I never saw what he did with the changeling. That means I have only Victor's word for it that he did anything but bring me back the same imposter baby.'

'That's okay. You can trust Father.'

'I hope so. But I'm not always sure.' She gripped my fingers so tight that my knuckles ground into one another. 'Be honest, Martin; you are my boy, aren't you?'

Jared

A gust of hot air hit them as soon as they stepped out of the tavern, wafting smoke into Jared's stinging eyes.

Beth led them through the maze of narrow streets. 'They told me it started over by the Circus.'

'They were mistaken. This whole area is left untouched by the fire.'

Jared froze. Flames licked from the workshops surrounding the Circus Maximus. Before his eyes, it consumed the length of the entire row of buildings, driven by a fierce wind. The curved end of the arena, in which only hours before they'd watched the chariot race, was now blackened.

'You were right,' Jared said.

'Don't get used to it.' Beth wrapped her arms around herself. 'This reminds me of when we first met.' She shook her head as if loosening the memory. 'I'm going to look from a different angle. We'll need it for the visualiser.'

Jared watched as the Roman citizens did their best to beat the fire back. Amongst the growing panic, one figure stood still, looking into the open doorway of a building.

He turned and smiled at Jared, a lit torch clasped in his hand.

'Who...who is that?' Jared asked himself, a nagging famil-iarity teasing him.

The man threw the torch into the building. It was his smile that gave him away. Jared had seen it before. He'd been a member of the Guardian Elite.

'Wait,' Jared called. 'What are you doing here?'

The guardian gave him a wave and disappeared into a nearby alley.

Jared ran after him, skidding to a halt a few metres away.

'Hello, Jared. Do you remember me?'

Jared did, but he wouldn't give him the satisfaction of an answer.

'I think you do.' The guardian held up an orb and ran a finger around the top. The air began to hiss and spark with flecks of red.

'Where did you get that?' Jared asked.

He rolled his eyes. 'A community full of geniuses, and you didn't think one of them would be able to follow your grandfather's work? Besides, it's not like he could take it all with him.'

Jared flinched at the mention of Edmond. 'Just tell me why you're here.'

'Not one for small talk, are you?' he said. 'I have to say, meeting you again hasn't been as satisfying as I'd hoped. You're pretty infamous in the Sanctuary nowadays.'

'Get on with it.'

'Fine. I have a message for you from Reverend Durand, and you'd better listen carefully. You're meddling with forces that should belong to God alone. Time travel is illegal. Should you choose to ignore that fact, there will be consequences.'

'What makes you think you have any say over what we do? The committee have no juristiction anywhere but the Sanctuary.'

'That's where you're wrong,' he said. 'We can follow the trail of energy your orb leaves. If you don't stop this sick little freak show you have going on, then we'll have to make you.'

'I'd be interested to see you try.'

'Interested, huh? Well, you're in luck. You're about to find out just what we're willing to do to stop your sacrilege.'

Unease prickled the hair on the back of Jared's neck.

The portal opened, but the guardian hesitated. 'I only saw you and the redhead. Weren't there four of you?' A smirk turned up the side of his mouth.

A chill ran through Jared. 'What...If you've hurt them...'

'You'd better run, Jared,' he said, stepping through the portal. 'Time isn't on your side.'

The Book of Durand

Growing up within the church, I met examples of kind, Godly men who worked hard for their congregations. My father was not one of them. Although he was a vicar, Father was neither a religious man nor a good one. He wore his faith like a cloak he could shrug on and off as it pleased him. He loved to quote the bible, but only the parts that fitted his own narrative, and would dismiss anything that didn't. That made him impossible to argue with. Ruthless. The first time I saw his true colours was not long after the world began to decline.

Perhaps if the Levelling had happened in the way it did in films, with blazing infernos and tidal waves, then things might have been different. But it didn't. Not for anywhere but Brook Green Valley, anyway. The rest of us were the metaphorical frog in a pan, and the world around us was being brought to a slow boil.

For the longest time we were able to ignore how the thermometer climbed and scorched the earth, writing off the failed crops as somebody else's issue. At the same time, the news reported coastal towns submerged in floodwater. God, it seems, is not without a sense of irony. It was only when the supermarket shelves were no longer stocked that we thought this might be an 'us' rather than a 'them' problem.

A small consolation was that attendance at my father's church had never been better. Religion became the anaesthetic of choice for the desperate, and his flock multiplied.

At first, he revelled in the attention. He preached salvation, never faltering as he promised that the righteous would be saved.

When the food deliveries stopped, his words began to lose their conviction. The hungry and frightened turned up at his church with open hands and left with nothing but his pleas to have faith ringing in their ears. Eventually, he stopped opening the church altogether. He moved my mother home and told his parishioners that he intended to nurse her back to health.

She flourished under his attention. It appeared that the three of us taking refuge from the world in our little house was just the tonic she needed.

When he was late home one evening, she sent me to look for him. She claimed to be worried, but I was under no illusions; I was her spy.

I found him around the back of the church, helping unload canned goods from a van.

'You're a good man, Michael. My parishioners will be grateful for this.'

'It's not much, but it's all I have to offer. Are you sure you don't need my help getting it into the church?'

My father shook his head. 'You've done enough.' He watched as the van disappeared down the road. Then he unlocked his car.

I must have made a noise, because he turned to look at me. He hesitated before saying, 'Help me with this.'

We loaded the crates into the boot of his car without uttering a word. There was no need. To him it was a simple equation. We could feed the parish for a day or our family for months. It was a matter of survival.

As I said, my father was neither a religious man nor a good man, no matter what he claimed. Maybe now I'm out of his shadow, I will be able to find my own faith again. It would be nice to have something to hold onto.

1. Guardhouse
2. Head Quarters and Commandant's Living Quarters
3. Ukrainian Guards' Living Quarters
4. Building for Sorting Gold and Valuables
5. SS Services
6. Barracks for the Domestic Staff
7. SS Living Quarters and Armoury
8. Fabric Storehouse
9. Barracks for Male Prisoners
10. Latrine
11. Refilling Station
12. Garage
13. Undressing Barracks
14. Storehouse
15. Latrine
16. Lazarett
17. Burial Pits
18. Gas Chambers
19. Cremation Grids
20. Prisoner barracks

Buildings
Burial Pits
Railroads
Wells
Gates
Earth Walls
Roads
Barbed Wire
Watchtowers
Wooded Area
Tank Barriers

Seb

It is a bizarre feeling to wake and find you are being watched. It is horrifying to realise that the eyes watching you are unblinking and dead. Despite that, Seb could not help but wonder at the softness of their blue. Even in death, Uzziel radiated kindness. Seb lay there for a while in Uzziel's gaze, insulated by exhaustion or shock from the horrors around him. But after a while Uzziel's stare became accusing. Seb should have done something to prevent his death, he seemed to say, or at least been awake to witness it.

Voices from outside penetrated the cocoon in which Seb had wrapped what was left of his sanity. Someone was walking along the length of the train, opening the doors and bellowing at the survivors within. When the door to his car opened, Seb blinked against the intense light.

'Everybody out!'

It wasn't the hoarse bark of the soldier that got Seb moving. It was the thought that Isaac might be waiting on the platform outside. He dragged himself to his feet, his bones aching from the night spent on the wooden floor of the cart. Looking round, the bodies of his fellow passengers remained unmoving. Seb couldn't bring himself to look closer.

As he stepped down from the car, he stared round, bewildered, at the hundreds of people crammed onto the small platform. Some clung to one another. Others tried to force themselves through the crowd, shouting the names of lost relatives.

'Get moving!' With brutal efficiency, the guards began to rain down blows upon their prisoners, barbaric shepherds moving their flock on. At every side people pushed and shoved, stumbling forward, trying to avoid the punishing thump of a truncheon.

Seb caught sight of the girl from his car and was relieved to see that both she and her mother had survived. 'Why are they shouting?' the little girl asked, jogging to keep up.

Before he could hear the mother's response, somebody tugged him from the torrent of passengers and propelled him back towards the train. For a moment, Seb let himself hope it could be Isaac, but that hope was quickly extinguished when he heard a gruff whisper from behind.

'Don't turn around. Just keep walking.'

With no other option, Seb did as he was told. When they reached the car that he had just stepped from, Seb was able to turn.

Shadows carved the man's face, even in the bright morning light. Beneath the sunken pads of his cheeks, the angles of his bones were clear. He wore a white armband with the word *Lagerältester* upon it.

Seeing Seb staring at it, he said, 'I'm the camp elder,' as though that somehow explained everything.

'What do you want from me?' Seb asked.

'Put this on,' the man ordered, ignoring his question and thrusting a piece of blue material at him. Seb plucked at it with fumbling fingers for so long that the man snatched it back and tied it himself, pulling it so tight that it pinched the skin of Seb's arm. Looking around, Seb saw the same material encircling the biceps of the men boarding the train.

'Now just follow my lead,' he said, signalling at the car.

Seb turned to his former prison, his dread rising at the

thought of entering it again. But before he could step up from the platform, shouts rose from the opposite end.

'They are going to kill us! Can't you see what's happening?' A woman, her frame so tiny it looked as though a guard could dispatch her with a single swat, pleaded with the people around her. 'Fight back or you're going to die!'

Panic spread through the crowd and they began to push back towards the cars.

'We are not cattle for them to slaughter!' she continued. 'Fight!'

A nearby guard, an angry red climbing from underneath his shirt collar and across his face, brought his truncheon down hard on her head. She disappeared into the crowd, a drowning woman in a sea of bodies.

Then she resurfaced. Dazed, she held her torn scalp together with her hands. Before she could continue with her plea, the guard picked her up around the waist and carried her towards a small building just inside the compound.

'She is being taken for medical attention,' another guard assured the crowd. 'The rest of you will be taken to the shower rooms to be deloused.'

Seb's new companion huffed.

'You don't believe him?' Seb asked.

'That woman is dead already,' he said. 'They're all dead.' The horror on Seb's face must have shown, as the man added, 'But you don't have to be one of them. Do as I say, and you will live. For now, anyway. Now grab his feet.'

He gestured towards Uzziel. Seb couldn't bring himself to look into those kind eyes as they lifted him from the floor of the cattle car.

The Book of Durand

The power winked out at sunset, as though it had been waiting for the most dramatic point to make its exit.

'What's happening?' I asked.

'How would I know?' Father rummaged under the sink for candles. He dotted them around the room as though we were about to hold a séance.

'Isn't it romantic?' Mamma said. But Father ignored her and she stropped from the room.

She returned minutes later, swishing the skirt of a crimson dress. 'Do you like it?' She beamed, and I couldn't diminish her joy by pointing out I'd seen it many times before. 'Your father bought it for me on our honeymoon.' She spun right into my arms, giggling as she waltzed us around the room. 'Did I ever tell you that story?' Although she danced with me, her gaze was fixed on my father. 'Your father had taken me on a cruise, and on our final night we were to dine with the captain. As I got ready, I felt a trail of kisses on my neck.'

'Was it Father?' I asked.

She flung her head back and let out a deep belly laugh. 'Of course it was. He presented me with a box, and this dress was inside. Do you know what he said to me?'

I did, but I asked her to tell me all the same.

'He said, 'A crimson gown for the woman who brings passion to my life.' Do you remember that, Victor?'

Father grunted something inaudible.

The sparkle around my mother dimmed. But then she flashed her most winning smile. 'Twirl me, Martin.'

I obliged, turning her below the arch of my arm, again

and again, until she let go, spiralling towards my father in a flurry of red silk and laughter.

'Dance with me,' she said, looping her arms around his waist.

He turned his face away from her. 'You've been drinking.'

'Don't be such a bore.' She reached up to hook her arms around his neck.

He seized her wrists before she could. 'For God's sake, Serena. There's no music. Just sit down and be quiet. Please.'

Mamma's dress billowed as she slumped onto the couch.

I think he must have felt bad, because he added, 'You look very pretty, but I need to think.'

As the world descended into an eerie dusk, alien sounds rose to take the place of the light. Gunshots sliced through the settling darkness. A nearby explosion sent ripples through the air, making my ears pop. The noise outside was accompanied by whoops and cheers, contrasting with the grave mood in our little house and making it all the more sombre. Worse, the noises were getting closer.

Father couldn't settle. He would sit, only to spring to his feet and pace to the window. Then he would repeat the process. Sit, spring, pace.

'We can't just stay here and wait for them to destroy everything we worked for.'

'Who?' I asked.

'Looters.'

'Ours is the only house along this track,' Mamma said. 'And we have nothing to steal. They wouldn't waste their time.'

'It's not the house that I'm worried about,' he said, shrugging on his coat.

Mamma didn't want to go with us to the church. 'I'll stay here and keep the house secure.'

Father's hand rested on the bulge at his hip, his pistol hidden beneath his jacket. 'Go and get changed, Serena. I want you with me, where I know I can keep you safe.'

Even in the dim light, I could see that her glow had returned. She was a princess defended by her brave knight.

As we drove to the church, I marvelled that the sun was still setting. Then I realised that it was not the sun at all. The supermarket, which loomed over the road as you entered the city centre, was on fire. Flames licked the night sky as anonymous figures stood silhouetted in front of it. Someone threw a bottle and it shattered against a blackened wall, causing the fire around it to leap and dance.

'Keep your head down,' Father said as we passed.

But curiosity got the better of me. Nearby, a man swung a baseball bat at a shop window. His companions piled in, before passing every type of electrical equipment back through to him. He piled them onto the pavement. Seeing me looking, he waved. I could hear him cackling as I ducked down in my seat.

When we reached the church, we were relieved to find the street deserted. Father rushed us down the pathway and up the steps to the entrance, slamming the heavy wooden door behind us.

'Take whatever you can carry.' My father handed us a plastic bag each before placing the candlesticks from the altar into his own bag.

'What? We can't steal from the church!' Mamma

dropped her bag to the floor and sat in one of the pews, arms crossed.

'Listen to me.' He knelt in front of her. 'You saw the chaos out there. Either we take them or somebody else does. We're protecting them.'

'How would they even get in?' I asked. My father had locked the door and dropped the long wooden plank across it for extra security. The looming stained glass windows had long ago been reinforced with a protective mesh as a deterrent to vandals. I thought we were as safe there as anywhere.

'Don't be fooled, Martin. People like that will always find a way in if they want to.'

A hammering at the front door stopped me responding. 'Father Durand, are you in there? Let me in, please!'

Mamma's eyes widened and her mouth formed a little 'o'. 'Is that Heidi?'

At the mention of her name, I was heading towards the door.

Father's arm sprang out to block my way. 'Stay away.'

I stared at him, slack jawed. 'But she's my friend.'

Technically she wasn't. She had always been kind to me, but if she hadn't been my childhood babysitter, I doubt she'd have even known my name. But I knew hers. Everybody did. From her golden hair to the blue of her eyes, she was the type of girl people noticed.

'Victor, she's a child. We can't leave her out there.' Mamma pushed past him and strode towards the door.

'And what about *our* child?' He snarled the words from between twisted lips. 'What if she isn't alone? Maybe she's being used as bait. Let's just think for a second.'

Part of me was pleased that he was concerned for my

safety. Still, I think even then I realised I was just a shield to mask his cowardice.

He marched over to the door and put his ear to it. If he was checking she was still there, he needn't have bothered. I could hear her whimpers from where I stood.

Only when he was satisfied that he could hear nobody else on the other side, did he speak. 'Heidi, are you alone?'

'Father Durand, thank God! Please let me in!'

'Are you alone?' he repeated.

'Please, Father, they will be here any second!'

He leapt away from the door as if it had burnt him.

I rushed forward. 'We've got to let her in.'

'If somebody is chasing her and she disappears, what do you think they'll assume?'

'It doesn't matter. They can't get in.'

He swallowed hard. 'I won't risk that.'

Even if I'd had the time to protest, I knew it would have been useless. Heidi's cry cut me off anyway. 'Please,' she sobbed, a last-ditch attempt to gain empathy from a man who I was not wholly convinced was capable of such an emotion. It made no difference.

I sat hunched against the doorframe, my knees to my chest. I knew it was pointless; she didn't even know I was there, and if she did, she would probably feel betrayed by my inaction. But still, I couldn't let her go through that alone. So, I sat with my palm resting on the door and made myself listen to every whimper.

It lasted for hours. I tried not to think about what was happening to her on the other side of that door, but her screams told their own story. The muffled shriek escaping a hand cupped over her mouth. The resigned weeping punctuated by a guttural moan. The broken tremor of a cry bubbling through blood. And the whole time her sobs were contrasted with the cackles and whoops and sniggers of the male voices around her.

I didn't think it was possible, but her silence was even worse than her cries. As the church was bathed in the morning light streaming through the stained glass, the voices retreated.

I knew she was gone long before we dared open that door.

She was sprawled on the church steps, the end of her fair hair turned crimson by her own blood. One unblinking blue eye stared accusingly at me over the crook of her arm.

My mother fetched her dress, which hung on the fence cordoning off the graveyard, and laid it over the top of her.

'Come away. There's nothing you can do for her,' Father said. When neither of us obeyed he added, 'You see, I was right. If we'd opened the door, we'd be dead, too.'

Mamma frowned at him. 'You may have been correct, Victor, but I think it's up to God to judge if you were right.'

Jared

'Wait for me!' Beth struggled to keep up. 'Or at least tell me what's wrong.'

Jared couldn't stop. No matter how his lungs burned and his legs ached, he wouldn't rest until he knew Nell and Aaron were safe. He skidded to a halt at the end of the street. 'Please. No.' The tavern was already consumed by fire.

Jared ran at the building. 'Nell! Aaron!' Strong hands held him back as he went for the door, the windows above it already glowing with the flames inside. Two men pushed him away. He did not need to speak Latin to understand what they were saying. It was hopeless, and if he went into that building, he would die.

A strangled whimper escaped Beth as she caught up with him. She dropped to her knees. 'No, this can't be happening.'

Jared tried to help her to her feet. She hooked her arms around his neck and sobbed into his chest.

'Maybe they went out,' she said. 'We don't know they were in there. And if they were, surely they got out before it...before it...' She crumpled into tears again.

'I don't understand. This shouldn't be.'

'My thoughts exactly.'

Jared turned to find Aaron standing on the road behind him.

'Thank God!' Beth threw her arms around his neck. 'We thought you were...'

Aaron untangled himself from her embrace and backed away. 'We don't have time for this.'

Beth cupped her hands over her mouth. 'Where's Nell?'

'They took her.'

'Who?' Beth asked.

'Soldiers. They rounded her up with a load of other people. We were dragging the cases from the tavern and they just grabbed her. I don't even know why. When I tried to stop them, I got this for my trouble.' Aaron ran his fingers over a purple lump already showing through the sooty streaks on his face. 'I couldn't do anything to stop them.'

Jared stepped towards him. 'It's not your fault. You didn't know this would happen.'

'My fault?' Aaron's voice was small, as though it was straining through his vocal cords. 'I know it's not. This is down to you.'

Beth put herself between the two of them. 'We can't start blaming each other.'

'He told us it was safe.' Aaron jabbed a finger at Jared. 'You two do what you want. I'm going to get her back.'

'We should stay together,' Beth said. 'Wait for us to gather anything essential and—'

'No, I'll do it myself. I've taken money from the case. I'll pay whatever they want.'

'We can help,' Jared said.

'I'm not sure you can. I can't help noticing the people I care about get hurt when you are around, Jared. I think perhaps, when this is all over, Nell and I will be better off going our own way.'

'That's not fair,' Jared said.

But Aaron had already stalked off into the night.

The Book of Durand

I'd always imagined the end of the world to be a quick affair, perhaps the result of a killer mist, an alien invasion...an asteroid. The truth was, for me, it was pretty boring. The annihilation of our species involved a whole lot of waiting around.

Out of interest, do you know how many different types of bean there are? Me neither, but I'm pretty sure we tried them all. At first, my father would attempt to disguise them amongst sauces and stews. But as our rations ran short, so did his effort. I'll be happy if I never see another.

We secluded ourselves away from the world, surviving on the little we had. I almost felt sympathy for my father during that time; he couldn't win. Mamma would chide him for our reduced circumstances, as though he had any control over them, but then berate him for leaving us to look for supplies. Then I would remind myself that the limbo in which we lived was a small penance for the way we had abandoned Heidi.

There was no question of Mamma accompanying him on these supply runs. She hadn't gone outside since that night in the church. While he was gone, she would pace the length of our little house, muttering under her breath. I gave up trying to calm her; better to stay out of her way. She reminded me of a clockwork toy, wound too tight and destined to snap.

Then, one night, Father didn't come home. Mamma ping-ponged between fury and despair, between ordering me out to look for him and clinging to me like a life raft.

When his key turned in the lock the next morning, she greeted him with angry tears.

'Where have you been?' she asked, tugging at his shirt.

He ignored her frustration and guided her to a kitchen chair. 'My love, listen to me. I've found us somewhere safe, somewhere they'll look after us.'

Her sobs stopped instantly. She had a knack for turning them on and off as required. 'Where?'

He pressed his lips together as though unsure whether to answer. 'Krakow.'

'Krakow? As in Poland? Well, why stop there? Let's set up camp on the damn moon.'

Father knelt in front of her, grasping her by the upper arms. 'Listen to me. It's not that far. And the arrangements are being made for us. We're being picked up tonight.'

My mother's eyes narrowed. 'Why us?'

He got to his feet. 'The people in this shelter are going to need religious leadership.' Puffing out his chest, he met my eye. I knew what he was thinking: *Why not me?* He was irritated that my mother would even question it. The only thing that surpassed my father's confidence was his vanity.

'But this is our home.' Her voice was small, childlike.

'Serena, this place is dying. We need to go where it's safe.' He stalked over to me and pulled me to my feet. 'Look at the boy. He's not afraid.'

It was true; I wasn't. But only because I expected his plan to come to nothing.

'We need to get packed. The car will be here in a few hours.' Father let out a laugh, a sound that had become a distant memory for me. 'Don't you see? God is saving us, just like I said he would.'

If that was true, I couldn't help wondering what we had done to deserve it.

Seb

'Galewski,' Seb's saviour said. 'My name is Marceli Galewski.'

Once he'd realised the guards were not suspicious of Seb's presence, Galewski had disappeared, returning in the late afternoon. It was the first chance Seb had to look at him properly. The odd scar nicked the angular lines of his face. Wrinkles surrounded his eyes and carved themselves down the length of his cheeks, the ghost of smiles.

Seb stuck out his hand. 'I'm S—' he began, but the dark look Galewski shot him truncated his sentence.

Realising this would be an obvious sign he didn't belong there, Seb dropped his hand back to his side. 'I'm Seb,' he whispered.

'Ah, well that is where you are wrong,' Galewski informed him. 'Your name is Reuben Posner.'

'I don't understand.'

'The less you know the better. That way, they can't force you to tell. But if one of them asks, which I doubt they will take the trouble to do, that's who you are. Have you got that?'

Seb nodded. 'My name is Reuben Posner.'

'Good,' Galewski said, patting him on the back. 'Because if you screw this up, they will kill you, and me, too.'

A horn rang out across the platform, piercing through the heat, and all work stopped.

'Can you sing, Reuben?'

Again, Seb stared blankly at him.

'They like us to sing as we walk to and from work. Perhaps it lets them persuade themselves we aren't as miserable here as they suspect. And make it enthusiastic,' Galewski added. 'They've killed people for less.'

They were led through the camp to the roll-call area. As they walked, Galewski spoke in snatched whispers, pointing out key buildings. Staff barracks flanked the yard on either side. Guards stood upon their roofs clutching machine guns, a warning to those with fantasies of escape. A sign announced in ten-inch letters that they were to surrender valuables on pain of death.

Standing in line with hundreds of other prisoners, Seb was torn between the urge to run while he had the chance, risking a bullet, or staying to take the consequences. It came down to neither option. The inspecting officers passed by him without question, as if he had always been present amongst their ranks.

Until the danger had passed, Seb did not notice that he had been holding every muscle tense, poised somewhere between fight and flight. The adrenaline still pumped through his blood as Galewski escorted him to the barracks. As they entered the large wooden building, Galewski pointed towards a bunk. 'You'll sleep there. I'm afraid we just get a cup of coffee in the evening,' he said apologetically, as if he had some control over the menu, 'but if you get the chance, take the food from the bundles the prisoners bring with them. The guards usually turn a blind eye.'

Galewski shifted from foot to foot, scuffing his heels on the sandy floor.

'I appreciate all you have done for me,' Seb said.

'The lights go out at 21:00,' Galewski said over his shoulder as he left. 'Rest while you can. You'll need it.'

It was then that Seb noticed a man sitting on a bunk nearby, watching him. Although he was not the only man in the room, he glowered openly, catching Seb's attention. A short greying beard clung to his face, covering the lower portion of his features.

With more courage than he felt, Seb said, 'Can I help you?'

'No, you can't help me. You know, you shouldn't be so quick to thank Galewski.'

'Why not?'

'Nobody in here does anything for anybody but themselves. We are all just trying to survive, Galewski included.'

'But—'

'But nothing. Galewski needed you. This morning a prisoner named Reuben Posner escaped by hiding in a transport of belongings being shipped out of the camp. Posner was about twenty years old with fair hair. Sound familiar to you?'

He could have been describing Seb.

'If the guards had found out that another prisoner had managed to escape, we would have all been punished, or worse. Galewski saved you so you could take Posner's place in the roll-call.'

Seb deflated but didn't want to show his disappointment. 'It doesn't matter. I'm alive because of him.'

'That's true enough. There are many who would have happily changed places with you today.'

Looking Seb up and down one last time, he made his way out of the barracks without another word.

'Just ignore him.' The words came from a man stretched out on one of the bunks. His short brown hair and oval face were unspectacular. But his grin unfurled like a flag, lighting his face with a sincerity that Seb had only seen in one other. He pushed thoughts of Isaac away.

'I'm Adolf Freidman. But considering our predicament, I just go by Freidman. No explanation needed there, I assume.'

'No, and I can't say I blame you. I'm...Reuben Posner,' Seb said, remembering his promise.

'Okay,' Freidman said. 'Your diligence has been noted. And now how about you tell me your real name?'

Right or wrong, Seb found himself trusting him. 'It's Seb.'

'Well, I'd like to say it's good to meet you, Seb, but I wouldn't wish Treblinka on anybody.'

'Who was that?' Seb asked, motioning towards the door.

'Tomas Silva,' Freidman replied.

'He doesn't think much of Galewski, does he?'

'He likes Galewski just fine. Tomas is a good man. One of the best. He's just seen too much not to be a realist.' Freidman hesitated. 'Tomas was married to a Jewish woman. He refused to let her be transported alone. They chose him for labour and sent her to the gas chamber.'

His words tied themselves in knots in Seb's mind. 'Gas chamber?' Although he'd heard of Auschwitz and the atrocities that had happened there, Treblinka had never been mentioned in any history book he'd read.

'Those are the rumours.'

'Somebody must know for sure.'

Freidman sighed. 'For all the different areas this place has, when you get down to basics it is split into two, the lower camp and the extermination area. And if you get sent to the extermination area, you don't come back.'

The image of the woman from the car, towing her little girl behind her, popped into Seb's head. Had she any inkling she was leading her child to her death, he wondered? Then a cold sweat covered him despite the summer heat. If Durand had sent Isaac through after him, which side of the camp had he ended up on?

That night, Seb lay staring at the ceiling of the barracks.

'Galewski was right.' Freidman's voice pierced the darkness. 'You should try and get some rest. If you're too hungry, I have some bread that I managed to—'

'No. But thank you.' As much as his stomach growled, Seb wouldn't take food from these men. Hollow cheek bones and scrawny limbs told him they needed it much more. 'I was just thinking.'

'About?'

'I don't belong here.' Seb thought back to the claustrophobia of the Sanctuary. It seemed a small price to pay now.

'None of us do,' Freidman said. 'Although I never did ask you what sick logic sent you here. Wait, let me guess. You're not Jewish?'

'No, I'm not.'

'You're a little young to be an academic or a priest.'

Seb considered lying, but he was already enduring hell to defend his right to be who he was. 'I fell in love with the wrong person. At least that's what they told me.'

'Oh. Enough said.' Freidman fell quiet. Then he added, 'Was your friend sent here, too?'

'I think so.'

'I'm sorry. I hope you find each other again.'

Seb rolled over and squeezed his eyes shut.

As he began to drift off, Freidman asked, 'I've never been in love. Was it worth all this?'

Seb didn't even need to think. 'Every second.'

The Book of Durand

One small bag each, that was all we'd been allowed. Even with my paltry belongings, I'd fretted over what to bring. So my father's anger, when he found Mamma stuffing swathes of material into his bag, came as no surprise. The zip snagged, refusing to close over the bulging mass of rose chiffon, crimson silk and buttercup satin.

'What are you doing?' he asked. 'That's my bag.'

'I can't leave them.' Mamma continued to tug at the zip, as though getting it closed would settle the matter and he wouldn't be able to force her to take them out.

'You're going to break it.' He took the bag from her and pulled out the coloured material like a magician pulling handkerchiefs from his sleeve. 'They're just clothes, Serena.'

She scooped the pile into her arms. 'They're my memories.'

Father sighed. 'Martin, pass me your bag.'

I held onto the handle a little tighter.

'Now.'

I handed it over.

'Let's see what we've got here.' He took each item out of the bag, inspected it, and put it to one side. 'Here we go,' he said, holding up my favourite comic books. 'You must have read these a million times.'

I'd never been one for books. I loved comics, though. The clarity of them, each character labelled as hero or villain, appealed to me. How naive I was; we both know nothing is that black and white. 'Yes, I have, but—'

'Then it's settled.' He dropped the comics to the floor and shoved my mother's dresses into my bag.

Mamma clapped. 'You don't mind, Martin.' It wasn't a question, so I didn't answer.

'Right, let's wait outside,' Father said.

'I'll miss this place.' I took a last look at the place we'd made our home.

Father sniffed. 'I won't.'

When the coach stopped outside our home, my father deflated. It wasn't the car he said he'd been promised. But he only allowed his disappointment to show for a second.

'See,' he said to us. 'Didn't I promise you door to door service?'

Mamma didn't look convinced. She took a step backwards when the doors opened, and she heard the wails of children coming from inside.

'It'll be fine,' Father said, placing a hand on the small of her back and guiding her onboard.

He looked at the driver and then pointedly at our bags. In return, the driver reclined in his seat, arms crossed over his chest.

We put our own bags in the luggage compartment, my father grumbling under his breath the whole time.

After he took a seat at the front, Father gave the driver a nod, signalling for him to continue.

In return, the man's eyebrows shot up. I could see why; who was my father to give him instructions? But still, the driver started the engine. Father glanced back at me with a smug grin. In his eyes, the balance of power had been restored.

The coach was full, so the only seat left was next to a greying woman, a few rows back from my parents. I don't think she was pleased with the company; she claimed the armrest as soon as I sat down, aiming her elbow at me as a warning.

We were jostled around the coach for about half an hour before Father began throwing furtive glances at the road signs.

Eventually, he got up and approached the driver. 'I think you've missed the exit for the airport.'

The driver didn't respond.

'Excuse me? Did you hear what I said?'

'We aren't going to the airport.'

My father let out a snort of laughter. 'You can't mean that you intend to drive. That's ludicrous. You plan to take us through Italy and Austria?'

He gave an exaggerated shrug. 'I don't pick the route; I just drive the bus.'

Father took his phone from his pocket. Reception had become so unreliable that my own had sat in my bedside drawer for the last six months. I hadn't even bothered to pack it.

He dialled a number a few times but received the same shrill tone. At last, he was rewarded with ringing.

He noticed that Mamma and I were watching him and took a few steps away, as though being slightly further down the aisle in the centre of the coach would somehow make his conversation private.

'You said it would be a plane.' He offered no pleasantries to the person at the other end. 'Of course, I'm grateful, but you can't expect—'

The beeping told me the person on the other end had hung up. Father stared at his phone in disbelief before slipping it back into his pocket.

'Everything okay, Victor?' Mamma asked.

'Fine. Everything's fine.' He patted her knee. 'The journey will just take a little longer than I'd hoped.'

As the day crept on, the heat inside the bus became unbearable. Rivulets of sweat ran between my shoulder blades and pooled at the base of my back. At first, the coach was alive with a chorus of complaints. Pleas were made to open windows; all but the tiny sliding ones at the top were sealed shut. Some passengers begged the driver to open the doors so the air could flow through as he drove. For a while he did, but we realised that the air outside was almost as hot and had the added discomfort of dust and sand.

Soon the coach settled into silence, each passenger dwelling in their own private misery.

When the first fat drop of rain hit the window, I thought I was dreaming. I sat staring as it multiplied, splatters covering the glass.

'Do you see that?' I asked the woman next to me.

She opened her eyes before clapping her hands together in excitement. 'I do! How lovely!'

The whole bus came alive as the spattering sound on the roof intensified.

Father peered back at me through the gap between the seats. 'You see, Martin. You see.'

I'm not quite sure what he meant by that. It seemed he was taking credit for the change in the weather, as though he had arranged it as part of a package deal for the trip. I doubt he was as keen to accept responsibility for what happened next.

'Let us off.' A woman, clinging to the tops of the seats to

steady herself, made her way to the front of the bus. 'My daughter needs to use the toilet.'

The driver let out a snigger. 'Well, you won't find one out there.'

'We'll make do. It will only take a minute.'

'We aren't stopping.' He flicked the windscreen wipers up a notch as the rain came down heavier.

'If that's the case, you should have provided a bus with toilet facilities.' She sneered at him through gritted teeth.

'I'll pass on your comments to the management.'

I heard my father whisper something to my mother. Then he stood up. 'Perhaps we can reach some sort of...' English was not his first language, and he searched for the word. 'Compromise.'

'Perhaps you should shut up and sit down.'

Mamma was on her feet beside him in seconds. 'Don't you speak to my husband like that!'

The woman wobbled and grabbed my father for support as the bus lurched to the right. 'You can't keep us prisoner on here.'

'Fine,' the driver said, pulling up at the side of the road. 'Do what you want.'

The doors opened with a swish. Even over the mass exodus of chattering passengers, I could hear the drumming of the rain.

Apart from the woman I was sitting next to, I was the only one left on the bus. Even the driver stood by the doors, trying to light a cigarette in the rain.

My father's head appeared at the steps, poking up like a meerkat's. 'Come on, Martin. It's glorious.'

I turned to my neighbour. 'Are you coming?'

She shook her head and turned to watch the children playing by her window.

I hesitated at the top of the steps. The rain, getting heavier by the second, flowed over the baked earth in angry rivers.

However, after several hours bouncing around in oppressive heat, I longed to feel it on my skin.

'Where are we?' I asked the driver as I got off.

He blew out a plume of smoke. 'Somewhere near Venice, I figure.' He tried to take another drag, but realising the cigarette was already too wet, stamped it out on the floor.

'Venice?' I'd seen pictures of it in magazines: canals and gondolas immortalised forever in colourful spreads. The patch of wasteland on which we stood was nothing like that.

When I looked around, my parents were nowhere to be seen. I walked towards a group of passengers who stood nearby, hoping to find them there.

'Don't go too far,' the driver called after me.

My parents weren't with the other passengers. I peered over their shoulders to see what they found so interesting and realised that it wasn't so much what they saw, but what they didn't. The land was scarred by a long ditch, which I assumed had once been a canal. Even as we watched, rainwater flowed around our shoes and splashed onto the ground below.

A crack of lightning split the darkening sky and sent the group heading back towards the shelter of the bus.

I knew I should have followed them. Already my shirt was plastered to my skin and my hair pasted to my face. But I couldn't resist tipping my head back and opening my mouth.

That's the last thing that I remember before my feet

went from under me. Earth and sky tumbled over one another until I came to rest on the riverbed.

I lay there, winded. Then I felt the gathering water pick me up. I tried to dig my nails into the hard dirt, but it was no use; I was wrenched away. My nose and mouth filled with a muddy sludge as the current dragged me along. Finally, I managed to grab hold of an old tree root and hung there in the water, a flag waving its surrender.

It was then that fingers gripped the tops of my arms as my father dragged me to my feet. He lifted my shaking body so that the other passengers could pull me to safety. I wanted to cry with relief.

As I felt him climb up next to me, I threw myself into his arms. But when I buried my face in his shirt, something felt wrong. His frame was slight and bony. I could feel his shoulder blades jutting from under the material of his shirt. And he smelt of tobacco. My father never smoked.

'You'll be okay, kid.' The driver of the coach peered down at me, his face etched with concern. It was he who had saved me, not my father.

He helped me to my feet, turning me from side to side to scan me for injuries. His face lightened as he realised that I was okay. 'I'm Glen,' he said, his name the only thing he had to give. He tussled my wet hair, an awkward attempt to comfort me.

I looked towards the coach and saw my father hunched within the shelter of the steps. He beckoned for me to hurry up and get on, not bothering to venture back out into the rain to retrieve me.

⁓

Jared

People hemmed Jared in from every side. They stepped on his heels and shoved him this way and that in their panic to get away from the fire. The flames leapt between buildings like dominoes. When Jared was certain they must have outpaced it, he looked up to see the wooden shack next to him begin to smoulder.

Beth was being propelled along the narrow street, and he grasped her hand. 'Stay with me,' she said, her body jerking as she was shoved this way and that.

Somebody grabbed him, a soul seeking an anchor in the torrent of people. 'Let go of me,' Jared said, feeling his tunic tighten around his throat.

Jared saw Beth mouth his name, her voice lost in the cries of the people as their hands were wrenched apart.

He prised the fingers from the back of his tunic. But he was too late. Already, he had lost sight of Beth. Sparks of panic ignited behind his eyes as he scoured the crowd for her auburn hair.

Then he saw her, clinging to a doorframe, fighting the tide to look for him. He was relieved that she still clutched the material they had bundled the visualiser within. Patting his tunic, he felt the bulge of the medilaser and orb.

When he finally reached her, Beth slumped with relief. 'Well, you took your time. What now?'

Jared looked to the horizon. Already it glowed. 'I think the fire has reached that side.'

'We can't go back.' She was right. There was no way they'd be able to fight the surge of people heading for the Palatine area.

'Okay. Then we go down.'

'What?'

'Help me lift this.' Jared hooked his fingers into the holes of the stone sewer grate, lifting it just enough for Beth to slide her fingertips beneath.

'Into the sewers,' she said. 'Not quite what I had in mind when you suggested Ancient Rome.'

'It leads to the River Tiber. We'll be safe down there.'

Beth didn't need convincing. She handed him the bundle of equipment to hold while she levered herself down. 'Let's find our friends and get out of here,' she said as she disappeared into the world beneath the city.

Seb

Every part of Seb ached. A muscle in his leg twitched, refusing to rest, as though fearing the consequences if caught.

He slumped onto his bunk, dropping a small package of bread next to him.

'What have you got there?' The prisoner a few bunks away sat with his legs pulled towards his chest, watching Seb through the valley created by his knees.

'Just some bread I found in the bundles.' Seb hesitated. 'Would you like to share it?'

The man flicked his tongue over his bottom lip. 'No. Thank you.' He laid down on his bed and squeezed his eyes shut.

Later, when Seb was on his way to the latrine, Freidman stopped him. 'What did you say to Chezkel?'

'Who?'

'The man you were just talking to.'

'Nothing. I just offered to share the bread I'd found in the prisoner bundles.'

Freidman rubbed his forehead. 'Seb, he's an informant.'

'What?'

'It's against the rules to take anything from the prisoners' bundles. He'll tell the SS.'

'I didn't know...Galewski said—'

'I know. Don't worry.'

'Don't worry?' Seb laughed, incredulous. 'What will they do to me?'

'Nothing. I'll have Galewski speak to him.'

'But—'

'Leave it with me.'

As Seb climbed into his bunk later that evening, hunger and nerves gnawed at his stomach. The heat was oppressive, shrouding him. Still, he pulled his blanket up over his head, a semblance of defence against the unknown.

When he heard the shuffling of feet and grunts of fear, he put his eye to the thin material. Through a mesh of threads, he watched shapeless figures drag someone from their bed. A clunk bought an end to the whimpering.

Seb could still make out the peaks and valleys of Freidman's sleeping silhouette in the next bunk. He considered hissing a warning but worried it might draw attention to him.

Instead, he nestled further under his blanket. His heart beat so fast that his blood pooled in his head, his pulse blasting in his temples. Only as the voices faded did it begin to slow. He didn't even try to sleep after that, thinking there was little point. So he was surprised to wake to the stretches and yawns of his fellow prisoners.

Tossing the blanket from on top of him, he slid from his bunk. The other men milled around, pulling on shoes and tidying their bunks.

The normality of the scene was probably why Seb didn't notice the boots at first, the way the men skirted around them so they didn't knock their heads on the soles.

When he did, he dropped back down onto his bunk, unable to tear his eyes from the horror before him. He looked from the loose laces, past the bare ankles and scrawny limbs, to the noose around the man's neck. A blanket covered his head, but Seb was almost certain he'd recognise the face below it. Bending double, he retched, splattering the floorboards with a watery bile, his stomach empty of anything else.

When the first SS officer entered the barracks, he regarded the hanging man with a dismissive grumble. He turned to a Ukrainian guard. 'Cut him down.'

Somebody touched Seb's elbow, and he flinched backwards.

'It happens here. Suicide, I mean. It happens.' Freidman walked to Chezkel's empty bunk and folded the bedding. 'We can't turn on each other or they'll win.'

The Book of Durand

When I took my seat on the bus, I was shaking. But it wasn't due to being wet through and smeared in mud. It was because I couldn't stop thinking about what might have happened had the driver not come after me. I'd never felt so alone.

The woman, who had viewed me with little more than disdain up until this moment, sat down next to me and gave my hand a squeeze. She didn't even comment on the fact that I'd taken her seat by the window.

'That wasn't just rain,' she said. 'That was a monsoon. I should know, I saw enough of them as a child. It's one of the reasons I moved.' She glanced over at my parents. 'Are you sure you don't want me to switch seats with one of them?'

I shook my head, knowing that they'd only decline the offer.

'Well, okay then,' she said, settling back into her chair and closing her eyes.

The combination of the heat and the wet clothing of the passengers made the coach so humid that it felt as if I were breathing underwater. As we started moving again, I'd hoped at least for some scenery to keep me entertained. That wasn't to be; the windows had completely fogged over.

I wrote my name in the condensation, my finger squeaking against the glass.

Looking back over my shoulder, I noticed my neighbour watching me through one eye. She clamped it shut when I caught her. Still, I used the sleeve of my shirt to wipe the letters away. How easily erased I was.

I longed for something to do, thinking of my stack of

comics abandoned on the hall floor, wishing I'd picked up just a couple on my way out.

Soon the boredom got to me, and my eyelids became heavy. I decided to nap and rested my forehead against the window.

A mixture of the adrenaline from my accident and the heat must have exhausted me, because I was asleep in seconds.

It was dark outside when the bus hit a pothole and my forehead hit the glass. I looked around for somebody to complain to, but nobody was interested in me.

The other passengers stared out of the window, some cupping their hands around their faces to try and get a better view. We were bumping along a dirt track flanked by lights. However, they were pretty ineffective. The darkness beyond fought back so that it was impossible to see past the sides of the path or the small section of dirt lit by the headlights of the bus.

I wanted to ask the woman next to me where we were, but she had her body twisted, chatting to somebody in one of the seats behind.

Then the bus stopped. Every eye went to the driver, but he just put on the handbrake and settled back into his seat.

I stood so I could look over the headrests. We had stopped in front of a large metal gate.

My father was leaning over the driver. 'What now?'

'Now we wait,' the driver said.

At first, the coach was silent. But soon a murmur broke out amongst the passengers, their comments echoing my own thoughts. Had we reached our destination? We'd left France barely a day ago; could we have already arrived in Poland?

The swish of the opening coach doors silenced us. That was the moment I first saw him, the man who would save my life, only to then ruin it.

'Welcome,' he said, pushing his glasses up the bridge of his nose, just for them to slide down again. 'I'm Doctor Edmond Pearse. Welcome to the Sanctuary.'

Chapter Three

The Book of Durand

Back then, they made up the rules as they went along. As part of the first wave of survivors to be admitted to the Sanctuary, we were privileged to be met by the illustrious Doctor Pearse. I mean, you certainly wouldn't get that now.

My father stepped into his path, hand outstretched. 'Victor Durand, pleased to meet you. This is my wife Serena and son Martin.'

'Um...yes, welcome.' Pearse gave my father's hand the briefest of shakes. He tried to head for the entrance to the Sanctuary, but Father sidestepped so that they again faced one another.

'We want to be of assistance here. Anything we can do to help, let us know.'

I nodded my agreement and glanced at my mother to see

if she was doing the same. She was staring, open mouthed, at the looming black building in front of us.

'And what is it that you do?' Pearse asked.

'I'm a reverend,' Father said.

'I see. Well, I'm sure the citizens will find comfort in your words as they settle in.'

Annoyance radiated from my father. He pulled me by the elbow and presented me to the doctor. 'We could be a useful family. We're multilingual, you know. Serena and Martin speak French, German and a little Flemish. The boy is fluent in English, too.'

Pearse stopped. 'And you?'

'Well, I speak French and my English is pretty good.'

'And what language are you speaking now?' Pearse continued walking and my father followed.

'French, of course.'

'I don't speak French.'

Father frowned. 'I don't understand.'

'But you do, and that's my point.' Pearse rolled up his sleeve. 'This tiny chip emits a signal that intercepts and translates the brain waves of anybody in it's vicinity. One chip is all that is needed for us to comprehend one another completely, regardless of language.'

I was in awe. I'd read sci-fi comics with universal translators pinned to lapels or clasped in hands. This was on another level.

My father wasn't nearly as impressed. 'Leviticus 19:28 tells us not to cut our bodies or put marks upon ourselves. Your chips seem somewhat...invasive.' I knew that wasn't his real issue. It was that Pearse's technology had voided what he saw as his trump card.

'Communication will be key to building our little society. If we can't understand one another how will we ever be able to, well, understand one another.' He smiled at me. 'You just need to focus on getting your family settled.'

My father puffed out his disappointment, but Pearse had already started towards the entrance. 'Follow me, please,' he said to the coach passengers, who were now milling around the outskirts of the building.

They gathered in front of the waiting doctor. 'This is the entrance to the Sanctuary, an underground town that sprawls over three metres beneath the city of Krakow. There are some who have called our construction of this safe harbour over-cautious, pessimistic and wasteful. They did not have the vision that those standing in front of me did; you who helped me to see this project to fruition, be that through the donation of funds or skills. This foresight has earned you the place you deserve within the Sanctuary.'

I turned to my father. 'But we didn't—'

'Shhh,' he hissed, telling me all I needed to know.

'And the nay sayers, the ones who claimed that all of this was unnecessary?' Pearse continued. 'I pray for them. Projects like the Sanctuary are now springing up all over the world. Nuclear bunkers in Beijing and Helsinki are being extended as we speak. Our team of scientists are advising them every step of the way, because they are in a race against time.' He paused. 'Enough of such depressing talk. Now you will begin your next adventure. Please follow me into your new home.'

My father pushed to the front of the crowd. 'Come on.'

Doctor Pearse looked startled when he turned to find my father so close. He craned his neck to address the crowd over his head. 'Watch your step and hold onto the rail on the way down.'

Mamma froze in front of me before she'd even gone down a single step. 'I can't. I'm sorry, I can't.'

'It's okay—' I began, but Father was already bounding back up the few steps between them.

'This isn't the time.'

'It's so dark. And how will we breathe down there?'

'I'm pretty sure they've considered that.'

'Is everything okay?' Pearse asked.

'Absolutely fine,' my father said, his smile fixed. 'She just has a slight problem with enclosed spaces.'

Pearse's brow furrowed. 'I'm afraid that comes with the territory of a subterranean town.'

'Of course.' Father leant towards Mamma and whispered in her ear. Only I, stood behind them, could see the way his fingers dug into her arm.

Silent tears streaked her face, but she nodded.

'Stay behind her,' Father told me.

Like I had a choice. The stairway was so narrow we walked in single file, each trying not to step on the heel of the person in front.

I won't bore you with what came next. The adjustments that we had to make. How we learnt to acclimatise to life with a third of the space and none of the distractions we enjoyed on the surface.

What I should tell you is that there was none of the tattooing and segregation that later became par of the course. It was only when the world above began to disintegrate, that life in the Sanctuary began to warp into something...different. But you don't need to know about that, yet.

Just understand that, at the beginning, it was simple. Hopeful. Even in my own family, life became easier. You wouldn't think the end of the world would have a silver lining, would you? But as my father led us below the earth into the Sanctuary, we left behind the controversy that had surrounded us for so long. Despite being hundreds of metres below the ground, the air felt lighter.

That was until the third day. We sat in the canteen, pushing a stew of greying meat around our plates. Father fidgeted in his chair, scanning the dining room. I thought that perhaps he was waiting for Doctor Pearse to make an appearance; he had talked relentlessly about needing an opportunity to prove himself.

That's when I heard a familiar clinking sound. My jaw clenched and I grasped the seat of my chair.

Mamma's fork hovered over her meal. She stayed like that, chest heaving, until Father broke the silence.

'Millicent, what are you doing here? Serena, look, it's Millicent.'

At his instruction, Mamma looked up. The two women stared at one another, but neither said a word.

'It's good to see you safe and well,' Father said. His voice had become shrill and strained with the effort of filling the silence.

Millicent gave her head a shake, as though realising she needed to speak. 'You too,' she said. 'All three of you. If you will excuse me, I'm late for a meeting.' She exited the dining room in a flurry of purple material and clattering bracelets.

As Millicent disappeared, Mamma let out a strangled laugh. The diners around us stopped their conversations and looked over at her.

'Are you okay?' Father asked her.

'Me? I'm fantastic,' she said, shovelling a forkful of stew into her mouth. She chewed it for the longest time before chasing it down with water. Then she dropped her cutlery onto her plate. She sat, her hands cupped around her face, shielding her eyes from our view.

'Mamma?' I watched as tears dropped from the end of her nose into her food.

'I'm fine. Eat up.'

I could hardly blame her for her reaction. My mother had assumed she was leaving her troubles in Menton. I doubt she ever suspected that they would be waiting for her at the other end.

Susan

My name is Susan Cole. My name is Susan Cole. She repeated it in her head, over and over. The fact that it was not her name wasn't what bothered her most; it was that it didn't suit her.

Susans were sensible. They made cakes for the bake sale and chaired the parent association. They matched their shoes to their handbags and would never have dreamt of dropping off their children at the school gates in their pyjamas. However, as all of the things on that list were no longer part of their lives, perhaps it didn't matter. She wondered what the Susans of the world would do with their time in this depleted world. She wondered if they regretted spending so much energy on such trivial things.

She shifted her weight from one side to another, crossing and uncrossing her legs. They'd only been travelling for a few hours but already she ached.

Fingers encircled her wrist and she flinched at the touch. Robert let her go and spread his palms in front of him. 'It's just me.'

He didn't meet her eye; he rarely had since that night. She understood: misplaced guilt. The trouble was, depending on how charitable she was feeling, she wasn't convinced his guilt was all that misplaced.

Susan was surprised how easily she'd taken to calling him Robert. They'd been using their new names in private since they'd learned them. It was a shame her memories weren't as easy to shed.

'What's wrong?' he asked.

She offered him a weak smile. 'Just a little backache.'

Healing bones hurt; that's what the doctors had said to her. An understatement if ever she'd heard one. 'I'm fine. Get some rest.'

He crossed his arms over his chest and settled back in his seat.

To distract herself from the pain, she stared out of the window. Travelling had once been one of the few shared interests that bought her and Robert together. On paper, they had so little in common. But the buzz they both felt when they planned a trip was enough back then. She'd loved sitting with her forehead pressed against the cool glass, watching the world pass by together. But now the glass wasn't cool, and the landscape wasn't beautiful. There was only so long that you could look out at the same dry scrubland. She wondered where the Venn diagrams of their lives would meet in this new world.

His breath deepened and was punctuated by snuffles that were dangerously close to a snore. If the other passengers noticed, they were diplomatic about it. Susan couldn't help the irritation rising within her, though.

She peered between the seats in front. An ear, a tad oversized for the fair head on which it sat, was on the other side. She flicked it.

The owner turned with his fist raised and nose wrinkled. 'Mom, cut it out.'

'What?' She sat back in her seat, pointing at Robert.

'It wasn't him. He's asleep.'

Right on cue, Robert's eyes flicked open. 'Who's asleep? I wasn't sleeping.'

'Really?' Susan asked. 'We must be having some serious engine trouble then.'

Her son smirked at her and she couldn't resist reaching through and tussling his hair.

'Mom, get off.'

'I can't help it; you're so darn cute.'

'You're so embarrassing,' he said, smoothing his hair. 'How much longer?'

'No idea,' Robert said.

'I'll ask Uncle Glen.' He shuffled across the empty coach seat.

Robert's hand shot out and grabbed him by the bicep. 'No!' He barked the word with such force that other passengers snapped from their daydreams and turned to look at them.

Robert gave them a strained smile before dropping his voice to a whisper.

'Geor...Luca, listen to me carefully. You can't ask Uncle Glen because there is no 'Uncle Glen'. He's just a driver. We don't know him any better than the other passengers on this bus. Have you got that?'

Susan wondered if he saw the irony in lecturing Luca considering he had been about to call their son by his real name.

'This is important,' Robert continued, his voice raspy with nerves. 'If we get found out, it won't just be us that gets in trouble. Glen will, too. You understand that, right?'

Luca nodded, but the sides of his mouth tugged down.

Susan hated to see him like that, but it was true. A silly mistake would put them all at risk. 'Dad's right. We can't do anything to mess this up.'

Luca returned to his seat without another word.

Guilt bubbled in Susan's chest; he was leaving everything and everyone he knew behind. She resisted the urge to reach her arms around the seat and hug him. Or tickle him so she could get just a small reminder of the carefree boy she used to know.

The bus passed through large iron gates, the top of which were laced with barbed wire. She tracked it as far as she could see; it looped the facility like an unholy halo. The sight of it made her eyes prickle with tears; they'd be safe inside.

The coach pulled to a standstill and Glen ordered the passengers off. 'I've got another pickup. Get a move on, folks!' he called as the dazed passengers collected their things.

Get a move on, she thought. They couldn't be the last words she heard from her big brother. The brother who had learnt to plait her hair when their mother had been too drunk to do it. The brother who had walked her to school every morning and cooked her dinner every night, who had escorted her down the aisle despite his own reservations about her marrying 'a toff'. That couldn't be it.

Pushing Luca ahead of her, she headed for the steps leading down from the bus.

She tried to catch Glen's eye as she passed, but he stared straight ahead. It was as she brushed his side that his little finger hooked onto hers for the briefest moment before he let go.

'Goodbye,' she said, refusing to look back in case she broke down.

As soon as their feet hit dirt, Luca pulled away from her, desperate to explore. She had to clench her fists to stop herself from grabbing hold of him and pulling him back to her.

'Don't go too far,' she called after him.

She turned to Robert but realised he was missing. Looking back at the bus, she saw him standing at the top of the steps. Glen whispered something into his ear. Robert nodded, but his lips were pursed in defiance.

When he joined them, she couldn't resist asking what he'd said.

'He told me that if I didn't look after his sister and nephew, he was going to ram my head so far up my...behind that I might dislodge the stick that's embedded there.'

A snigger escaped her. 'Oh no. Sorry about that. You know he doesn't mean it.'

The awkward silence that followed suggested that he didn't. 'He is never going to forgive me, is he?' Technically he had asked her a question, but she knew it needed no answer.

She gave one anyway. 'Probably not. But don't you think it's more important that you forgive yourself?'

He looked her square in the face. 'I can't do that. Not until I know that *you* have.'

She forced enthusiasm into her words. 'Well, I guess it's your lucky day, because I have.' It wasn't a lie. She had forgiven him. But she would never forget. When she had needed him most, he hadn't been there. When looters broke into their home, he could have tried to fight them, to defend her. Instead he had chosen to run and save himself. He had been right to do so. There was nothing he could have done, not against that many men. But still, it was a hard thing to forget.

'So, can we leave all this bad feeling behind us?' she asked. 'This is supposed to be a fresh start.'

He pinned the sides of his mouth into a smile, a mechanical motion that held no warmth. 'I can. And, sick sense of humour aside, I know we owe your brother our lives.'

He wasn't wrong. Glen had been searching the details of the passengers for months to find a family they could impersonate. The Coles had been the best fit he could find. Robert Cole was a renowned architect, no doubt the reason they had been invited to join the Sanctuary. Although her own husband had not gained such heights of success, he could fill the role well enough to avoid suspicion.

'So, what now?' she asked.

In answer, a man stepped from the entrance. He sported an impressive tan and teeth straight from a Colgate advert.

'Subterranean life seems to agree with him,' Robert said. 'Nice to know there will still be time for a spot of sunbathing hundreds of metres below ground.'

'Shh!' Susan said, slapping him lightly on the arm. Still, she was happy his mood had improved.

Luca gravitated back towards them, and Susan pulled him to her side. Her breath seemed to come easier when he was near to her.

The man began to speak. 'Good afternoon and welcome to the Sanctuary. I am David Malone, one of the benefactors who made the vision of Edmond Pearse, the extraordinary gentleman to my right, a possibility. Now, if you will follow us, we'll lead you into your new home.'

'American,' said Robert. His tone was smug, as though the fact that he and David Malone shared a nationality was more than an accident of geography. Despite the fact that it was her homeland that now offered them sanctuary, quite literally, she couldn't shake the feeling that he still believed his roots superior to her own.

'Apparently even the apocalypse makes your lot unavoidable,' Susan said.

'Hey,' Luca said. 'That's not nice.'

She ran her fingers through his hair, sweeping the blond locks from his face. 'Don't worry, my love. My genes are bound to overpower your father's.'

They filed down a narrow wooden staircase. The ceiling seemed impossibly low, and as they descended, the air felt thinner.

'How are you doing?' she asked Luca, squeezing his shoulder.

'I'm fine, Mom. I'm not a baby.'

It was pointless explaining that looking after him made her braver. And she wanted to feel brave right now.

When they reached the bottom, they were led down a tunnel lit by sconces. They passed mannequins arranged in various mining scenes. Glen had told them the Sanctuary used to be a salt mine and then a tourist attraction, so it wasn't too much of a surprise. Still, the shadows cast on their lifeless faces gave her the creeps.

Droplets fell from the roof of the tunnel.

'Have we sprung a leak?' Robert asked, wiping water from his forehead with the back of his hand.

Doctor Pearse turned. 'No, it's just condensation. The main living areas of the Sanctuary are climate controlled, but we need to preserve energy. Besides, a little water never hurt anyone.'

He led them to a large wooden door. Before he pushed it

open, he flashed them a grin. 'Welcome to the Grand Chamber.'

Susan blinked against the white light that flooded the tunnel. She had to stand and allow her eyes to adjust before she could follow Pearse down a set of stone steps.

'What is this place?'

'It used to be a chapel. Now it will serve as the main assembly point for the Sanctuary,' Pearse replied. 'Please,' he said to the group, 'feel free to look around.'

Susan ran her fingertips over the bumpy surface of a carving. When somebody touched her elbow, she turned, expecting to see Robert or Luca. She jumped to find Edmond Pearse smiling at her. 'Doctor Pearse.'

'Call me Edmond, please. I didn't mean to startle you. I just wanted to say, it's a pleasure to meet you,' he said, his hand outstretched.

Robert stepped in front of her. 'The pleasure is ours,' he said, shaking Edmond's hand. 'What you've created here... it's breathtaking.'

'Thank you. We are rather proud of it.' He spoke to Robert, but his eyes were trained on Susan.

'I can't wait to get started,' Robert said. 'I know I can offer some great suggestions for how we can extend the infrastructure.'

'Sorry? Oh yes,' Edmond said, his glasses bobbing as his brow furrowed. 'No doubt you will be a great help to us. And of course, we are excited to hear the plans your wife has.'

'Me? For what?' Susan felt the blood rush from her face.

'The hospital, of course,' Pearse turned. 'David, come and meet one of our most prestigious arrivals.'

Malone flashed a smile as he reached for her hand.

'Susan Cole is a leader in the field of vascular surgery, and we are honoured to have her join our team,' Edmond said.

Susan choked on her words before she managed to spit them out. 'The honour is mine.'

David squeezed her hand a little too hard. 'Your reputation precedes you, Mrs Cole.'

'Doctor Cole,' Edmond corrected.

Susan felt sick. 'The stories are exaggerated, I'm sure.'

'You're too modest,' Edmond said. 'We must catch up soon.'

He walked away, leaving them in awkward silence.

'I too look forward to seeing what you can do,' David said. 'Now, if you'll excuse me.'

Susan and Robert stared after them.

'I'm supposed to be a vascular surgeon?' Susan's words spilt out louder than she intended.

'Shut up,' Robert said, offering a frozen smile to the people around them.

'What am I supposed to do if they need me to operate on somebody? Wing it?'

Robert spoke through clenched teeth. 'Stop panicking. We'll think of something.'

Seb

A train rattled past the platform and Seb stepped forward.

'Not that one,' Freidman said. 'It doesn't stop here. The Malkinia train transports prisoners from the labour camp back to the Treblinka penal colony.'

'There are other teams working here, too, aren't there?' Seb pointed to his blue armband. 'Otherwise, why would they go to the trouble of labelling us?'

Freidman's eyebrows bobbed. 'Are you thinking of asking for a transfer?'

'I'm hoping a friend of mine might be here.' That was a lie. Seb hoped Isaac was back at the Sanctuary, that Millicent's pleas had saved at least one of them. But if he was there, Seb needed to find him.

'It's possible he was selected for a work group on the other side of the camp, I suppose.' Freidman didn't sound convinced. 'And yes, there are other teams. The red team strip the prisoners of their clothes and take those who can't walk to the lazarett.' He pointed at a small enclosure with a cross flying above it.

'It looks like a hospital.'

'That's what they want you to think. It's just a cover for the pits below. But wooden walls can't keep in the gunshots.'

Seb winced.

'The gold team sort the valuables. They also search the arrivals for anything that they've tried to hide...especially the women.' Freidman flushed and quickly changed the subject. 'The hair cutters shave the prisoners' heads. The forest team camouflage the fences and the path that leads to the extermination area. So yes, your friend could be amongst one of the other teams.'

'It all sounds very...efficient. I'm sorry, that makes it sound as if—'

'I think that's the perfect way to describe it. A little too efficient, actually.'

'What do you mean?'

Freidman hesitated. 'Your train was the first we'd had in weeks. Everything is slowing down.'

'That's great. Maybe this will soon be over.'

'Maybe. But if there is no work left, what happens to us? I doubt the guards are going to pat us on the back and send us home. Not after what we've seen.'

'Oh.' If Seb had his way, he wouldn't be around to find out. But he couldn't leave Isaac behind. 'I need to get into the other areas to see if my friend's there.'

'There's not much chance of that. The guards don't exactly let us wander.'

'But there is a chance?'

'Nothing is impossible. You see him.' Freidman nodded towards a man painting the numbers onto a clockface. 'That's Jacob Wiernik, the camp carpenter. His work takes him into every area. Maybe he could ask around for you.'

Seb watched as Jacob added the hour and minute hand in black paint, stopping time at six o'clock forever. 'What's the point in that?'

Freidman shrugged. 'To keep the arrivals calm, I guess.'

'Do you really think a clock will do that?'

'No. But look around you. This is all fake.' Freidman was right. Ticket windows and timetables gave the impression of a working station. Signs directed visitors to the booking office and the refreshment room, and informed them of platform changes. None of it was real. 'Would you have been quite so compliant if you knew Treblinka was going to be your final stop ever?'

'I guess not.'

The rumble of the approaching train turned to a screech as it pulled in. While passengers swarmed from the cars and they waited for the path to clear, Seb noticed a guard at the side of the platform, picking out survivors and ordering them to one side. 'Where is he taking them?'

'Who knows? Probably selecting men to replace the ones that have been shot or starved to death.'

Freidman clambered into a car. While Seb's eyes were still adjusting to the gloom, he heard him say, 'Poor kid.' He was knelt beside a boy, the child's arms still wrapped around his mother. Their limbs had already begun to stiffen. Even in death they were reluctant to let go of one another. 'I don't think I'll ever get used to seeing the children.'

'I don't think I'll ever get used to any of it.'

'No. But you have to try, or you'll go insane. Are you ready?' Freidman asked.

'Never,' Seb said, climbing on board.

Jared

Jared's world, which moments before had been filled with smoke and flames and screams, became still. The dull circles of light cast through the grates bathed the sewer in an eerie dusk.

The waste from the city, heated both by the stifling summer temperatures and by the fire above, assaulted them from every side. It was thick and meaty and felt as if it was invading his every pore. Jared tried not to think of the science behind it, the inescapable truth that he was breathing in particles of the faeces in which they stood.

Beth retched. 'That's foul.'

'It's better than the alternative,' Jared said.

'No doubt. Which way?' Beth asked, like she was assuming he had a plan.

He considered pointing out that he was making it up as he went along. Instead, he told her to follow the direction of the water.

They didn't talk as they made their way through the huge arched tunnel. Usually this would have been Jared's preference. But after all that had happened, it felt like torture. 'Do you think this is my fault?' His voice sounded too loud as it rebounded back at him.

'Don't be absurd. And neither does Aaron. Not really. He's just worried and needs somebody to blame.'

'I could have given him that if I'd had the chance. I saw somebody I knew. A guardian from the Sanctuary.'

Beth was quiet for so long that he was sure she thought he was insane. Finally, she said, 'How is that possible? You told me that there were only two orbs. We have one and your grandfather took the other.'

'That's right,' Jared said, resting his hand on the swell of the orb hidden inside his tunic. 'But apparently they managed to replicate his work.'

'Who was it?' Beth stopped, placing a hand on Jared's arm so he did the same. 'You're shaking.'

Despite the heat, Jared realised he was. 'Adrenaline, I suppose, and probably shock.'

'There's something else.'

'Yes. The guardian I saw was a bit of a bully, somebody I would really rather forget.' Jared moved the conversation on, not wanting to go into details about all he'd endured, because then he'd have to remember. 'Anyway, he said he was sent by Victor Durand, a nasty piece of work who cloaks bigotry with religious piety.'

'And you think this Durand had something to do with the fire?'

Jared nodded. 'I don't know how they managed it, but somehow they changed the date the fire started by days.'

'That would have changed the course of events for a lot of people though, wouldn't it?'

'I don't know,' Jared said. 'I guess it remains to be seen how different this timeline is from the one I was expecting.'

'I'm sorry.'

'Why?'

'If I'd let you go back to the Sanctuary before we came here, none of this would have happened.'

'There was no way we could have known that. Besides, the only people to blame are the Durands and—' Jared stopped. 'Do you hear that?'

'It's the river.' Beth walked faster, her feet sloshing through the dank sewer water. As they neared the mouth of the tunnel, the gloom gave way to an early dawn light.

It was only as it illuminated them that Jared noticed the gash marring Beth's shoulder. 'You're hurt.'

'Just a scratch.'

He fished the medilaser from inside his tunic. She gave no resistance as he closed her wound.

'I need you to do something for me, Beth.'

'Anything.'

'I want you to stay he—'

'No way.'

'Listen to me. You stay here and guard the orb and the visualiser. Without them, we're stuck here.' He took the bundle from her and tugged out Edmond's pocket watch by the chain. 'I'll be back by midnight.'

'You can't know that. This is stupid. We should stay together.'

'I promise you; I'll be back.' He looked at the fading streak where her wound had been minutes ago. 'I won't let them hurt anybody else,' Jared said. 'I'll find Aaron and Nell. Then we will pay a visit to the Sanctuary. This needs to end.'

The Book of Durand

It was a week before the next bus load of citizens arrived. Despite being new myself, I felt knowledgeable, superior even, to the scared group that Pearse shepherded in.

'You like watching people, don't you? You always seem to be skulking in the shadows.' I hadn't heard Malone approach from the tunnel behind me.

'Sorry,' I said, turning to head back to our unit.

'Wait.' He rested his hand on the opposite wall, blocking my path. 'It was an observation, not a criticism. Stay and keep me company. I've heard this speech more times than I can remember. I could use a distraction.'

'Okay.' I turned back to the Grand Chamber, where Pearse addressed the new arrivals. I could feel David's eyes studying me. 'What's your name?'

'Martin.'

'Not much of a talker are you, Martin?

I shrugged. 'Words are overrated.'

'Really? Tell me more.'

I could hear my father's voice in my head demanding that I walk the line and say what he wanted to hear, but I was in no mood to listen. 'Well, just look at that lot, lapping up every syllable. At the end of the day, Pearse and the others will look after themselves first, no matter what they tell us.'

Malone's eyebrows shot up. 'So cynical for one so young.'

I chose not to comment.

'I think you underestimate how many people care about you in the Sanctuary, Martin.'

I laughed, but it was heavy, harsh, like the grating of

metal on metal. 'Really? Well, that's all right then.' I was embarrassed to realise that tears stung my eyes and crowded my throat. I swallowed them down, a solid lump of anguish.

Malone didn't say anything for the longest time. When he did, his voice was flat. I preferred it; it sounded more honest. 'You're right. At the end of the day, you can only ever rely on yourself. And if your family is anything like mine were, then they aren't to be trusted either.'

My brain took one word from his sentence and high-lighted it in neon. Were.

'Your family are dead?'

He sniffed, his nose twitching in distaste. 'Maybe. Probably.'

'You don't care?'

He looked surprised by this question, as though he'd never considered it. 'I don't think about them at all, to be honest. They gave up on me a long time ago. It was only right I returned the favour.'

I couldn't help rolling my eyes at this. The end of the world was in full flow, and he stood there in a well-cut suit. 'Oh yeah, you must have been such a disappointment to them.'

He smirked. 'Money didn't impress them. Besides, if I've been successful, it's in spite of them, not because of them. I haven't seen them since I was little more than a teenager.' He fell silent and I thought maybe I'd misjudged him, that perhaps his air of indifference was just a shield. Then he added, 'The friends you choose are your real family. The one you're born into is just a matter of luck, and some of us are dealt a bad hand.'

'I thought you said that you should only rely on your-self?' I said, a little smug.

'Oh, I stand by that. But friends can be...useful.' He nodded towards the crowd. 'Perhaps you should consider making some.' He clapped me on the back as he walked past me into the chamber. 'I'll see you around, Martin.'

I scanned the crowd. Every eye was trained on Pearse. Desperation leaked from their pores. They were all looking for some kind of saviour, something to cling to. One another, religion, and now the Sanctuary. I didn't begrudge them their hope. It's just that the constant fear and anxiety had begun to bore me a long time ago. I didn't see how any of these people could hold my interest, let alone be useful to me.

With one exception. A boy, about my age, sat slumped against the side of the chamber. He fidgeted with something at his side. I walked over to him to get a better view of what he was doing. As I neared him, he stopped and looked at me for a moment, before carrying on. Apparently, I was not considered a threat. How wrong he was.

I crouched down next to him and watched as he wore a ridge into the salt rock with the buckle of his bag. He'd already inscribed a G and was working on the next letter. 'What are you doing?'

'I think that's pretty obvious.' His mouth twisted into a sneer as he spoke. I liked him immediately.

'Okay, then. Why?'

'Why not?'

I couldn't argue with his logic.

'What's your name?' I asked.

He let out a little snort as if I'd said something funny. 'Luca.'

'I'm Martin.'

'Well, Martin, is this place as boring as it looks?'

'Worse,' I said. 'I can show you around if you want.'

He shrugged but got to his feet. 'I may as well find out what I've got myself into.'

Susan

Robert rifled through the boxes that filled the unit they'd been allocated.

'What are you looking for?' Susan asked.

'Information. Anything that will tell us what exactly it is your brother has got us into.' He shuffled papers before discarding them on the floor.

'You can't blame Glen. He didn't know.'

'Who do I blame then?' His words were cutting, a challenge.

'Keep it down; he'll hear you.' Susan walked to the bedroom, where Luca was unpacking his things, and closed the door. When she had explored his new room with him, she avoided looking at the boxes that contained Luca's things. The real Luca. The family had sent their things ahead, probably with no inkling that they wouldn't arrive to claim them.

Robert held a certificate up towards her. 'Glen told us that Robert Cole had earned an invitation to the Sanctuary for his architectural work. But they aren't interested in him, are they?'

Susan wondered if this was what really bothered him. He had liked the idea of being the superstar; his own architectural career was mediocre at best.

'Now we're stuck down here with...' He faltered, rubbing his hands over his face. '...with no explanation for what happened to the real Cole family.'

'We know what happened to them. Glen just didn't pick them up.'

Robert rolled his eyes. 'You don't believe that any more than I do.'

She stared at him open-mouthed. 'Glen would never hurt anyone. Especially not a child.'

'Really? He's threatened me more than once over the years.'

'That's just banter, and you know it.' Tears threatened at the insinuation.

Robert sat next to her and draped an arm over her shoulders. But it didn't feel comforting. It felt cold, mechanical.

'I'm sorry, you're right,' he said. 'It's just if they find out that we're not who we say we are, then some uncomfortable questions are going to be asked.'

'An hour ago, you were telling me not to panic, that it was going to be all right.'

'And it will be,' he said. 'We just have to find as much information out about the Coles as we can so that we can keep up the cover story for as long as possible.'

'Then what?'

'I'm not sure,' he said with a weak smile. 'Who knows, maybe by that point we'll have proved ourselves so useful that they'll show us mercy.'

A knock at the door made them both jump, and for a moment they sat staring at it.

'I'll get it.' Robert peered through the crack in the door. 'Can I help you?'

A short balding man regarded him over the top of his glasses. 'No,' he said. 'But your wife can. I'm Doctor Reed.'

Susan wanted to vomit. Instead, she braced herself and walked towards the door.

Robert widened it so she could see out.

'Nice to meet you. I'm Susan Cole.'

He didn't return her smile. 'I thought as we would be working closely together, I should be one of the first to welcome you.'

'That's very kind.'

He flapped away her comment. 'And when can we expect to see you at the hospital?'

'Soon, I hope. We need a little time to settle in, to get our son adjusted to all this.'

He grumbled to himself. 'I suppose that's a reasonable request. But there is much to do, and I'm keen to get started.'

'As am I. It was so nice of you to introduce yourself, but I have to go and help my son unpack.'

Reed opened his mouth to add something as Susan closed the door.

'Sure,' she said to Robert, with her back pressed against the wood. 'Everything is going to be fine.' He didn't rise to the sarcasm coating her words.

She forced a smile when she heard the click of Luca's door. 'Hey, buddy. How's the unpacking going?'

'I didn't have much to unpack. The rest of it's not mine.'

'Yeah, but there might be something interesting in—'

'It's not mine. I doubt the real Luca would want me going through his stuff.'

Robert puffed out a long breath and massaged the bridge of his nose. Then he sat down on the sofa, patting the cushions in a sign for Luca to join him.

Susan had no desire for another instalment of the lecture she knew was coming, so she busied herself with unpacking a box of books and slotting them onto a shelf. She turned one of the books over. 'Vascular and Endovascular Surgery: The

Specialist's Companion.' She wondered if the 'For Dummies' series did a book on the same topic.

'Listen to me carefully,' Robert said. 'You *are* the real Luca. The only one that matters any— Are you okay?'

Susan was by Luca's side before the book she'd been holding hit the floor. 'Luca? Can you hear me?' She watched as his pupils, one moment so large they bullied the soft brown from his eyes, contracted to the size of a pinprick. He swayed towards her before his muscles began the rhythmic pulse she'd become too familiar with.

'Help me,' she said. They lay him on his side on the floor.

His head jerked and Susan heard a solid clunk as his temple struck the leg of the coffee table.

'Move that,' she said.

However, the instruction was unnecessary as Robert was already shoving it into the middle of the room. 'It'll just be the excitement of the day,' he said over his shoulder. 'Once everything has settled down, he'll feel better.'

'And if he doesn't?'

'Then...' He threw his hands up. 'Then we say it's a new condition that he's only developed since we entered the Sanctuary.'

Susan felt a sob building up in her chest. It was as much of a surprise to her as anyone when it turned out to be a laugh. She scooted backwards on her bottom and sat with her back against the wall, trying to swallow her giggles.

'What is wrong with you?' Robert asked. Luca had become still beside him, and he rubbed the boy's shoulder.

She tried to contain her laughter, but the more she gulped it down, the more tears pooled at the corners of her eyes. 'I was just thinking, how lucky it is that it's the child of a renowned vascular surgeon who develops epilepsy.'

Robert threw daggers in his glare. 'I don't find that very funny.'

Susan cupped her hands over her mouth but still hiccups escaped. 'Believe me, neither do I.'

Seb

As they arrived for the evening roll call, the tension in the air set Seb's nerves jangling.

'Those of you who arrived today, line up this side,' the guard said, raising his right hand. 'The rest of you this side.'

Seb went to move, but Freidman grabbed his arm, giving his head an almost imperceptible shake.

Agitated, the guard barked the order again. 'New arrivals to the right, current prisoners to the left!'

The men looked at each other but none of them moved.

'I don't know which, but one group or the other is going to end up in the lazarett,' Freidman whispered.

The guard signalled to his comrades, and a wall of grey marched towards them. 'Perhaps you need a little persuasion.'

A flurry of men broke off in either direction, but Seb and Freidman stayed with the others and backed towards the building behind.

While they edged away, Seb noticed a lone figure moving forwards. The guard barely registered Tomas's presence as he walked towards him. It was only when Tomas broke out into a sprint that he screamed for help.

Seb saw a glint as Tomas pulled something from under his shirt. Then he lunged at the guard, striking him on the neck. No, not striking, Seb realised, as the guard clutched his throat and blood seeped from between his fingers. Stabbing.

Prisoners and guards alike froze as the man fell to his knees. He fingered the blade protruding from his neck, and as blood began to pump from his wound, he pawed at the trousers of his nearest comrade. Fear seemed to leave his body along with the blood that pooled around him, and he slumped forward.

'We're going to pay for that,' Freidman said.

The sound of gunfire shocked the prisoners into silence, limbs frozen in a depraved game of musical statues.

The only man to move was Tomas. He stretched his arms wide, chest exposed. 'Come on then. I'm ready to be with my family.'

The guard nearest to him was happy to oblige. Picking up a shovel discarded by one of the work teams, he approached Tomas from behind and brought it down hard on his head. Tomas's skull caved with a sickening crunch. For a moment he staggered, bringing his hand up to the side of his oddly flattened head. Then he fell to the floor, lifeless.

The air suddenly felt too thin, like Seb couldn't draw enough into his lungs. 'We should run.'

'We'd be dead before we even hit the fence,' Freidman said.

'Manchuk, what is this?' An officer strode from the direction of one of the storage buildings.

The guard tossed the shovel onto Tomas's body. 'He killed Kovalenko.'

Freidman nudged Seb in the ribs. 'Keep your eyes down. That's Kurt Franz, the deputy commander.' Even in his hushed tone, Seb could hear the tremor in Freidman's words.

Seb looked at the officer, who now stood over the two bodies. He knew there were no age limits on cruelty. His dealings with the Durands had taught him that. But in his black uniform, Franz looked like a child playing dress up.

Franz turned to the SS officer nearest. 'Kuttner, bring Galewski to me now.'

The crowd parted as the officer strode towards them.

'Why Galewski?' Seb asked.

'He's the camp elder,' Freidman said. 'Uneasy is the head that wears the crown.'

The guards turned to the crowd, ready to search, but there was no need. Galewski stepped forward from the ranks and walked towards Franz, stride steady.

Franz looked Galewski up and down. 'Fifty lashes.'

The guards grabbed Galewski's arms, but he shook them off. 'I can walk.' He made his way to a nearby bench and lay with his torso against the stone.

Franz spoke into his ear: 'You will count every lash. If you go wrong or hesitate, we will go back to number one.' He nodded for the guard to begin.

The whip sliced through the air. 'One.' Galewski grunted. 'Two...' Seb looked away, his shoulders jerking in sympathy with each slash.

'You're barely marking him,' he said to the guard. This was a lie. Galewski's back was crosshatched with bright red welts. 'Harder.'

By the end of the punishment Galewski's skin had been transformed into a bleeding mass of raw meat, but he did not falter in the counting once.

Finally, Franz grabbed Galewski by the hair and yanked back his head. 'Any more violence against my men and your camp elder will be shot,' he promised the horrified prisoners. 'And the rest of you right after him.'

'Are we done?' Galewski asked.

'Not quite,' Franz said, letting go of his head. He turned to the guards. 'Select ten men and shoot them.'

'No.' Galewski tried to get up but didn't have the strength.

The guards began to yank prisoners from the group. Seb fixed his eyes on the dusty earth and prayed. Shiny boots stopped just paces from him.

'Please, no.' The prisoner next to Seb fell over his own feet as he was hauled to the front.

'Look at them!' Franz walked along the line of ten men. 'One of ours, ten of yours.'

Terrified, a couple tried to run. Most accepted their fate. The conclusion was the same. A hail of bullets rained down on them, and in seconds it was over.

Jared

Jared stalked through the city. Pillars of smoke blighted the horizon in every direction. He was thankful that, for now at least, the streets he walked were untouched. He feared this had changed when he heard shouts from nearby. By the time he got there, people had gathered, blocking his view.

A group of men were being led in a line, their hands bound. Stones and rubbish struck them, and they cowered away.

All that is except for one. Aaron walked at the back of the line. Scraps of rotting food showered him, but he didn't even flinch.

'What's going on?' Jared asked the man next to him.

From the tirade of Latin that the man gave, Jared managed to pick out one word. Christianus.

'No!' Jared pushed his way through the crowd. 'Aaron, listen to me! They're going to execute you.'

Aaron's eyes flitted towards him, but he kept walking.

Jared kept pace with him, citizens grumbling as he pushed past them. 'Aaron, they think the Christians are responsible for the fire. If you don't get away now, they will torture and kill you.' It chilled him to remember the accounts he had read whilst preparing for the visit. Men ripped apart by dogs, crucified or used as human torches; Jared wouldn't let that happen to his friend.

'Just shut up, Jared. These are the men who took Nell. They're taking me straight to her. Once we're together, we'll find a way out.'

'That's a stupid plan. We'll find her together. I won't risk losing you, too.' Jared scoured the streets around him for something he could use as a weapon and found nothing. He ran his thumb over the medilaser. It was capable of cutting flesh, but the last thing Jared wanted was to start dissecting the citizens. Instead, he aimed it at a nearby statue of the Emperor Nero and flicked it on. The bronze began to glow as he guided the beam across its throat.

A woman next to him, seeing what he was doing, began to shout. 'Maleficus! Maleficus!'

The people around Jared surged away, screeching in terror, as the head of Nero's statue rolled onto the street.

The guards leading the prisoners marched towards Jared, spears aimed right at him. He easily cut through the wooden shaft with the medilaser. They dropped the stumps to the floor and followed the retreating crowd.

The prisoners, seeing the destruction and panic Jared had caused, tried to escape. However, bound together in a long line by both hands and feet, they fell to the floor in a heap.

As Jared approached, some tried to crawl away. Tethered to their companions, they got no further than the edge of the road.

'I'm not going to hurt you,' Jared said, but they couldn't understand him, so his words did nothing to calm them.

Jared grabbed Aaron's arms and used the beam of the medilaser to slice through the rope entwining them. The man next to him, seeing what Jared had done, raised his own hands. Jared freed him and every other man who followed. Soon, all the prisoners were fleeing in different directions.

'Aaron, please,' Jared said. 'Let's find her together.'

'I was wrong to blame you, Jared. Maybe it's me. I'm a jinx.'

'No, none of this is your fault. But I know who is responsible. This fire was no accident. Come with me, and I'll explain who is really to blame.'

They moved fast, just in case the emperor's guards came back with reinforcements.

'Are you going to tell me what you meant?' Aaron asked.

'Yes, when we're somewhere safe.' Jared had taken several steps before he realised Aaron wasn't following.

'No. Now.'

'Okay. The fire wasn't an accident. Somebody lit it on purpose.'

'Who?' Aaron's face darkened.

'The man behind it is called Victor Durand. He's—'

'Oh, here we go again. I know who he is, Jared. A member of the committee back at the Sanctuary. You've told me about him time and again. Can't you just accept that you made a mistake? Not everything revolves around that place, you know.'

'You don't understand. This time it does.'

'And how exact—' Aaron froze. 'What is he doing?'

Jared turned and saw a man clasping a burning torch. He tossed it into one of the wooden shacks. The timber ignited in a dramatic woosh.

Aaron ran at him. 'Why did you do that? That was somebody's home.' He punched the man, and his jaw snapped together in a sickening clunk. He slid down the frame of the burning building, his hands raised to protect his face, and pleaded with them in Latin. Nero was the only word they could pick out.

'It looks like you were right about one thing,' Aaron said. 'Someone lit the fire on purpose.'

'Yes, there was a rumour that Nero ordered Rome to be burnt. But not in the area where the tavern was and not then.'

'I give in. Tell me how you know it wasn't this guy who started it.' Aaron stamped a foot in the direction of the cowering man, and he scarpered away.

'That's easy. Because I know the person who did it and he basically confessed.'

'You saw him here?'

Jared nodded. 'He disappeared back through a portal before I could stop him.'

'In that case, I think I need to meet him for myself. Once we've found Nell, we're going to the Sanctuary.'

The Book of Durand

I didn't want to be there. I'd tried begging and sulking but neither had worked; at that time, they were the only weapons I had in my arsenal.

'We've been handpicked, invited personally,' my father had said. 'It would be rude not to go and see what it's about.' No, that wasn't a slip of the tongue. He'd said 'we' not 'you'.

So I sat in the pews with the other boys, all of us around fourteen, listening to how we were 'the future and the best hope of the Sanctuary'. I know, ironic.

It was Caleb Moss who spoke to us. You remember him, right? The one you left for dead.

'Tasks will include learning practical skills such as sewing and woodwork, but also those that will be needed to survive on the surface: orienteering and first aid, for example.'

I tried to focus. Whenever my attention wavered, my father would elbow me or hiss his disapproval.

And the whole time, I couldn't shake the feeling I was being watched. You know what I mean: eyes creeping over your skin like probing fingers. I don't know if I was more or less disturbed to realise that it wasn't my imagination.

David looked away the first few times, but eventually he winked at me, as though we'd been playing a game and I'd won.

After that, I kept my eyes trained on Moss.

When the speech was finished, the parents circulated with their children.

My father gave an audible gulp, which made me look up

to find David approaching us, the full force of his beaming smile directed at me.

'Mr Malone...' Father said, his hand outstretched.

'David, please.' He turned his attention to me. 'So, what did you think of the talk, Martin? Has it inspired you to sign up to the Elite?'

He remembered my name; this surprised me. 'Not really.'

'Martin!' Red spots climbed from beneath my father's collar and pooled on his cheeks.

'Don't give him a hard time,' David said. 'I want to hear his honest opinion.'

'Honestly, I don't want to be a drone. I can see how it might work for this lot, but it's not for me.'

My father spluttered his disbelief. 'I'm so sorry. He doesn't know—'

'He knows exactly what he's saying,' David said. 'And he's right. Some people are made to be minions. Others are made for leadership, and that's exactly why we need you, Martin. Think about it; just because you start as a private, doesn't mean you have to remain one.' He leant in and lowered his voice. 'Now, if you'll excuse me, I'd better go mix with the minions.' He clapped me on the shoulder as he passed. 'Oh, and Victor, I have a job that I'd like your help with. If you're still willing, that is.'

'Absolutely.'

'Great. Let's chat once this is all wrapped up.'

My father's grin was so wide that I could see his back teeth. 'Did you hear that? Leadership. It's in your DNA.' The panic he'd shown before had disappeared. With his chest puffed and with a grin wide enough to split his face, he looked giddy. 'I knew it. This place needs me. Us.'

I couldn't share his enthusiasm. Not then. Unease was bubbling within me. I couldn't shake the feeling that, no matter what I'd said, David would have claimed that in the Elite, with him, was where I belonged.

Susan

'You did what?' Susan asked.

'I told David Malone who we are. Well, who we aren't, anyway.' He said it as though he were telling her he'd picked up milk on the way home, rather than that he'd admitted to one of the most powerful men in the Sanctuary that they were imposters.

'But why? Why would you do that?'

He grasped her by the tops of the arms and gave her a little squeeze that she assumed was supposed to comfort her. It didn't.

'Because we can't go on like this. Sure, we could hide away until we are found out and banished, or worse. Or we can take control of the situation.'

'But you haven't put us in control. You've done the opposite of that. At least we still had the option to leave if we wanted, to tell them we'd decided this life wasn't for us.' She shrugged her arms free. 'You've taken away what little choice we had left.'

'Choice?' He spoke through gritted teeth. 'Take our sick son out into that wasteland or wait for them to discover the truth and execute us. Some choice.'

'Yes, you said it yourself, Robert, the word 'or'. Pretty much the definition of a choice. The options may not have been great, but they were ours. Now you've handed any control we had over to him of all people. Why?'

He pushed past her and slipped on the shoes he'd left by the door. 'You wouldn't understand.'

'Then explain it to me.'

'I needed to do something to protect my family. He

understands that. After all, isn't that the point of this place, to preserve what we have left?'

Susan groaned. 'You're an idiot.' She spat the last word at him. At first, she felt silly, directing such a schoolyard taunt at him.

But when his face darkened, she knew it had made the required impact. 'Say what you want about me, but at least I'm doing something to sort this mess out.'

Adrenaline pulsed through her body and she gnawed at the cuticle around her thumb nail. 'We need to pack. You start and I'll find Luca. I'm not sure what I'll tell them but...where are you going?'

He knelt, tying his shoes. 'David wants to see us. Both of us.'

Susan's eyes widened. 'What does he want?'

'To talk. To help.'

'Dear God, can you be that stupid? He'll have the guardians waiting to drag us away.' She was already picturing it, a guardian either side, her feet trailing behind her as they hauled her out with everyone watching. Would they tell Luca first, she wondered? Or would they kill her and break the news to him later?

'You're just dismissing this because it was my idea. If you'd come up with it, you'd just expect me to fall in line.'

The hypocrisy of his words made her splutter. 'I moved to America for you, gave up my career. But even if that were true, which you know damn well it isn't, it's not an idea you've suggested. You've already done it.'

He waved away her protest. 'Anyway, we are meeting him in the old museum. We better get moving.'

As they pulled the unit door closed behind them, she

considered stopping to lock it but decided not to bother. Soon, everyone would know who they weren't and that hardly anything in the place they'd made their home belonged to them. Not even their names.

She followed him robotically through the tunnels. As they reached the doors to the museum, he stopped. 'Whatever happens, we'll get through it. Together, we can face anything.'

She didn't dignify his comment with a response. What was the point when her opinion meant so little to him anyway?

The door screeched as he pushed it open. Most of the exhibits were covered in sheets. They had slipped from a few, exposing the glass cases below.

'I was beginning to think you'd changed your mind about meeting,' David said as he leant against a large rock-crushing machine.

Susan glowered at him, before turning to survey the room. 'Why did they keep all of this stuff?'

'Because it's part of the Sanctuary's history,' David said. 'And none of us are anything without a past. Besides,' he said, picking up a hammer from a nearby tool bench, 'look at the workmanship on these tools. It would be a sin to waste them.'

'I was just telling Susan that you've offered to help us,' Robert said.

'That's right.'

'And why would you do that?' Susan asked.

David gave this some thought. 'Because I've done things that I'm not proud of to survive, too. It's human nature, and I don't think that should come with a death sentence.'

Susan hesitated. 'Well, thank you. What did you have in mind?'

'In all honesty, I have no idea. I don't think we can pass you off as Susan Cole long term. For now, we can only delay the inevitable.'

'How do you plan to do that?' Susan asked.

David didn't answer her. Instead, he nodded at Robert.

'This will only hurt for a minute,' Robert said, pinning her hand to the belt of the rock crusher.

'What do you mean?' she asked, wriggling from his grasp. 'Let me go.'

'Are you intending to help with this or not?' David asked.

Susan thought he was talking to her until she saw somebody step from the shadows. The reverend.

'Help me,' she said. 'I want to leave.'

David passed him the hammer. 'What's it to be?'

Durand looked into her eyes as he raised the hammer over her hand. 'Remember, this is for your family.'

The Book of Durand

Whilst I tried to build a life for myself, my parents filled their days with accusations. Father swore that he had no idea Millicent would be in the Sanctuary until we saw her. Mamma did not believe him for a second.

The ease with which they fell back into old patterns saddened me, but it was no surprise. I, too, took up old habits. Wherever possible, I disappeared into the background, making myself as inconspicuous as a piece of worn furniture.

On the day that changed things, I was attempting to sneak past them and out of the unit. Sneak is probably the wrong word, because if I'm honest, I doubt they'd have cared what I was up to. I just didn't want to be drawn into their drama.

'I can only assume that the diocese arranged her place here as they did ours,' Father said. It appeared the same argument was doing yet another loop. 'You know how generous she was with her donations. It makes sense that they'd have allocated her a place.' He reached out a cautious hand and placed it on Mamma's shoulder. 'You have to believe me; I had no idea she was here.'

She regarded his hand the same way she might a mosquito landing upon her and slapped him away just as viciously.

'I don't have to believe anything you say. You're treacherous and manipulative and I would have been better off on the surface without you.'

Father noticed me heading for the door. 'Look, you need to stop this; you're upsetting Martin.'

'*I'm* upsetting Martin?' Her voice was a whisper, the calm before she unleashed the storm. '*I'm* upsetting Martin?' She launched herself at him, her tiny fists beating on his chest.

'Serena, please!' He pushed her backwards onto the sofa. She sprang to her feet, grabbing at anything within reach that could be used as ammunition. Cushions, plastic dishes and clothing were launched across the room. It didn't sate her anger, though. In fact, it seemed to rile her more. There was no satisfying smashing of crockery or shattering of glass; it is hard to express frustration in a place designed so that nobody can cause harm.

Fists balled at her side, hair wild, she let out a furious wail.

Then the lights went out.

Her cry was snuffed out with them, although I didn't notice at first; it was replaced so seamlessly by the shrill whine of a siren.

'What's going on?' I asked, feeling my way through the darkness. Finding my mother's bony wrist, I clung to her.

She shook me off. 'Victor, where are you?'

'Right here.' Father drew us both to him.

'I'm frightened,' she said.

'Don't be,' he replied, although he didn't qualify this comment with any reassuring reasons.

We stood like that, huddled together, the whole time the darkness blanketed us. Without any light from a window or from beneath the crack of the door to guide us through our unfamiliar surroundings, we did not dare to move. We were shrouded like that for so long that the muscles in the back of one of my legs began to tic in protest.

When the lights finally flicked back on, Mamma stepped out of my father's embrace.

'What happened?' I asked. Nobody answered and, because my own ears still rang despite the muting of the siren, I chose to believe that they didn't hear me.

Father went to the door and jiggled the handle. 'Locked,' he said, though that fact was already obvious to us both.

Mamma busied herself with picking up the things she had thrown, as if the light had also bought reason. She froze, a cushion clutched to her chest, when the tannoy announcement began. 'All citizens are to proceed to the Grand Chamber.'

When we stepped out of our unit, we joined a stream of people all heading in the same direction. They speculated about the cause of the alarm.

As we filed into the Grand Chamber from our various tunnels, most citizens filled the pew nearest them. Not Father. He tugged Mamma forward towards the front.

I felt fraudulent sitting there, like a regular guest sitting amongst family at a wedding. My father, however, sat bolt upright, head held high. He was exactly where he wanted to be.

It took only ten minutes to seat all the citizens; you have to remember that the population was much smaller then. But we were left there, with no word as to the reason, for far longer.

Finally, Pearse and Malone entered from a door at the back of the chamber.

They stopped there, their heads so close together that I strained to hear them over the babble behind us.

'I can't. I just can't,' Pearse said. He removed his glasses and rubbed the bridge of his nose. It looked to me as if he was verging on tears.

Father gave me a sideways glance, his eyebrows arched. He was as intrigued as I.

'Then don't.' Malone gave Pearse's arm a comforting pat. 'Let me take on this burden for you.'

Pearse faltered. He looked over the crowd, and for a moment his eyes met mine. He quickly looked away. 'You're sure?'

'Edmond, you can't do this all alone. Let me help you.'

Pearse nodded.

Malone took his place behind the lectern. 'Fellow citizens, I address you today under tragic circumstances. On the surface, over a hundred metres above our very heads, the city of Krakow has fallen victim to an earthquake. Reports are still coming in, but it appears the damage has been...catastrophic. My thoughts are with those of you with family still on the surface in this region.' He paused, waiting for the murmuring voices to stop. 'We regret the need to have actioned emergency protocols so soon, but your safety is paramount. The reinforced units are the safest place for you in such circumstances. Saying that, the spectacular design created by Doctor Pearse and his team withstood the quake impeccably.' He turned to Pearse and began a round of applause that was echoed by citizens across the chamber.

'You may ask, 'what now?' Our plan remains the same, although our timeline may be somewhat accelerated. With conditions on the surface deteriorating so rapidly, we will need every one of you working to your full potential.

'But for today, at least, let's take some time to reflect on the losses sustained above and to appreciate how lucky we are to be safe down here. Thank you.'

As soon as Malone stepped from the lectern, the room erupted. Islands of grief sprang up around the chamber and condolences were offered.

Father didn't join in, though. He shooed me from the pew so he could get out. Then he headed for Malone. Through habit rather than forethought, I followed him.

'Can I help?' my father asked, trailing behind Malone.

'We have it all under control.'

'But...'

David stopped. 'But what?'

My father lowered his voice. 'I've proven myself useful, haven't I?'

'Very. And you can be sure, when I next need your particular skill set, I will be in touch.' David must have noticed my father's shoulders slump, because he added, 'I mean it, Victor. I think you, and the rest of your family, could be a real asset to the Sanctuary.'

Father beamed as David walked away. 'You see, Martin. Class recognises its own. I've got a good feeling about this.' He walked towards my mother, who was still seated in the pew.

'Doesn't this bring perspective to everything, Serena? All of those lives lost. Shouldn't we do everything we can to build a happy life down here?'

Her arms were wrapped tightly around her. 'I don't have a lot of choice, do I? I can't exactly leave you.'

He knelt next to her and cupped her face in his hands. 'My love, don't talk like that. Until death do us part, remember.' He held a hand out to me and I took a seat at the edge of the pew. 'We're a family. All three of us are safe and together. There are people on the surface who would kill for this opportunity.'

Little did we realise, somebody already had.

Chapter Four

The Book of Durand

'Luca!' I did an awkward half run, not wanting to look too keen, to let on just how desperate I was for company. 'Didn't you hear me calling you?'

'No,' he said, jamming his hands into his pockets.

'Well, I've been chasing you since the cafeteria.'

He wrinkled his nose. 'Why?'

'I don't know. I thought we could hang out.'

Luca strode on without looking at me.

'Maybe I could show you the lake,' I added. My words were framed with rasping breaths. 'Could you just stop and talk to me for a minute?'

When he looked at me, I understood his reluctance.

The eyelid on his right side was swollen and shiny, leaving just a slit for him to see through.

'Wow, what happened to you?'

He tutted. 'Walked into a door.'

'Did...did someone do that to you on purpose? Was it your father?'

Luca's face flushed with colour. 'Don't you ever talk about my father like that. Ever. Do you hear me?' He clenched his fists by his sides.

'All right. I'm sorry.'

He puffed out his breath and the tension in his frame disappeared with it. 'Good. Well, make sure you don't.'

I shadowed his steps as he continued down the tunnel. 'Where are you going?'

'I don't know. To walk, to burn off some energy.'

'My father made me join this programme called the Guardian Elite. Apparently we'll get to do orienteering, camping, all that kind of stuff. Maybe you could give it a try.'

He didn't say anything for a while. 'How do I join?'

'I'm not sure. I was invited.'

He gave a little snort. 'They'll never want me.'

'Why not?'

'They just won't. I'm not exactly a team player.' His top lip twisted when he said the word 'team'.

But still, ten minutes later we were following David as he orbited the dining room, chatting to the new arrivals.

After we got under his feet one too many times, he stopped. 'We already have a full class. Perhaps when we extend the—'

'Please!' The word had more force than I'd intended, and I lowered my voice, embarrassed. 'You're the one who suggested that I make some friends.'

'I did, didn't I?' He clicked his tongue as he stared at the pair of us. 'Who are your parents, Luca?'

Luca stood a little taller as he began to reel off facts. 'My father is Robert Cole. He was top of his class at Harvard. His designs changed the way people thought about green architectural designs.'

'Oh, really,' Malone said. 'That was my line of work, too. It didn't do us any good though, did it? We're all still stuck here.'

'No, I guess not.' In just two sentences, David managed to flatten the first bit of enthusiasm I had seen from Luca.

'And your mother?' David asked.

'My mother?' Luca's brow wrinkled.

'Yes, you know, that woman who's been hanging around your unit.'

'She's just...my mother,' Luca said.

David smirked. 'A worthy role, too. But we both know that she's far more than that.'

Luca flicked a sideways glance in my direction. I shrugged in return.

'I see,' David said, although what it was he saw I had no idea. Not then, anyway. 'Forgive my rudeness. You seem the loyal sort, Luca. And we can always make room for loyal people in the Elite. Isn't that right, Martin?'

It wasn't a lie. I know now that was how David operated, manipulating the lost and broken with half-truths and promises. Luca and I were exactly the type he looked for, broken boys who would follow his every command. And, although David might not have been around to complete his project, when he disappeared, my father was only too happy to make his vision a reality.

~

Seb

The men perched on the edges of their bunks, listening to Zialo Bloch's story. When Freidman had introduced them, Zialo had been friendly enough. Still, Seb had grown wary of those who held court with such ease. He had experience with silver-tongued leaders who would smile at your face while plunging a knife in your back.

'The German troops took the people of Warsaw by surprise, striking at dawn.' Zialo's sunken eyes glimmered. 'But they resisted. The people fought fiercely. Using only their small stockpile of weapons, their bare hands and their ingenuity, they managed to reclaim key posts within the ghetto an—'

A sneer from a nearby bunk sliced through the good mood.

'You have something to add, Kuba?' asked Zialo through clenched teeth.

'Just don't forget to tell them how it ends.'

Zialo pressed his lips into a hard line.

'Have you forgotten that part?' Kuba asked. 'Let me help you. Three days later the Germans massacred a thousand Jews in the main square. That is where resistance gets us.'

'You would rather give up and die here?' Zialo asked.

'No! I would rather live! And the best way to do that is to keep our heads down and wait for the allies to come.' Kuba's voice softened. 'I for one don't want to end up like Tomas Silva. But many of us will before tomorrow is over.'

A panicked chatter broke out amongst the men.

Zialo shushed them. 'Have you heard something?'

'Do you think just because I'm the barracks leader that

they bother to tell me anything? No. But experience tells me that it won't end there. Ten men won't satisfy them. I doubt a hundred will.' Kuba swallowed and his Adam's apple bobbed. 'Personally, I'm going to do whatever I can to make sure I am not amongst that number. Now, get ready for lights out, all of you.'

Soon darkness covered the room and Seb listened to the breathing of the men hemming him in from every direction. He envied those who so easily welcomed the escape of sleep. Hungry and thirsty, he longed for rest, but his brain refused to cooperate.

Even the short snippets of sleep he managed were plagued by nightmares. Perhaps it was dehydration that guided his unconscious mind to the lake in the Sanctuary. He saw his own hands, holding Jared under the water. Nausea churned his stomach as the boy thrashed against his grasp. The familiar cackle of Martin Durand echoed through the cavern.

Seb awoke, heart pounding. When the drumming in his ears subsided, he heard whispers from the other side of the barracks. Abandoning the idea of sleep, he went to investigate. Kuba let out a ragged snore as he tiptoed past his bunk.

A small gathering of men huddled around Zialo's bed at the other end of the room.

'Kuba was right about one thing; they won't leave it there. But that doesn't mean we give up. Now's the time to resis—'

Seb accidentally nudged the dimmed lamp with his foot, sending the shadows dancing. The men fell silent.

'Who's there?' Zialo asked.

Seb stepped from the gloom. 'I'm sorry...I just...'

'How much did you hear?'

'Not much,' Seb said. Which was true. But he wanted to hear more, to know there was hope that he might escape this place and somehow get home.

Zialo turned to Freidman. 'Is he trustworthy?'

Freidman paused long enough for the hammering in Seb's chest to begin again. 'I think so.'

'Please. If you're planning to resist, to escape, I want to be a part of it. I don't belong here.'

'None of us do.' Zialo puffed out a sigh. 'Well, if Freidman is willing to vouch for you, that is good enough for me.' His eyes lingered on Freidman, who gave the slightest of nods. 'Okay, I guess you'd better come and sit down.' Zialo motioned an empty space on the bunk next to him. You know Sadovitz, Salzberg and Korland?' he asked, pointing to the other men.

Seb said he did, although he had no memory of seeing them before.

'And Marcus, of course.'

A boy, no more than fourteen, was huddled at the end of the bed, his knees pulled to his chest as though he were trying to make himself as small as possible.

'So we're agreed,' Freidman said. 'Salzberg, will it be safe for us to meet at the tailor shop tomorrow?'

Salzberg nodded. 'I'll make sure any workers I don't know well are sent on errands.'

'Then it's settled. We meet there and tell Galewski we can't put the rebellion off any longer. We have to act now while there's still time.'

'Does anybody know how he is?' Seb asked.

Sadovitz nodded. 'He'll live. For now. And in this place, that's the best we can hope for.'

Zialo got to his feet. 'Get some sleep. We're all going to need it.'

When the dawn light seeped through the wooden boards, a mixture of fear and excitement meant Seb still hadn't slept. When the guards entered, whipping the feet of the men who didn't rise fast enough, Seb was already standing at the end of the bed.

As they reached their roll-call point Kuba went up and down the line, counting the men from his barracks. He looked grey, pointing to each one with a shaky finger, stumbling over the numbers. Before he even got to the end of the second row Franz marched towards them, flanked on either side by two Ukrainian guards. Galewski trailed behind.

'It looks like Kuba was right,' Seb whispered. 'He's not finished with us.'

The three men travelled down the rows, looking into each anxious face.

'It's no good,' Franz said. 'I can't choose. Besides, it might be easier for the men to stomach if their camp elder made the selection, don't you think?' Franz slapped Galewski on the back and he flinched away.

'Fine,' Galewski said, but even from where he stood Seb could see the way the sides of his mouth tugged down. 'Freidman, come to the front.'

A gasp of disbelief went up in unison. Freidman looked around him, confused.

'I said come to the front,' Galewski repeated.

'But...' Still Freidman did not move.

One of the guards reached for his gun and marched towards him. Seb squeezed his eyes shut and waited for the shot.

From further down the row, Seb heard a familiar voice. 'Why him?' Zialo asked. 'He's strong. He can be useful.'

In equal measure, Seb wanted to applaud and shake him. The lazarett was the only likely outcome of speaking up.

It appeared Franz agreed. 'If you are that concerned for him, then you should go with him and hold his hand.'

'Where?' Zialo asked.

Franz smirked. 'I think you know.'

Scanning the crowd around him, Zialo seemed to be sizing up his options.

'Zialo, you heard the man,' Galewski said. 'Get to the front.'

Seb was surprised to watch both men walk to the front without further resistance.

'I think we need one more,' Franz said.

This time Galewski hesitated, the heat of his stare drifting over the ducked heads of the men. 'Reuben.'

Seb kept his eyes on the dirt.

'Reuben Posner,' Galewski said, a little louder.

That name, it was like an itch in Seb's brain, making him shuffle through the faces of the men he'd met since he'd arrived.

'Reuben Posner, come to the front,' Galewski said, irritation coating his words.

Then it clicked. That was him. He was Reuben Posner. Seeing no other option, Seb did as he was told.

'You can lead the way,' Franz told Galewski.

Seb joined the line of men as they followed the camp elder. Galewski had to pick someone, Seb knew that. And why not him? They barely knew one another. Still, it stung that Galewski had saved him only to send him to the extermination area.

Susan

Susan cradled her broken hand as she half-jogged to keep up with Marney. She imagined it was how most of the people in Marney's orbit felt. And not just because of her slender limbs and determined stride. Formidable. That was the word that popped into Susan's head when she thought of her. Intelligent and beautiful, she made Susan wish she'd worn something tailored. Although she'd been eyeing up the real Susan's boxes, she couldn't bring herself to look inside. Rummaging through her clothes would feel like the final insult.

Marney breezed through the door of the old museum, leaving Susan hovering on the threshold, wondering if she should follow.

'Laura, I'd like to introduce you to Susan Cole. She'll be helping out with a few lessons.'

Laura looked up but continued emptying the contents of a glass cabinet. 'Not if we don't get this place ready, she won't.'

Susan chewed on her thumbnail. 'Can I help?'

'Sure,' Laura said. 'Grab a box.'

'As much as I'd like to stay and help,' Marney said, 'I need to get back to the hospital.'

Laura winked at Susan. 'A likely excuse.'

'Don't make me feel bad,' Marney said.

'I'm just teasing. You've done more than enough already.'

Susan watched Marney disappear through the door. 'She seems friendly.'

'She is.'

Susan gave Laura the once over. Oversized shirt, which

could possibly have been made for a man, and ballet pumps. Much more her style.

'She's a bit intimidating, though. Nobody can really be that perfect, can they?'

'Marney is. But don't worry, she's lovely. Besides, I didn't think the great Susan Cole could be intimidated by anybody.'

Susan deflated. 'You've heard of me, then.'

'Oh yes. My father couldn't contain himself when he told me you'd volunteered to help out at the school.'

'Your father?'

It was only a beat, but Susan noted Laura's hesitation. 'Edmond Pearse.'

'Doctor Edmond Pearse? As in the Sanctuary founder?'

Laura turned back to the cabinet. 'The one and only.'

'Well, I guess you're from a pretty intimidating legacy yourself.'

'Yes, but I'm very much the black sheep of the family. Anyway, what led you here? I thought you'd be off saving lives or something.'

Susan held up her bandaged hand. 'Until I'm healed up, I want to be as useful as possible.'

'How did you do that?'

Susan pushed aside the memory of Durand brandishing the hammer and of Malone promising her it would be worth it. The worst one of all was Robert; the way he'd kissed her tear-stained face, comforting her as though he hadn't been key in creating her pain. 'I'm really clumsy,' she said.

Laura smirked. 'Not a great trait for a surgeon.'

'I don't open with that fact when I meet my patients. Marney and the others have the setup of the hospital under

control. But David said education would be our responsibility, too.'

'Yes... But I thought he'd want you in the main school.'

'I asked for this assignment. All of the kids deserve to be educated.' It wasn't a lie. But it also helped that she would be working away from the hospital staff and the pressure that they might realise she didn't have a clue what she was doing.

'Agreed. Well, I am happy for any help I can get.' Laura took a book from a nearby shelf and tossed it to her. 'Welcome onboard. You should find the curriculum easy enough.'

Susan ran a finger across the title. Higher Level Combined Science. One lesson ahead, she told herself; that's all she needed to stay.

Jared

They approached the Circus Maximus under a cloak of darkness. Not that it was needed in the end. Fires still raged across the city, leaving the damaged Circus area deserted.

'It's too quiet,' Aaron said as he peered out from the side street.

Jared could understand his unease. Compared to the dim alleys they'd stuck to, blazing torches flanked either side of the road leading to the Circus Maximus.

When they'd taken just a few steps down the middle of that street, Aaron stopped, his hands cupped over his mouth.

'What's wrong?' Jared asked.

Aaron's voice opened and closed wordlessly before he managed, 'Don't you see?'

Jared followed his gaze to the torch. Within the flames was the unmistakable silhouette of a human being.

'They're burning people,' Aaron said. 'Why don't you look more shocked?'

Jared didn't know how to answer that. He was disgusted, terrified, angry. But shocked, no. 'You were never supposed to see any of this. You or the guests who eventually visit. A couple of days scoping out the city, capture a few memories of the fire, and they were supposed to be gone before all this even started. All of the thrills with none of the horror.'

'What do you mean?' Aaron asked.

'It's said that Emperor Nero spread the rumour that Christians started the fire to cover the fact that he did so himself so he could rebuild Rome to his liking. This...' Jared nodded towards the blazing body. 'This is just one of the vicious ways he chose to 'punish' them.'

'You learnt about it when you researched the era?'

'Yes.'

Aaron stared down the road lined with human torches. 'You shouldn't do that,' he said. 'You don't get to choose which parts of history are remembered. History shouldn't be sanitised, or how do we learn from it? If your guests want to visit, they should see the truth. These people deserve that much.'

Jared could see what Aaron meant. And it wasn't because he worried that his guests would shy away from details such as this that he didn't show them. It was because he feared they'd want to see it for the wrong reasons.

He wasn't sure how to explain all that though, so he just said, 'Okay.'

'No!' Aaron sucked in a sharp lungful of air as if winded. 'You don't think... Could Nell...'

Jared shook his head. 'She's like a sister to me. Unless I see it with my own eyes, I'm not even considering the possibility she's gone.'

'You're right. Besides, I think we'd know. We'd feel it somehow.' Aaron kept his eyes trained on the road as they walked. 'Just a sister. I thought maybe you had, you know...'

Jared frowned.

'You're actually going to make me say it. Okay. I thought maybe you were in love with her.'

'I love her,' Jared said. 'She and Beth have been my world for over four years. Just not like that.'

'Well,' Aaron said. 'I must admit I'm a little relieved.'

The razed workshops at the circular end made it easy for them to sneak in.

'Where are the cells?' Aaron asked.

'The other end of the racing track.'

Aaron sighed. 'Of course they are.'

They kept close to the stands, hoping the shadows might offer some protection from the approaching dawn.

When they reached the other end, Jared pointed. 'Down there.' A row of small, barred windows looked out into the arena at ground level. 'You start at the other end.'

Jared dropped onto all fours and peered into the cell below. 'Nell, are you in there?'

A gasp came from within before a hand clutched his wrist. Jared couldn't understand what the man said to him. He didn't need to. His beseeching eyes said enough.

'I'm sorry,' Jared said. 'I can't help you.'

He crawled to the next cell, then the next. Each time he looked in, more voices added to the chorus of pleas from below.

'Jared, she's here,' Aaron said.

When Jared reached them, Nell's face, round and pale, looked up from the gloom. 'You came for me.'

'Of course we did,' Aaron said.

'There were wagons with caged lions in them. I think they are planning to feed us to them.' Nell let out a sob. 'Did you know that was really a thing?' Her eyes were wild.

That was exactly the point of having cells that peeked up into the arena, Jared realised. They wanted the prisoners to see what was in store for them.

'We're going to get you out,' Aaron said. He searched around for inspiration. 'Jared, do you think the medilaser will cut through these bars?'

'To be honest, I was as surprised as anybody when it managed to cut through that statue,' Jared said. 'But we can try. Stand back.' Jared aimed the beam at the metal, and it began to glow. Then it hissed before dripping to the floor.

'It's working,' Nell said.

However, her cell mates didn't share her enthusiasm. Seeing the laser melting the iron, the chatter of the people behind her turned to screams.

'Shhh!' Nell begged them. 'The soldiers will hear you.'

'Come on, Jared,' Aaron said, as though he had any control over the time it was taking. The second bar fizzled onto the cell floor.

'One more and I think I can slide through,' Nell said.

Jared focused the laser again, but this time it wavered and dimmed. 'Please, not now.'

The barking commands of a soldier could be heard from beyond the cell. As the voice got closer, the prisoners backed towards the far wall.

'Try again,' Nell said, casting terrified glances over her shoulder. 'Please.'

Jared flicked the medilaser back on, and this time it burst into life. The metal bar burned orange and melted away.

'Grab my hands,' Aaron said, pulling her up towards the window.

Nell wriggled her tiny frame through the opening with little effort, but just as her torso was free, she stopped. 'He's got my ankle.'

Jared looked through the remaining bars to see a soldier trying to drag Nell back through. Holding the medilaser in front of him, he switched it on. Nothing happened.

Nell kicked back, her foot landing square on his jaw. 'Get off me!'

The soldier fell backwards, and she was free.

Together they ran.

The damaged end of the Circus Maximus was in sight before Jared risked looking behind him. Nobody was following.

Nell slumped to her knees.

'Come on,' Aaron said, trying to haul her back to her feet.

'No. Something's wrong.' She reached over her shoulder, feeling the area there with a shaking hand.

Jared's breath caught in his throat. An arrow protruded from Nell's back. Another whooshed past his ear, landing in the dirt in front of them. 'Let's get her up.'

They ran with the girl they both loved carried between them.

The Book of Durand

I was watching a sitcom once, back when television was a thing. It was filled with canned laughter and slapstick gags that were as unfunny as they were implausible. But one of the characters said something that got me thinking. He told his friend, who was expecting his first child, not to worry because 'two ugly people make a pretty baby'.

It made me wonder if the opposite was also true. Even as they approached middle age, both of my parents were stunning. When they entered a room, they demanded the attention of everyone in it. Maybe that's how I became as ugly as I am.

I don't mean on the surface; my looks are as inoffensive as magnolia paint. The only striking feature I have is my different colour eyes, and I guess one of them is stolen from the twin I absorbed.

No, I mean underneath. Below the surface, I know I'm just layers of ugliness accumulated like decades of dust. Though I'm pretty sure if you tried to clean my layers of dirt away, you'd find nothing beneath worth polishing.

Evie sensed this as soon as we met. She looked at me like a rabbit might regard a fox, never letting me out of her sight, always ready to flee.

What? Yes, that Evie. Did you think she blinked into existence the moment you two met? You really do think the world revolves around you, don't you?

Anyway, like I was saying, she had a sixth sense about these things. She bristled when I was near. I think that's why I was so desperate for her to think I was good. If I could prove this to her, my biggest critic, then perhaps I was worth saving after all.

So, I made it my mission to move within her orbit. If she visited the lake, I made sure I was nearby, trying my best to make it look coincidental. I ensured our dinner schedules coincided. David helped with that after he noticed me staring at her; he liked to tease me, saying that he couldn't get in the way of young love.

Perhaps, had I been happy to continue to watch her from afar, things wouldn't have turned sour.

The problem was, I wasn't the only one drawn to her. And so, my only friend became my biggest competition. On the plus side, Luca was more confident around new people than I was. Without him, I doubt I'd ever have talked to her. My plan seemed to be to linger around her and hope we got to know one another through some process of osmosis.

However, Luca walked right up and introduced himself. I watched, mouth gaping open, as she laughed at something he had said.

Shuffling from foot to foot, I waited for an introduction. At last, they seemed to notice I was there.

'This is Martin,' Luca said, his voice devoid of enthusiasm.

'Hello,' she said, as though she hadn't seen me every day for weeks. 'I'm Evie.'

'I know.' The words slipped out; I hated myself sometimes. Most of the time.

Her brow furrowed. 'You do?'

'Yeah. I think we might have the same meal sitting.' I tried to sound casual.

When I looked at Luca, he was smirking, but he had the decency not to comment.

'Have you found anything interesting to do round here?' he asked her.

'Not really,' she said. 'Mostly I just hang around the lake and read. I can't believe I'm saying this, but I miss school.'

The gap between them shrank and they turned away from me as they spoke. Panic welled in my chest at the thought of being excluded. It pushed out three words, three words that I regret to this day: 'Truth or dare?'

Neither of them answered at first. They just passed a knowing smile between them.

'Dare,' Evie said at last.

This took me unawares. I hadn't thought as far as actually coming up with a dare. But as I studied the floor, wracking my brain, inspiration struck. 'You're going to visit Saint Kinga in the chapel.'

Her hand sprang up and she held her palm an inch from my face. 'No way. I'm not doing anything to the church.'

'Calm down. I'm not daring you to do anything that can't be wiped away with a tissue.'

Luca's mouth twisted in disgust. 'That's gross.'

'Lipstick,' I said, before they had any more time to explore that thought. 'You are going to put lipstick on Saint Kinga's wedding day statue.' I smirked. 'It's only right she looks her best for her big day.'

'I don't even wear lipstick,' Evie said, as though this were the biggest obstacle in her task.

'Yeah, but your mother does.' It was hard not to notice. While other people in the Sanctuary struggled by with necessities, Ruth Malloy always had a full face of makeup.

An hour later, we were scarpering away from the Malloys' unit.

Unfortunately, we ran straight into the path of Evie's stepfather.

'Hello, Mr Malloy,' Luca and I said in unison, a little too brightly.

He frowned in return. 'What are you three up to?'

'Nothing,' Evie said, clutching the lipstick behind her.

'Is that right?' He studied each of our faces. 'Then why don't you show me what's in your hand?'

Evie unfurled her clasped fingers. 'I was just borrowing it.'

Malloy sighed. 'You shouldn't be going through your mother's things.' He picked up the tube and took off the top. He twisted the bottom to reveal a pearly pink nub. 'Besides, you don't need this rubbish. You, my dear, are a natural beauty.'

Evie didn't comment. Instead she kept her eyes on the floor. When he put his finger under her chin, in an attempt to turn her face to his, she ducked away from his touch.

He wound the lipstick back down again and put the lid back on with a click. 'Put it back before she notices,' he said, handing it to her. 'And Evie, don't be in such a hurry to grow up, okay?'

She took the lipstick and headed down the tunnel. I followed after her.

'Bye, Mr Malloy,' Luca said, before jogging to catch up with us. 'Your dad seems pretty cool,' he said to Evie when he caught up.

'Stepdad,' she corrected. 'And no, he's not. He's a dick.'

'Oh.' I could tell Luca didn't know what else to say.

I, however, could have spent hours swapping notes with her on terrible parents. I hoped I'd get her alone, so I'd have the chance.

We reached the tunnel that led to the chapel.

'This one,' Evie said, pointing to one of the statues that flanked it.

'No way, the dare was—'

'This one or nothing.' Her words came out as a growl.

'Okay,' I said. 'This one it is.'

When I looked at Luca, I arched my eyebrows in a 'what's got into her?' motion. His shoulders gave a near imperceptible jerk. But neither of us were willing to say it out loud.

We kept lookout as she performed her dare. When I turned to check out her handywork, I found that Saint Kinga had been given a wide clown mouth.

'You were right,' Luca said. 'You know nothing about makeup.'

She wrinkled her nose at him.

Footfalls echoing down the hall sent us racing for cover. We dived into one of the recesses and slunk down behind a mannequin pushing a wheelbarrow.

The footsteps continued past us and disappeared.

'We nearly got caught,' Evie said. But she was smiling again and that made me happy.

'Maybe it was Saint Kinga's ghost, come to get revenge.' Luca put on a stupid spooky voice and finished it by tickling Evie's sides. I've never wanted to punch someone more.

'Whose turn is it next?' I asked, trying to change the subject.

'Definitely yours,' Evie said.

'Okay.' I tried to sound nonchalant, but my tongue suddenly felt too big for my mouth. 'What's my challenge?'

'To steal something from the museum,' Luca said.

I didn't like the sound of that. 'Yeah, because I want to get chucked out,' I said, praying they'd reconsider without me having to refuse.

'Just something small,' Luca said. 'Like a hat or a trowel or—'

'A weapon,' Evie interrupted.

'Oh yeah, because they leave those lying around,' Luca said, not bothering to suppress his chuckle.

But her face darkened and cut his laughter short.

'It's a stupid idea,' I said. 'It will be locked up.'

'Not necessarily,' Evie said. 'My mother told me that another school is being set up in there. They have been moving lots of the exhibits to make room.'

'For who?' I asked.

'I'm not sure. But I hope it's a girls' school,' she said.

'Why? You can learn everything you need from your mother, can't you?' As soon as the words were out of my mouth, I knew I'd said the wrong thing.

'You're an idiot,' Evie said.

'Fine,' I said, in an attempt to change the subject. 'I'll do it.'

The deserted museum was in an unused part of the Sanctuary. The whole time we walked towards it, I prayed it would be locked.

But the doors creaked as I pushed them open. I was startled when I was faced with the waxy head of a grinning mannequin. Evie and Luca giggled behind me, taking delight in my fear.

I stepped forward so that the mannequin and I stood nose to nose. Its glass eyes glistened with the dim light from the tunnel behind me. To me, they looked like they brimmed with tears.

'At least you don't think this is funny,' I said, snatching his cloth hat from his head.

I ventured further in, dragging the sheets from exhibits as I went. Clouds of dust erupted around me and I instantly regretted it. Gritty air filled my lungs and I bent double, spluttering into the darkness.

'Hurry up,' Luca hissed from the door.

When I was able to breathe again, I looked at the exhibits I'd uncovered. It was a mining scene, as generic to the Sanctuary as the hundreds of others lining the various tunnels. The only difference was the tool belt one of them wore around his waist. It was difficult to make out the different instruments in the gloom, but I traced my fingers over the soft leather until I came across something metallic. I prised it from the belt and held it up to my face, noting the outline of a knife. It was small, but the handle curved as if it were made for my palm. Satisfied with my find, I headed back towards the door. But as I neared it, the room flooded with light. I scrunched my eyes shut as they burned in protest. The knife clattered to the floor by my feet.

When I dared open them again, a guardian stood in front of me.

'What are you doing in here?' He scouted around the room for accomplices, and I was surprised when he found none. 'Is anybody else in here with you?'

'No?' I hadn't intended it to be a question, but I had no idea where my friends could have gone.

'I know you; you're an Elite recruit. You know you could fail your induction because of this?'

'Please, don't tell anybody. I was just curious.'

'You know what curiosity did to the cat, don't you? Stay out of here; there is dangerous equipment lying around.'

'I didn't realise,' I lied. I looked to my feet to see where the knife had landed, but it had disappeared into the same abyss as Evie and Luca. I have a pretty good idea where it ended up, though. Deep in the back of Evie's stepfather.

Susan

A lump formed in Susan's throat as she entered the room. All the members of the committee were seated around the table, interspersed with random citizens of the Sanctuary.

Only one of these citizens was familiar to her. Durand didn't acknowledge her as she sat down. Still, a cold chill consumed her at the sight of him, and she cradled her broken hand in her lap.

'That completes the dream team for today,' David said.

The legs of Edmond Pearse's chair screeched as he shuffled it further under the table. 'I've got a lot to do. Could we get started?'

Susan wondered if the tension she felt between the two men was just a product of her own unease.

David's eyebrows bobbed. 'Do accept my apologies, Edmond. If the running of the Sanctuary is becoming inconvenient to you, I'll happily step in.'

Susan thought she'd happily slap the smirk from David's face on Edmond's behalf if he'd only ask.

But Edmond ignored his remark. 'Of course not. But there are new arrivals waiting. I don't think they need us adding to their stress by delaying their admission for yet another meeting about red tape.'

'You say red tape. I say essential logistics,' David said. 'I've invited a few key members of our community to represent the views of the citizens.'

Susan noted the way the reverend, who sat opposite, beamed at this description. In contrast, she sank lower in her seat. She was pretty sure she knew why she was there, and it had nothing to do with sharing her honest opinion. Whatever David had in mind, he was stacking the deck in his favour. He knew too much. It left her with no choice but to agree. What, she wondered, did he have on the other citizens sitting around the table?

'Fine,' Edmond said. 'So what is it that you are so keen to say that it can't wait until the next meeting?'

David paused as if steadying himself. 'I believe there's a need to bring some organisation to the Sanctuary.'

'Organisation? To what end?'

'Security, for a start. The citizens far outnumber the guardians. We need a more...strategic means of keeping tabs on them.'

Edmond said nothing.

David continued. 'Thanks to your forethought, we already have the means to do this. A chip is already inserted for communication and identification purposes upon arrival. I have spoken to Aleksey, and he has assured me that it will be a simple process to extend its uses.'

Edmond glared at Aleksey. 'Did he? And what kind of extension did you have in mind?'

'Well, first of all, tracking the citizens. I suggest, as the most vulnerable members of our community, we start with the children. Wouldn't it be better if we could keep tabs on where they are at all times?'

Just weeks ago, Susan could imagine herself signing Luca up to this wholeheartedly. The winding tunnels, the earthquakes: she would have jumped at the idea of knowing where he was at every moment. Now the thought of David having tabs on their every movement only made her sick. There really would be no escape.

'No,' Edmond said. 'I think that sounds like a police state.'

Susan wanted to hug him.

David sighed. 'That's a little melodramatic, don't you think? In fact, Aleksey tells me that this is a function that you built into the initial prototype.'

'Yes. But as a precaution for when we start sending groups to the surface.'

'Well,' David said. 'This is no different. Now we can ensure the citizens are safe, wherever they go.'

Millicent, who up until then had looked uninterested at best, suddenly perked up. 'Not the committee members, surely. We may have classified business to attend to.'

Edmond studied her. 'We don't have anything to hide. If the citizens are told they must sacrifice privacy for safety, then we should lead by example.'

'Perhaps it could be on a voluntary basis for members of the committee,' David said. 'Those who want to be part of the programme are encouraged to do so.'

Reverend Durand cleared his throat.

'The same allowances will be extended to citizens with sensitive roles,' David added.

Sensitive roles? Susan thought. *More like those not wanting to get caught carrying out barbaric acts.*

'Is that it?' Edmond asked. 'Because I'm ready to cast my vote now.'

'Actually, no. I think it would also be helpful to know which sector each member of the community belongs to.'

Edmond took off his glasses and rubbed the bridge of his nose. 'There are no sectors.'

David shook his head. 'That's where you're wrong. Of

course there are. Every member of the community is here because they are either a benefactor who invested in your vision, a scientist who made it reality...or they are a trade who took part in the construction.'

'I don't get your point,' Edmond said. 'What does it matter? We're one community now.'

Aleksey waved a finger at Pearse. 'David may be onto something here. There are those, such as you and I, who put years of our lives into the building of the Sanctuary. Why should somebody who just happens to be the family member of some hired help get the same privileges that we do?'

'Because that's what we agreed we were building here,' Edmond said. 'A fair and equal society. It's not about what's happened in the past, it's about the future we're building together.'

'I totally agree,' David said. 'And we need a way that the citizens can contribute to that community, safe in the knowledge that their efforts will be rewarded. History has proved that communism doesn't work. If people are just handed everything they want on a plate, then what incentive will they have to better themselves? The people should be rewarded, based on their merits.'

Susan's head whirled. On paper, she and her family would benefit from such a system. But 'merits' was the word that played over in her head. Because she had none. Not by their standards. It didn't matter that in their real lives Robert had worked hard to gain a position in a small architecture firm. Nor that her art work was garnering a modest amount of attention. Those weren't the terms they were there on. And once it was discovered, at best they would be starting from the bottom.

Edmond spread his palms on the table. 'But we won't be starting on a level playing field, not when we proclaim some citizens to be better than others.'

'Not better,' David said. 'Different.'

'And what is it you are suggesting?' Edmond asked. 'We single the workers out with a yellow star emblazoned on their arms?'

David groaned. 'Could we please discuss this without the theatrics?'

'Edmond, listen,' Aleksey said. 'It would be a simple system. On a day-to-day basis, the citizens will barely register it's there. Everybody will be designated to a sector upon entry to the Sanctuary.' He pulled up his sleeve to show Edmond a small S raised in an angry red on his skin. 'S for STEM. It won't just be the trade sector.'

Edmond sat back in his chair. 'I see my opinion is irrelevant. You've begun the process already.'

'No,' Aleksey said, pulling his sleeve back over his hand. 'This was just a test. Nothing has been decided.'

Edmond looked at Millicent. 'You can't agree with what he's saying, not when your company managed the build of this place. All those people are here because of you. And you would let him categorise them as second-class citizens.'

Perhaps it was sexist, but as Susan looked from Millicent's excessive jewellery to her flowing skirts, she couldn't think of anybody less suited to running a building firm.

Millicent hesitated. 'I don't think David is saying that. Perhaps we would benefit from some form of hierarchy.'

'As long as you lot are at the top, of course,' Edmond said. 'I can see we are just going to go around in circles. So I'll tell you now that it's a no from me.'

'Good idea,' David said. 'Let's put it to a vote.'

'I didn't—'

David addressed the group. 'Raise your hand if you are happy to enforce a little bit of organisation on the Sanctuary.'

All around the table, arms shot up. It appeared that only Susan and Edmond objected. But she felt David's eyes boring into her and slowly lifted her hand.

Edmond got to his feet.

'Aren't you going to wait for the votes to be counted?' David asked.

'I won't have any further part in this,' Edmond said, and he stalked from the room.

Susan wished, with every fibre of her being, that she could follow him.

~

The Book of Durand

'This is so beautiful,' Evie said.

She wasn't wrong. We were sitting on the floor of the cave and I shone my torch over the ceiling. The crystals that were embedded within it fragmented the light like the sequins on a disco ball. They danced across her face, and I had to stop myself reaching out and tracing their path with my fingertips.

I'd been there plenty of times and it always took my breath away. Her presence magnified that.

But I didn't say any of that, of course. Instead I said, 'It's nice. You know it's made of halite, right? That's just kitchen salt.'

She sniffed. 'You really know how to drain the romance out of a place.'

Romance. My heart leapt at the word. I think I knew, even then, that she wasn't referring to me. But it gave me hope, and hope can be a dangerous thing.

'How did you find it?' she asked.

'When we were down here orienteering with the Elite.'

She snickered. 'Oh yeah, Luca told me about them. They sound like a load of bigots, if you ask me.'

'Well I didn't.' It came out sharper than I intended, but her reaction annoyed me. Being part of the Elite made me feel included, wanted. I hated to think of them trashing it.

The smirk dropped from her face and she changed the subject. 'Have you met Pearse's grandson yet?'

'Not really; I've seen him around. He's seems a bit of a weirdo.'

'He's okay. At least he's different from the rest of the

boring people around here. Maybe we should, I don't know, try and include him.'

Sorry? Yes, she said you were 'okay'. That's hardly a declaration of love. If you are going to sit there grinning like that, I'm not going on.

'Thank you for sharing this with me,' she said.

I shrugged. 'You've seemed really sad lately.' I debated adding to my sentence, not wanting to ruin the moment with depressing talk. But I went for it. 'Is anything wrong? I'd like to help, if I can.'

'You can't,' she said, a little too quickly. 'It's just my stepfather.'

'Yeah, my dad's an ass, too.'

'The good reverend?' She cocked her head to the side. 'How so?'

'I don't know. The usual, I guess.'

'Right.' She started to get to her feet.

'He barely notices I'm there most of the time,' I added, wanting to keep the conversation going.

She sat back down. 'There are worse things than being invisible. I think I'd like that.'

'Oh yeah. That would be your superpower of choice, would it? Sounds a bit dodgy to me. I'll be listening out for strange noises when I'm getting changed.'

She laughed. 'Don't worry; you're safe.'

'Shame.' I regretted saying it as soon as the word was out.

She shifted uncomfortably. 'Well, what would your superpower be?'

'That's easy, mind control. Everybody would have to do exactly what I wanted.'

'Nah, that's not for me. I wouldn't want that kind of power over somebody.'

'Even if it means getting everything you want?' I asked.

She got to her feet, wiping her hands on her jeans. 'Even then. You, sir, need to learn you can't always have things your own way.'

'Maybe. At least until I get bitten by a radioactive spider, anyway.'

'I think that'd just have you shooting webs out of your butt. Thanks again. For bringing me here, I mean.' She shone her torch at the glistening ceiling for a final time. 'I can't wait to show Luca.'

Seb

As they walked, Seb realised the path they were taking led them to the barracks. 'I'm sure you can handle it from here,' Franz said as he peeled away from the group.

The guards waited at the door and Galewski ushered the men inside.

'What's going on?' Seb asked as soon as they were out of earshot.

'Typhus is rampant in the extermination area,' Galewski said. 'Franz asked for some men to take the place of the dead.'

Freidman bent over, his hands on his knees, as he laughed with relief. 'Don't do that to me. I thought we were finished.'

'Don't celebrate too soon,' Zialo said. He turned to Galewski with narrowed eyes. 'Everyone knows if you're sent to the extermination area, you don't come back. And still, you chose us.'

'Or me, at least,' Freidman said.

'Yes, because this has to end. Don't you see? The only way we are going to put together a resistance that has a chance is if we can unite the two sides of the camp.'

'Go on,' Zialo said, still looking unconvinced.

'With you two over there, I can assign you to lead work groups. When the time comes to fight, I can make sure there is a member of our organising committee on every team.'

'Organising committee?' Freidman asked. 'That's a bit formal, isn't it? Maybe we n—'

'Organisation is what we need.' Galewski's skin looked

clammy, and he sat down on a nearby bunk. 'Because if we don't get serious about this, none of us are getting out alive.'

'What about me?' Seb's voice was small, strained, so he cleared his throat. 'As far as you knew, I was nothing to do with the resistance. But you still chose me.'

The group fell so silent they could hear the soldiers outside bickering.

'True. But I knew it was what you wanted,' Galewski said.

'Wanted?'

'That's right.' Freidman grasped at the explanation with enthusiasm. 'I told Galewski that you wanted to see if your friend was on the other side of the camp.'

'Oh.' Seb wasn't sure he believed them, but the alternative was accepting that they considered him expendable.

The door thudded against the wall of the barracks. 'Get a move on,' one of the guards called.

'Gather your things together quickly,' Galewski said.

The journey to the extermination area took the prisoners down 'the tube', a long enclosed pathway covered on all sides by tree branches. Beams of sunlight pierced the camouflage and danced across the faces of the men.

The guards walked behind them, chatting amongst themselves. Still, Seb was very aware of the rifles they held.

They soon passed a brick building that, from the Star of David on the gable, looked as though it was used for worship. A dark curtain was drawn across the front, and stitched into the cloth was something written in Hebrew. 'What does that say?' Seb asked.

Freidman stopped. 'This is the Gateway to God. Righteous men will pass through.'

'They allow a synagogue here?' Seb asked, surprised by this show of empathy.

'No,' Galewski said, making a wide arc around the building. 'It's just more trickery. That's a gas chamber.'

Seb stared, thinking of the comfort the new arrivals must have taken at the familiarity of it. The horror they must have felt when they realised the truth was unimaginable.

'Their cruelty knows no bounds,' Freidman added, mirroring his thoughts.

'Keep moving,' the guard said, jabbing his rifle butt into Seb's shoulder blade.

They were heading straight for a wooden shack. 'What is this place?' Seb asked.

'Your new boss works here,' Galewski said. 'I'm assigning you to the carpentry team.'

Seb thought of the man on the train platform, diligently painting the numbers onto the clock face. As if he'd been conjured from his memory, the carpenter stepped from the building and walked in the opposite direction.

'Jacob,' Galewski called after him. 'Jacob, wait.'

Jacob looked at them from beneath bushy eyebrows. 'I don't have long. There's a lot to do.'

'Exactly,' Galewski said. 'This is Seb, your new assistant.'

'I don't need an assistant.'

'You just said you had lots to do. He can help you with the new guard rooms.'

'Okay, let me rephrase that. I don't want an assistant. I've got enough to do without worrying about training up some kid.'

'Please, I promise not to get in your way.' Seb stuck out

his hand. Jacob glared at it until Seb dropped it back to his side.

'You see,' Galewski said, already walking away. 'Perfect. I'm going to show Zialo and Freidman where they'll be working.'

The group departed, leaving Seb alone with Jacob. 'Doesn't look like I have any choice, does it?' Jacob's thick moustache bobbed as he spoke. 'Well, if you're coming with me, you'd better get a move on.'

Seb half-jogged to keep up. 'So how does this place work?'

Jacob shrugged. 'Much like the lower camp. Each man is assigned to a group, and that group answers to their capo.'

'You're my capo then?'

'No. Let's get this straight. I'm nobody's boss. I don't want to be responsible for anybody. You just try to look useful and don't get under my feet. Got it?'

Seb didn't have the chance to answer before they reached a gate in the perimeter fence.

'He'll be working with me today,' Jacob told the guards, jabbing his thumb towards Sea.

Seb cast a glance back towards the gate. A guard trailed behind, but he wasn't even watching them.

'They just let us out?' Seb asked.

'With supervision. We've got to collect wood.'

'But...I mean, have you never thought about running?'

Jacob pulled up sharp. 'Will you shut up? Are you trying to get us shot? If we ran, they'd shoot us. And then ten prisoners, just in case anyone else got the same—'

A flurry of movement from the other side of the fence drew their attention.

'New arrivals,' Jacob said, although there was no need. Already naked women, arms crossed over their chests, raced past them on the other side of the fence. Their route took them past a building, and from where they stood, Seb could see a soldier hidden in the shadows.

'What's he up to?' Seb asked.

'Nothing good,' Jacob said, rifling through his tool bag. 'That's the Ukrainian barracks. Best to mind your own business and focus on the work.'

The way the soldier loitered in the shadows reminded Seb of a book he'd once read on arachnids. The trapdoor spider would spin a door of its own silk and cover it with vegetation. Then it would wait. The insects that ambled by wouldn't see it coming.

The author of that book had included a children's rhyme next to the picture. At the time, Seb had barely noticed it. Which was why he found it strange that it came back to him with perfect clarity.

Trapdoor spider, hiding underground.

He lurks in his tunnel, not making a sound.

The arrivals clutched towels and soap against their skin, props in the charade that they were going for a shower. The hidden guard's eyes were locked on one particular woman now. Seb could see why. Dark hair against porcelain skin, she was definitely striking.

He crouches down and there he'll wait,

'Til footsteps make the ground vibrate.

But Seb knew that was not what had caught the guard's eye. It was the way she held herself. If she was embarrassed by her nakedness or scared of the screaming men, she refused to show it. She held her head high and walked at a measured pace, with no clue about the fingers curled around the doorframe ahead of her.

He springs from his hole when you come into view.

And with a single snap, he makes a meal out of you!

Rough hands dragged the woman into the barracks.

'You shouldn't watch,' Jacob said. 'There's nothing we can do.'

But Seb found himself unable to look away.

Moments later, the door burst open and the woman raced out again. The guard appeared in the empty doorframe, clutching his groin with one hand and pointing at the fleeing woman with the other. Uniformed men reached for her as she passed, grasping the empty air where she had just been.

Without hesitation, she launched herself at the three-metre-high fence. She hooked her fingers into it. Seb could only imagine the pain as the wire dug into her bare feet. She paused at the top when she saw the twisted barbed wire. Looking at the crowd of guards gathering below her was all the incentive she needed, and she threw her leg over the top. A couple of guards tried to follow her, jamming their heavy boots into the chain of the fence. Others ran for the gate that Seb and Jacob had passed through.

She landed, knees bent, on the other side. Taking no time to inspect her wounds, she ran for the forest. A guard planted his boots on the soil seconds later. He repositioned his rifle on his shoulder and ran after her.

'She's going to make it,' Seb said, taking a step towards her.

'Don't do anything stupid, boy,' the guard supervising them growled. 'I'll shoot you if I have to.'

Seb froze, unable to do anything but watch.

The gap between the woman and her pursuer was closing fast. If the guard reached out, he would be able to brush her skin with his fingertips.

However, it was not his hand he raised but his gun. He was so close that it smacked against her elbow. Seizing the opportunity, she grabbed the rifle barrel and tried to wrestle the gun from his grasp.

As Seb watched her fight, the exposed flesh of her breasts against the steel of the weapon, he didn't think he'd ever seen anyone more heroic.

Then there was an explosion, and the woman and the guard stood motionless. Certain that she had been hit, Seb forced himself to keep watching. If nothing else, he would make sure others heard of her bravery.

As the couple performed the last turn in their morbid tango, Seb saw that the guard's lower jaw was missing. A few defiant teeth clung to the underside of his upper jaw. Seb's stomach lurched at the sight of those molars.

The woman shook the dead man free from the rifle. She stared at it as if disbelieving the carnage it had wreaked.

By now another guard had made it over the fence and was heading for her. With no other option, she aimed the gun with a shaky hand. The recoil sent her tumbling backwards, denying her the satisfaction of seeing the bullet land squarely in his chest.

One of the guards who had opted for the gate darted past Seb. Seeing him approach, she aimed and fired. Nothing happened. She tried again and heard just the impotent click of the trigger. She pulled the trigger again and again, a desperate sob escaping her. Tossing the rifle to the ground, she sprinted for the tree line. She only made it a few metres before the guard reached her. He grabbed her hair, snapping her head backwards. She opened her mouth and howled. But it wasn't fear that Seb heard in that cry. It was fury. Turning to her captor, she clawed at his face with nails already bloodied from the barbed wire.

Another guard soon reached them and held her back, his arms locked with hers. Seb looked away as they delivered the first punch.

Seb had forgotten about the guard at his side until the man spoke. 'Brave girl.' His rifle was still held down at his side and Seb realised he could have shot her at any time. 'But they will make her pay for that,' he added.

Seb had no doubt that was true. But he knew it wasn't the sick punishment they chose for her that he would remember. It would be the warrior he saw scaling that fence and fighting for her freedom.

Susan

History is full of stolen children. They might not have been printed on the back of milk cartons, but Susan knew it was true. Her great-grandfather once told her about the Hitler Youth, children poisoned against their families and moulded into Nazis. They might not have been kidnapped, well not in every case, but they were gone all the same.

'The adults couldn't even speak freely in their own homes,' he'd told her. 'Not when the Nazis had turned their children into mini spies.'

As Susan did up the top button of Luca's Guardian Elite blazer, his fresh chip still an angry red on his hand, she got the urge to ask: *Can I trust you to keep our secrets? Are you still* my *child?*

Jared

Despite the way her feet dragged along the bumps of the cobbled streets, Nell felt weightless between them.

'Hold on, Nell. Not long now.' Jared couldn't see anybody following them, but they'd learnt the hard way that it didn't mean they were safe. They ducked into an alleyway. The sound of leather slapping against stone silenced them.

Nell groaned.

'Shhh,' Aaron said, smoothing back her hair.

The soldiers passed them, and Jared sank with relief.

'What do we do?' Aaron asked, leaning Nell forward. 'She's losing so much blood.'

Jared couldn't think. Stress pulsated through his veins and throbbed at his temples.

'I'm going to pull it out,' Aaron said.

'No! You'll cause more damage.' Jared knew there was no good option. 'I'm going to snap off the shaft so we can move her more easily.' As he tried to break the wooden shaft, Nell let out a yelp.

Aaron cupped his hand over her mouth. 'I know it hurts, but you've got to be quiet.'

Jared reached into his pocket for the medilaser, praying for a miracle. It blinked on for a second, just long enough for him to scour the wood, allowing him to snap the shaft. 'This thing's useless now,' he said, dropping it back into his pocket. 'Let's get her up. It's going to take hours to get back to Beth.'

'Jared.' Aaron didn't have to add more than the shake of his head he gave.

'There's no other choice.'

'I'm okay,' Nell said. 'Don't worry about me.' The rasp in her breath told Jared she was anything but.

They hauled her onto their shoulders again, steeling themselves against the whimpers she gave. Still, they'd been travelling for over an hour before she complained.

Nell's words were clouded by an ominous bubbling. 'Please, can I rest for a minute?'

'Just a little longer. When we get to the riverbank, there will be some cover from the trees.'

As soon as they heard the rushing water, Nell begged, 'Please, Jared.'

'Beth is only a short walk down the bank now. Don't you want to see her?'

'Maybe after I rest for a while.'

They leant her against a tree trunk. The bloody tinge to her teeth was clear to them both. Aaron wrapped his arm around her and nestled in close.

'That's better,' she said between gasps. 'This is lovely.'

Jared looked at the moonlight shimmering on the water. 'Yes, it is.'

She smiled at him. 'This will do nicely.'

'You're going to be all right,' Aaron said. 'We'll take you somewhere they can fix this.'

'I think it's too late for that, but don't worry about me.' She coughed and left a splatter of red down the front of her white tunic. 'Jared, I was thinking about your book. The one you wrote while we were trying to help Aaron. You were right.'

'I was? How so?'

'This isn't the end. I just get to go ahead first this time.'

Jared shuffled up next to her, book ending her between the two of them. 'You are a wise woman, Nell.'

'Don't worry,' she said, her voice a whisper. 'I'll check it out before you three get there.'

Aaron kissed the top of her head and together they watched the river.

Chapter Five

The Book of Durand

I wish I could say my reasons for what I did that day were any deeper than old-fashioned jealousy. The truth is, I was furious when I saw them there. They sat together on the bench, overlooking the lake at its highest point, their heads so close they might have been touching. I'll admit that I lost it.

'How come nobody thought to tell me we were hanging out?' It was an accusation, not a question.

Luca was on his feet before I even reached them. 'Now isn't a good time, Martin.'

'I bet.' I squared up to him, our faces so close that I felt his breath on my cheek. 'I'm clearly interrupting something.'

'Actually, you are.' I hadn't noticed until then, but Evie had been crying. Her eyelashes were heavy with tears and she swiped at them with the sleeve of her dress.

This should have cowed me. It should have embarrassed

me to have interrupted such a private moment. But it didn't. For some reason it enraged me more than if I'd caught them kissing. Perhaps it was because she'd chosen to go to him instead of me.

'Truth or dare?' I spat the words at him.

He didn't answer.

'Truth or dare?' I repeated.

The look of exasperation they exchanged sparked a new level of rage. Their judgement was yet another thing they shared that didn't include me; well, not in the way I wanted.

'Dare it is then.' I said, jabbing at him with the heels of my hands. 'Jump into the lake.'

His fists balled at his sides. 'I told you, I'm not playing.'

I shoved him as hard as I could, leaving his back pressed against the barrier encircling the lake. 'Don't be a chicken.'

'You aren't in charge of us.' It was Evie who said it, but that made no difference. I knew the defiance had started with him.

A guttural growl escaped me; I hadn't known I was capable of such a sound. Then I barrelled into him, full force.

The splintering of wood bounced around the lake and Luca disappeared over the edge. Droplets of water showered me as he hit the water, head first.

Gravity threatened to send me tumbling after him. I teetered at the edge, flapping my arms like an insane cartoon character. My collar choked me as Evie yanked me back towards the safety of the walkway.

'You idiot,' she screamed. 'What have you done?'

Together, we peered over the edge.

Luca had already broken the surface. Between splutters of water, he was actually laughing. 'I guess I won that round.'

Relief consumed me. It was fleeting, though.

The smile fell from his face as his muscles began to jerk.

'Luca?' Evie's question turned into a scream. 'Luca!'

His face sank below the water.

I turned in circles, looking for somebody to help us.

The splash told me Evie had taken matters into her own hands. She disappeared beneath the surface after him. Seconds later, she erupted in a panic of coughs and splutters, Luca's head cradled in the crook of her arm.

I was elbowed out of the way as a pair of guardians raced past me. They threw open the gate at the bottom. The first one hesitated at the edge of the lake, before jumping in feet first.

Evie flinched away from the splash he caused but continued to paddle with one arm towards the edge.

The second man waded in and they heaved Luca from the water.

Evie looked lost, stood there empty handed. When she noticed me watching, she wrinkled her nose in disgust. I couldn't blame her.

Seb

Seb had heard the guards grumbling about an inspection and they'd ordered the area cleared, whether the tower was finished or not. It must have been somebody important visiting, as Marcus had been assigned to help them.

Not that he'd done much of that. As they walked across the camp, he'd dragged his heels, moving at a snail's pace. At first, Seb had hung back with him, hoping for news of the lower camp. But the single word answers that were grunted in response soon wore holes in his patience, and he strode to catch up with Jacob.

'I wonder what's up with him,' Seb said.

'Not me,' Jacob said as they approached the tower. 'I have enough of my own problems without making him one of them. Herman will be here soon to supervise while I fetch some wood. You and our little ray of sunshine can finish off the far wall and clear this area.'

They'd been working only a short time when Marcus slumped against the wall of the barracks, his eyes fixed on the dirt.

'Could you pass me the hammer?' Seb asked.

Marcus stared at Seb's lips, his eyes scrunched as though trying to focus.

It was only then that Seb noticed the yellow tinge to his skin. 'Are you okay?'

Marcus clambered to his feet. He swayed as he scanned the ground around him 'I'm fine. What did you need?'

Seb knew he was lying; sweat dripped down the boy's face, but still he wrapped his arms around his body as chills ran through him. Even in the short time he'd been there, it had been made clear to Seb that illness, or any kind of weakness, would not be tolerated in Treblinka. Admitting to it would take you one step closer to the pits. 'The hammer,' Seb said.

Marcus headed towards the tool bag. After only a few steps, he stopped, as though an imaginary wall blocked his way. Then he fell.

Seb knelt over him. 'Can you hear me?' he asked, shaking Marcus's shoulder.

The boy didn't respond.

'What happened?'

Seb looked up to find Jacob standing above them. 'I don't know. He just collapsed.' The relief Seb felt at seeing his mentor fled when he noticed Herman just behind him.

~

Susan

Susan's lungs burned as she ran. She knew it was bound to happen eventually. With Luca, the next fit was just a matter of time.

Relief flooded over her when she saw him propped up with pillows, alert and waiting for her.

'Are you okay?' she asked, brushing the hair away from his face.

Marney smiled at her from the other side of the bed. 'About time you got here,' she said, winking at Luca.

'The boy could have drowned.' Susan hadn't noticed Doctor Reed standing at the far end of the room. Just the sight of him made her want to run and hide.

'That's a bit extreme,' Marney said. 'The guardians pulled him out almost immediately.'

'Oh. So you're telling me his head wasn't under the water he just spent the last hour coughing up?' Reed's tone was laced with sarcasm.

Marney didn't answer.

'What happened?' Susan asked.

'Nothing,' Luca said. 'It was just a stupid prank.'

'I think it was just kids being kids.' Marney hung Luca's chart back above his bed. 'Apparently Martin Durand pushed him in the lake.'

'The reverend's son?' Just the mention of Durand sent chills through Susan.

'It was a joke,' Luca said. 'Just keep out of it, okay.'

Susan wanted nothing more than to stay as far away as possible from Durand and his whole family. Still, she couldn't let her son be treated like that. 'But if—'

'If I may interrupt, I think a more pressing concern is this fit he had.' Reed looked at her with narrowed eyes. 'Has that happened before?'

'No. He's always been perfectly healthy.'

'There are plenty of relatively harmless things that could have caused it,' Marney assured her. 'A temperature, for instance. But just to be sure, we will take some blood.'

Luca squirmed. 'Mom.'

'He's not a fan of needles.'

'Sorry, buddy,' Marney said. 'I'm afraid it's pretty unavoidable if we are going to get to the bottom of this.'

'It only hurts for a second,' Reed added, rummaging in the trolley for the equipment.

'Can you take my blood instead? Surely if you're looking for something genetic...'

Marney shook her head. 'It doesn't work like that, I'm afraid.'

'As you well know.' Reed studied her through narrowed eyes.

Susan looked away. 'I'm sorry. I guess I'm not thinking straight.'

'I know exactly how you feel,' Marney said. 'Every time one of my girls scrapes a knee it just about knocks ten years off my life. Now come on,' she said to Luca. 'I promise, it'll be over in no time.'

The Book of Durand

Father stirred the teaspoon around the cup for what felt like an age.

'We're going to be late!'

He laughed at me. 'We've got twenty minutes before we need to leave. Take this through to your mother and hurry her along.'

When I entered her bedroom, I was annoyed to find it still dark. Mamma grumbled and pulled the blanket over her head when I switched on the light.

I set the cup down beside her and tugged back the covers. 'Mamma, get dressed. We have to get going.'

'Five more minutes?'

'No, we'll miss it.'

She shuffled up the bed and propped herself up with pillows. 'Don't you worry,' she said. 'I would never miss this.' She picked up her cup and slurped the tea. 'I've just been so tired lately. But I'll do better, I promise. Now, go and get your things together while I get ready. Today's all about you.'

Half an hour later I was still sitting in the living area, waiting.

Father came out of the bedroom with Mamma's teacup in his hand. 'I'm sorry, but I don't think she's going to make it to the ceremony.'

I pushed past him and found Mamma still propped against the pillows, fast asleep. Her mouth hung open as she let out a gentle snore.

'Don't be too hard on her,' Father said, resting his hand on my shoulder. 'I think she really did want to come.'

'It doesn't matter,' I said, although it did, of course. She'd promised. 'Let's go.'

As we entered the chamber, Father stopped and scanned the clusters of citizens.

'We're going to be late,' I said.

He ignored me.

The parents of the other recruits stood anchoring their children to their sides. An arm slung around a shoulder, a hand on the nape of the neck: it was easy to see where they belonged. They fitted together like puzzle pieces.

'Please, there's no time.'

'What? Martin, stop being so dramatic. They're hardly going to begin without you.' He raised a hand when he saw Captain Moss. 'Caleb, do you have a minute?'

Then I was alone, drifting between the little islands of family unity around me. I was relieved when David called us to the stage.

Calling it a 'passing out parade' was a little exaggerated. We lined up on a raised platform in the Grand Chamber, me and the rest of the original recruits.

Other than a spread of drinks and nibbles at the back of the room, everything was as it always was. That didn't matter, though. It wasn't about pomp and ceremony. I felt like I was becoming a part of something bigger.

'I owe you all, not just my congratulations, but also my thanks,' David said, addressing the adults in the pews. 'You have raised young men with the moral fibre needed to allow the Sanctuary to flourish and thrive. They are a credit to you.' He paused to allow a mumble of self congratulation to pass among the small audience. 'But, of course, today is really about your children, although you may not consider them children any more. Each of the young men in front of you has earned the rank of private. If their hard work and determination continues, I have no doubt that some day one of them will end up as my boss.'

The audience tittered. All except for my father, whose familiar guffaw I could pinpoint without even trying.

David nodded towards Caleb, who joined him on stage.

'Well done, boys,' Caleb said as he uncovered the table at the back, revealing five piles of clothes in a rich Yale blue.

'Captain Moss is a man of few words,' David said. He picked up one of the bundles of uniform and held it towards the audience. 'Today your boys become elite.' A ripple of applause bounced around the chamber, making the audience sound far larger than it was.

Each recruit stepped forward, accepting his uniform along with an obligatory handshake and leaving the stage. Only I remained when the door at the back of the chamber opened. My mother tried to sneak in, but the sound of her heels echoed around the chamber. She gave me a little wave from the back.

'Martin Durand,' David said.

My legs seemed to work of their own accord as I made my way across the stage.

David clasped my hand. 'I'm very proud of you.'

I'm sure I was grinning like an imbecile.

David walked to the edge of the stage closest to us. 'Please show your appreciation to the first members of the Guardian Elite.'

The parents clapped and cheered, and for a moment the world looked bright.

But it was a fleeting moment. A crash came from the

back of the room. My mother steadied herself on the table at the back, a tray of hors d'oeuvres spilled at her feet.

'Well, I'm glad we decided against using the breakables,' David said. 'Please, enjoy what is left of the refreshments.'

The crowd laughed, and I felt my face burn.

When I got over to her, Mamma was swaying on her heels. 'I promised you that I wouldn't miss it.'

I looked her over. She'd mis-buttoned her shirt so that one side hung down at an angle. Worse than that was the way she was blinking, like her eyelashes were too heavy to allow her to keep her eyes open.

I scanned the room and noticed my new comrades whispering as they watched us.

'I'll take you home,' I said.

'I'm fine; I just got a little dizzy.'

I wanted to yell, scream at her, that I didn't care if she was fine, because it wasn't about her.

'This is your day,' she added.

'And you're ruining it.' The words were out of my mouth before I'd registered them.

The sides of her mouth dropped and part of me wanted to make it better. But another part of me was pleased that I'd said it. It felt like a valve had been turned, releasing the pressure. So I continued. 'Did you have to drink? Today of all days?'

'You think I'm drunk? Where would I even—'

'I don't know, and I don't care, because you clearly have. You can barely stand.'

She swallowed back tears. 'I'm sorry if I've embarrassed you. I should go.'

When the door closed behind her, I turned to my father.

'I guess we should go after her,' Father said.

'Can't we stay for a little while?' I asked.

Father didn't answer. He was beaming at David as he approached. 'I'm so sorry about that, David. Serena hasn't been well.'

'Please don't mention it. You are a saint to look after her the way you do.' David draped an arm across Father's shoulder, leading him away from me as they passed whispers between them, my mother forgotten.

The other Elite had already donned their caps, their bright blue heads like beacons as the parents milled between them.

I took a couple of steps towards them.

Then I followed Mamma out of the door. I needed to check she was okay. She was, after all, my responsibility.

Jared

They stepped through the portal and, just like that, they were back in the Sanctuary. Nothing had changed. Jared touched his palm to the smooth salt rock. Just the feel of it made a cloying claustrophobia bubble inside him.

'Are you okay?' Beth asked.

Jared could be honest and say that no, he wasn't. He could tell her how already the air felt thinner and his limbs heavier, like the place had a mind of its own and it was trying to keep him rooted to the spot. However, explaining that the walls of the disused tunnel that they'd arrived in were already beginning to shrink in on him wouldn't be helpful. They needed him to be in control, even if every fibre of his being told him he was not.

She'd been upset enough. Telling her about Nell had been one of the worst things he'd ever had to do. The wail she'd released seemed almost inhuman. She'd only calmed when he'd promised her that the Durands would pay.

So, instead, he settled on, 'I'm fine.'

'Well, where do we find this guy?' Aaron asked.

Jared could see how tightly wound he was and almost pitied the person on the receiving end of that energy. Almost. 'I think, before we rush into anything, we should find out what we are up against. Millicent's unit is close to here. The tunnels should be empty at this time of night.'

They took only a step or two before Beth stopped. 'If it's empty, then who is that?'

Jared listened. 'I can't hear anything.'

'There were definitely footsteps.'

'Well,' Aaron said, 'let's get moving before whoever it was comes back.'

Jared stuck his head into the communal area that joined the different sectors of the Sanctuary. It was just as he remembered. One of the stone tables even had a chess board set up on it, as though the players had been interrupted mid-game.

'There's nobody there,' Jared said, waving for them to follow.

Blinkered, Aaron headed straight for the tunnel that Jared pointed to.

Beth, however, gasped as she took in the huge glittering cavern around them. 'This is...wow. It's beautiful. Nell would have loved this.' Her chin dimpled and she covered her mouth to stop the swelling sob.

Jared had tried to comfort her. But it was difficult when his own grief threatened to consume him. Besides, everything he said felt clumsy.

'We'd better keep moving.' He searched for something to plug the awkward silence. 'Nell came here once, before we met you. Did she tell you that?'

'Yes,' Beth said. 'Although, she never mentioned any of this.'

'Well, she didn't see much of it. Just my grandfather's unit...and the inside of my wardrobe.'

'Your wardrobe? Now, that will require some explaining, when we have more time,' she said, picking up the pace. 'I know you have mixed feelings about this place, but it's breathtaking.'

Jared was surprised to hear her describe it so. It had been so long since he'd looked at the Sanctuary in that way. He thought of the day his grandfather had taken him to the lake and the first time his mother had led him into Saint Kinga's chapel. It was such a long time since he'd thought of the Sanctuary as anything but suffocating that he was surprised to feel pride swell inside him. 'This is nothing. You should see the rest of it.'

Beth smiled. 'I'd like—' A strange voice cut her sentence short.

'I know I heard something.'

Jared and Beth froze. Even if they made a dash for the tunnel, they wouldn't get there in time.

'Uh oh,' another voice echoed. 'Somebody must have broken curfew.'

A panicked heat swept over Jared as he looked around for the nearest place to hide. But he was too late.

'It's not a problem. I'll check it out.' The guardian's eyes widened at the sight of them.

It wasn't the familiar blue of the uniform, or even the fact that he recognised the person wearing it, that surprised Jared the most. It was that the guardian was a woman.

'Sienna?' The voice echoed from the tunnel. 'Is it clear?'

Her comrade's words stirred Sienna from her trance. 'Yeah. There's nobody here.' She pointed towards the trade tunnel and mouthed, 'Go'. Then she turned on her heel, blocking the path of anybody who sought to follow her. 'It looks like whoever it was has gone back to their unit.'

'No worries,' the voice from the tunnel replied. 'We'll check the locator. They'll get the spanking they deserve.'

'I don't know about you, but I'm not sure it's worth the paperwork,' Sienna said.

'There's only paperwork if we log it. I'm sure we can handle it ourselves.'

Jared hung at the mouth of the tunnel, watching her. It had been around five years since he'd sat in Marney's classroom, listening to Sienna argue about equality. How, he wondered, had she ended up as a guardian?

Susan

'You wanted to see us?' Robert asked.

'Ah, if it isn't my friends the Coles,' David said. 'I did indeed. Come on in and take a seat.'

Susan wanted to say no. She wanted to claw at his face and make him pay for what he'd done to her. But she knew she wouldn't, because it had worked. For now anyway. Reed had stopped cornering her in the dining room. She no longer had to make polite excuses to avoid invitations to the hospital. The injury David arranged had at least provided breathing room.

That didn't mean she intended to be polite to him, though. 'What do you want?'

'Straight to the point as always,' David said. 'It's what makes us so alike. We're both direct.'

'I think we all know you are anything but.'

'It's a matter of perspective, I guess,' David said. 'Look, I'm going to sit even if you two aren't.'

Robert and Susan glanced at each other and then sat on the sofa opposite him.

'Can we get on with this now?' Susan asked.

'We're doing away with the niceties, I see. Okay,' David said. 'There's something I would like your help with.'

Susan let out an incredulous laugh. 'Why would—'

Robert raised his hand to silence her. 'We are happy to help, if we can.'

Disgust pooled in Susan's chest. 'Don't speak for me.'

'What is it you need?' Robert asked, talking over her.

'I need somebody out of my way.'

Robert drew in a sharp breath.

'Just temporarily,' David added.

'When you say 'out of your way'...' Robert's voice trailed off.

'Nothing life threatening. Just a few cuts and bruises.'

Incredulous, Susan looked from one man to the other. 'Are you kidding? You can not actually be considering this.'

'Let's just hear—'

'No, Robert. He's asking us to—'

'I've been very patient with you, Susan.' The snarl in David's voice told her his mask was slipping, and she had no desire to see what was below. 'But if I'm honest, this self-righteous attitude is wearing thin. You left the real Coles for dead.'

'We didn't—' Robert began.

'Enough. You can plead ignorance all you want. But we all know, the moment you stepped onto that bus in their place, that's what you did. So please don't play the tortured martyr. You are just as ruthless as I am.'

He was right, and Susan knew it. She had spent so many nights making up fairy tales about what might have happened to the Coles. The fact was, if they hadn't been dead before she took their place, then chances were the earthquake had finished the job.

'I've done things to survive that I'm not proud of,' David said. 'I'm not judging you. So perhaps I could ask for the same courtesy.'

'What is it you want us to do?' Robert asked.

'I need to win this election. It's the only way we can secure all our positions here. There's somebody who I am pretty sure will do everything that he can to stop that from happening.'

'Who?'

David pursed his lips. 'Edmond Pearse.'

The Book of Durand

They say when you fall in love you get butterflies in your stomach. I think it's the same when you meet somebody who will change your life, as though some part of you knows. I guess my father would have said it's the soul. Sorry, I got a bit deep there, didn't I?

But that's how I felt that day, when I first saw you. A strange sensation crept over my skin, like an itch that wouldn't disappear. I followed you as you were led through the Sanctuary by your mother. Did you even notice me, I wonder?

How greedily you dominated the attention of those around you. Your mother couldn't go a minute without touching you, checking on you. Especially after Julian's little performance in the dining room. God forbid that you be upset in any way. Never mind the rest of us. What's it like to be so central to somebody else's life?

In the dining room, I sat a few tables away. David didn't look at me as he passed; he looked through me as though I wasn't there. It was you his attention was focused on. As though you didn't have enough people trapped in your orbit. I still don't understand what it is they see in you.

He placed a bowl of ice cream in front of you, and in return you chirped questions at him. Still, he studied you with a bemused smile.

And just like that he shifted. I don't know how I knew, but I did. Sure, he was still kind to me. But I knew I wasn't number one any more. You took the only person who cared about me, who thought I could be anything but a disappointment.

I've never experienced love at first sight, but I know it's a real thing. You know how? Because I hated you from the first moment I saw you, and if one is possible then the opposite must be, too.

Perhaps that's not a smart thing to admit to you, being that you hold my life in your hands. But it's true, and I think honesty is something you appreciate.

The day you arrived, Jared, you became my nemesis. The irony is that, just like everyone else, you didn't even know that I existed. But I fixed that, didn't I?

Seb

Herman scooped Marcus off the floor and stalked away so fast that Seb struggled to keep up. When he looked back to see if Jacob was following, the carpenter was where they'd left him, banging a nail into the watchtower with more force than necessary.

'Please, wait,' Seb said to Herman's back.

When the guard turned to face him, Seb's words deserted him. 'I...We...'

Herman turned away and continued across the camp.

'We can look after him until he's better,' Seb called, cursing his brain for working so much slower than his tongue.

If Herman heard, he ignored Seb's pleas.

When they reached the path leading to the tube, Herman made a sharp turn towards the barracks. 'Galewski,' he called to the camp elder, who stood by the well.

Galewski's eyes widened. 'What happened?'

Herman ignored his question as he thrust the boy towards him. 'I wasn't here.'

'Let's get him inside before the guards see.'

As Galewski carried Marcus into the barracks, Kuba followed them in. 'Don't bring him in here! We'll all get sick.'

Men began to gather. 'Get back to work,' Galewski said. Most obeyed, but a few, Zialo and Bloch included, lingered by the door.

Galewski laid him down on his bunk. 'How long have you been ill, Marcus?'

Marcus was conscious, but his unfocused eyes rolled. 'Just today.'

'The truth,' Galewski said, scanning the men in the barracks.

'A little while,' Freidman said. 'We didn't want to get you involved. If they found out you were keeping it from them... You've already made enemies amongst the officers.'

'How have you managed to hide it?'

Freidman shrugged. 'We share out his duties where we can. Between us, we smuggle what food we can to him. If we know the guards are away from their stations, we let him rest in the barracks.'

'You haven't done him any favours,' Kuba said. 'Do you think they'll be merciful when they find you've been covering for him? We are supposed to report any illness.'

Zialo squared up to him. 'Just shut up.'

Kuba held his eye, but then slunk towards his bed. 'I don't understand why you all can't just follow the rules. Do you think I like the idea of informing on a child?'

Galewski shot him a glare. 'There will be no informing.'

Kuba said nothing.

'Do you hear me? The guards are not to be told anything until I've had time to think.'

'Just keep me out of it,' Kuba said, lying down on his bunk.

Marcus grabbed Galewski's hand. 'Don't tell them I'm ill. You know what they'll do if they find out.'

They all knew. Those unfit to work were shot.

Galewski sighed. 'You've collapsed once. What if nobody is around next time? Or worse, if it happens in front of one of them?'

'It won't; I will make sure of that,' Marcus begged, sweat plastering his hair to his forehead.

'Okay,' Galewski said. 'For now, we'll keep it between us. Get some rest. You're going to need it.'

Marcus closed his eyes.

Galewski turned to the watching men. 'Keep an eye on him.'

'Where are you going?' Seb asked.

'To get some help.'

Marcus was still sleeping when Galewski returned an hour later, followed by a man who clasped a medical bag. 'Doctor Chorazycki has agreed to look at him,' Galewski said.

'Won't they miss you?' Freidman asked.

'Maybe. But they need me too much to kill me.' Chorazycki pulled back the blanket covering Marcus. After the briefest examination, he tutted. 'It's definitely typhus,' he said, pointing out the rash covering Marcus's torso.

'Do you have any medicine that might help him?' Galewski asked.

'Medicine? If they catch me giving their drugs to prisoners, they'll think up a whole new level of hell to send me to.'

Galewski nodded. 'I know the risk you've taken even being here.'

Chorazycki released an exasperated puff of air.

'I will see what I can get hold of. But Galewski, this problem is bigger than one boy.'

'What do you mean?'

'This won't be an isolated case. The lice that have infected him will spread. They probably have already. This is just the beginning.'

Seb's skin crawled. 'Is there anything we can do to stop it?'

'The guards are already spraying the buildings with disinfectant. Not that it will do much good in the conditions we live in.'

A murmur broke out amongst the remaining men in the room and, as if regretting his words, Chorazycki bit his lower lip.

'We should tell the guards,' Kuba said, still on his bunk, his arms looped around his knees. 'They might be able to help, or at least prevent it spreading further.'

'Nobody says a word,' Galewski said. 'I just need time to think.'

Susan

When Luca was a toddler, he'd dragged a cup of scalding coffee onto his tiny body. It left a map of red welts across his skin. Although Susan didn't think it bothered him, a small patch of skin on his shoulder was still a darker shade of brown than the rest of his body. Accident or not, she saw it as a constant reminder of her carelessness and had never felt so guilty over anything. Up until that point, anyway. Not just because it happened, but because it seemed to happen in slow motion. Although it could only have taken him a fraction of a second to grab the handle and tip it over himself, to her it was storyboarded in taunting frames that clicked over like the minutes on a digital watch. Her brain told her that she should have been able to reach him, to stop the fiery liquid from sloshing over his milky skin.

That is how she felt as she watched Robert preparing to leave. Somebody else she loved was making a huge mistake, one that would create scars, and there was nothing she could do to stop it. She'd reasoned, cried, hollered, but she still couldn't reach him. Not that it stopped her trying.

She followed him from room to room. 'You can't do this.'

He continued to ignore her.

'Robert, will you please speak to me?'

'And say what? You're acting like I have a choice. David was right. You get to be self-righteous and sit in judgement on the rest of us. Glen, David, me, we made the tough decisions so that you didn't have to. To protect you.'

'We both know protecting me hasn't always been your first priority.' Susan regretted the words as soon as they were out of her mouth. Staying to defend her that night would have made no difference to the outcome. It would just have meant they'd have both been beaten. But she'd seen his face as he'd backed out of the door. He wasn't running for help but away from the danger.

'I think about that night all the time,' he said. 'Every time I look at you. When I ran, I didn't just lose your trust. I lost the man that I thought I was. But I can protect you now. If roughing up Edmond Pearse a little means that you and Luca will get to stay here, then that's what I'll do.'

'Robert, I shouldn't have said that.'

'Why not? You're right. I was a coward. Now let me be the husband and father the two of you deserve.' He kissed her on the forehead. 'I won't let you down again. Tell Luca goodnight and that I love him.'

Half an hour after he left, the lights blinked out just as David said they would.

'Mom!' Luca cried from his bedroom. 'What's going on?'

She felt her way to his door, arms stretched out in front of her, and shuffled onto the bed next to him. 'I'm not sure. But the big brains here will have it under control.'

They lay there in silence. It wasn't that they had nothing to say. It was that there was too much. Justifying the endless lies had become impossible, so it seemed easier to say nothing at all.

Only when Luca's breathing fell into the steady rhythm of sleep did Susan sneak from the room. She got into her own bed fully clothed, the darkness making her usual routine impossible, even if she'd had the energy.

When Robert got home, slipping through the door under the cover of the black out, she squeezed her eyes shut. It was a pointless act; he couldn't see her anyway. Perhaps it was herself she was trying to fool, an excuse not to hear what he'd done.

He looped his arm over her and pressed his face into her hair. The only clue to his tears was the gentle jerking of his shoulders.

Susan tried to ignore it. But somehow that muted cry was worse than any howl he could have given. 'Are you okay?' she asked finally.

Robert stilled and she heard him swallow his tears. 'He just wouldn't stay down. Every time I hit him, he got back up.'

'You don't need to tell me the details. I just need to know you're all right.'

'I'm sorry, but you need to hear it from me before anybody else tells you.'

Susan rolled over. 'Tells me what? Oh, Robert, what have you done?'

'He just kept getting up over and over again. I had no choice; he kept coming for me. I think I killed him.'

The lights blinked on. As Susan sat up, she noticed a rusty smudge on her forearm. She grabbed Robert's wrists, and as he opened his palms, she gasped at the blood covering them.

'Get up. Wash your hands.' She looked down at her t-shirt, bloodied fingerprints covering it, and started to strip it off. 'Change your clothes.'

She picked up the discarded jeans and jumper and shoved them all into the washer, jabbing at the on button with a shaking finger. The whirring sound bought Luca to his door.

'What's that noise?' he asked, rubbing the heel of his hand into his eye.

'The power just came back on,' Susan said. 'It started the machine again. Go back to bed.'

Susan didn't look to see if he'd done as she'd told him as she went into the bathroom, closing the door behind her.

Robert plunged his hands into the sink. The blood on his knuckles, that had already started to crust, flaked into the water and turned it pink.

'There's no way they could have known it was me,' Robert said, although she suspected more for his benefit than her own.

'I'm sure you'll be fine.' She wished she could sprinkle her voice with some level of conviction.

'I'm scared, Susan.'

So was she. But not just that they'd be caught. Ever since the night the looters had broken into her home, she couldn't shake the suspicion that she didn't really know the man she was married to. As she watched him scrub Edmond Pearse's blood from beneath his fingernails, she was certain of it.

The Book of Durand

I knew he was watching me. And I knew it was my chance to impress him.

David had addressed us as a group, calling us 'the future of the Sanctuary'. But it was my eye he held as he talked, me he focused on.

We were practising our sparring skills. Caleb told us that our ability to defend ourselves would be key to deciding whether we were fit to visit the surface or not. He had frowned and lowered his voice when he said, 'There could be people up there who wish you harm, and I won't always be around to help you.'

None of us asked for further details; there was no need. The rumours were so ingrained amongst the citizens that they'd become bedtime stories to us. 'Stay away from the surface,' they'd say. 'Nothing awaits you there but death. If the storms don't get you, the cannibals will.' Although they might have caused a few nightmares, the stories meant we never disobeyed.

Still, the thought of being selected to go to the surface excited me. Adventure was short in our closeted world. More than that, to be chosen over everyone else, to be seen as the first choice, just to be *seen* after being invisible for so long...well, that was more than I dared hope for.

Seb was selected as my sparring partner. We were a good match for one another in height and build, but that was where our similarities ended. Where I was olive-skinned, he was pale, my hair dark and unruly, his blond and thin. We were living negatives of one another.

Before that day we'd done little more than shadow

boxing, dancing around one another a good twelve inches out of reach. That was to be the first time we were actually allowed to make contact.

'Remember, we are just jab sparring today,' Caleb warned us. 'No hooks or uppercuts. Spread your focus: offensive, defensive and countering.' He paused. 'And boys, there are no winners today, so keep it friendly. Now, touch gloves.'

We did as he said, a show of sportsmanship before the match began; the last such demonstration from me that day.

Before we'd begun, I'd hoped I had an advantage. I'd done some boxing training with one of the youth groups at my father's church. We'd been there for just a short time before we'd had to move again, but still, it was something.

This felt different, though. Then I'd only been hitting the bag.

Now that an actual person was in front of me, the gloves I was given were heavy and clumsy and slowed me down. Every time I jabbed towards him, Seb moved out of the way with ease. Not one punch landed.

Or perhaps it was nothing to do with the gloves. Perhaps he was just better than me in this, as he was in so many other things. I should let him have that; he deserves it after what I did to him.

'Is that the best you can do?' Seb asked, his words mangled by his mouthguard.

'Just getting started,' I lied. The sweat already covered my back.

Seb wasn't having the same problem. A punch landed on my temple so hard that, even through the head guard I was wearing, I saw stars.

'Ohh, that one looks like it hurt,' Seb said, but he pressed his lips together to suppress a smile.

'Not at—' A gloved fist slammed into my ribs. It deflated my lung and I doubled over, wheezing.

When I'd caught my breath enough to stand, I noticed that David was looking over at us, a frown knitting his brow. That was the worst of it; not my humiliation, but him witnessing it.

'Sorry,' Seb said, patting my shoulder as I dragged in deep breaths. 'That was too hard.'

He was right, it was. Caleb had warned us to pull our punches, that we weren't to put power behind them. I could have told him and got Seb sanctioned. But the truth is I didn't want to; I preferred to handle the matter myself.

'Let's leave it for today,' he said, taking off his helmet. 'I'll grab you some water.'

I guess my sweaty red face had pricked his conscience.

It was then I noticed that David wasn't watching me any more. He was watching you. Instructing, in fact. He modelled how you should hold your hands high for protection. When you held them limp, curled under your chin, he stood behind you and adjusted your awkward limbs.

I was furious.

And there, heading towards the water bottles lined up at the side of the room, was Seb, the source of my shame.

That first thud, as it made contact with the back of his skull, was so satisfying. All my rage from the previous days came flooding out. Evie's disgust. Luca's refusal to accept my apology for pushing him into the lake. I pummelled him again and again, my fists matching my pounding heartbeat.

He had the sense to fall to the floor and cover his head.

Besides, Caleb pulled me off before I could do any real damage.

When the guardians helped him to his feet his eyes rolled in his head.

Caleb patted his cheek. 'Seb, can you hear me?'

He didn't answer. As they carried him towards the infirmary, holding his weight between them, the toes of his trainers squeaked along the floor.

'What were you thinking?' Caleb asked.

'He started it.'

'You realise I've got no choice but to suspend you?' he said.

My shrug must have irritated him, because he added, 'And of course, I'll be talking to your parents.'

My stomach twisted at the thought of their reaction.

But there was one balm to the sting I knew I was about to receive: the hint of the smile that played on David's lips as he passed me.

Jared

Jared shuffled through the names of scientists in his head, an old strategy to keep himself calm. He hadn't realised he'd been mumbling them out loud until Beth leant in close.

'Are you doing okay? If we need to leave, just say. We can come back when it's not all so raw. If Nell were here, she would say the same.'

'Would she?' Aaron asked. 'I think she'd want us to finish this.'

Jared couldn't deny the idea of running was tempting. Every cell in his body told him to escape while he could. But to Beth he said, 'I'm fine. I need to get this over with.'

Living in the Sanctuary had nearly crushed him. Now it had played a big part in taking away somebody he loved. There was a huge part of him that wanted to allow it to implode, destroyed by its own self-righteous vanity. But there was still something, some invisible cord, that tied him to the place. If only he could see it, he'd cut himself free.

'This is Millicent's unit.' Jared hammered his palm against the door. 'Hurry up.' He cast a wary look over his shoulder, praying the guardians wouldn't hear.

'Is there someone else we could try?' Beth asked.

'My mother. But...But I'd rather not. Not yet.'

The door opened a crack. An eye, circled with purple liner, peered from the other side. 'Well, there's a face I didn't expect to see again.'

'I promised,' Jared said.

'You did. But that was over a month ago.' Millicent opened the door fully. 'You'd better come in.'

Jared found himself hesitating at the threshold of her

unit. He told himself to snap out of it, that the units were not really any more enclosed than the rest of the Sanctuary. Still, his senses screamed at him to run, that this was all a trap, and once the door closed behind him, he wouldn't be leaving.

Millicent stood with her hand on her hip. 'Are you coming in or not?'

'Yes.' Jared stepped inside.

Beth ran her fingertips over the polished top of a dresser. 'You have a lovely home.'

'It's filled with nice things,' Millicent said. 'But that doesn't necessarily make it a nice place to live.'

'Well, you should have seen the last place I called home,' Beth said. 'It makes this place look like a palace.'

Jared would never admit that he'd looked up Lady Elizabeth Harding, but temptation had got the better of him. She'd appeared in several family portraits, right up to her death at a ripe old age. Dark haired and willowy, she couldn't look less like their Beth. Not that it mattered. Still, he was surprised to hear her talk of her past so openly.

'I've seen my fair share of hardship,' Millicent said. 'And the most important lesson I've learnt is that it's the people who make a home, not the treasures you hide within it.'

Beth's eyes flitted up and down over Millicent and a smile played on her lips.

'You don't agree?' Millicent asked.

'Oh yes, believe me, I do,' Beth said. 'I was just thinking that it's easy to declare that treasures are unnecessary when you have so many to start with.'

Millicent sniffed and signalled for the three of them to sit.

Ignoring the offer, Beth continued examining Millicent's ornaments.

'So, you finally came back to us, Jared. Truth be told, you're lucky there's anybody left to come back to.' She scanned the group. 'I see you're missing a member, too.'

Beth flinched. 'We...we lost Nell.'

Jared felt Millicent's eyes settle on him, as though she were waiting for him to elaborate. But he knew if he did, he would unleash an overwhelming torrent of accusations and anger. So instead, he stared at his feet, the skin through his sandals blackened from the dusty streets of Ancient Rome.

'No. We didn't,' Aaron said. 'She was taken from us. And Jared thinks you might be able to help us find the man responsible.'

'I'm sorry to hear that. I really am.' Millicent turned to Jared. 'By somebody from the Sanctuary?'

'Yes,' Jared said. 'A guardian. He may not have made the shot himself, but without his interference, Nell would still be here.'

'Who was it?' Millicent asked.

Jared sighed. 'He was in the Guardian Elite at the same time as I was. I don't remember his name. I try not to think about them at all if I can help it.'

'Well, there are a few candidates then. David had a knack for scooping up lost children and moulding them in his image. I'm afraid Durand just built on that cruelty.'

'I remember. If my grandfather hadn't saved me, I might have ended up just like them.'

'No,' Beth said. 'You are a good person. He wouldn't have been able to twist you like that. There is no way you would try and burn innocent people in their beds, to watch them imprisoned and tortured because of what you did. I think these men must have been broken before Durand got to them.'

Jared hoped that was the case, but he couldn't shake the fear that in another life, he might have stood shoulder to shoulder with the Guardian Elite.

'I'm sorry for what they did to you...but not surprised.' Millicent smoothed her skirt, as though imposing order on it might somehow do the same for her thoughts. 'I told you a little of Victor Durand's vile punishments back in Brook Green Valley. But I don't know if I truly put across just how evil he is.'

'I think we have a good idea,' Aaron said, his voice trembling.

'You're hurting; I can see that,' Millicent said. 'So are the citizens of the Sanctuary. Even I had no concept of the depths that man would sink to. And I...well, I know him better than most of the people here.' She gnawed at her lip. 'He has no empathy. No tolerance.

'Some of the newest citizens wanted to practise their religion openly. Victor asked them politely to covert. Then he told them to. When they still refused, he said he would make them appreciate just how good they'd had it in the Sanctuary.'

Jared's stomach twisted. 'How? Did he...did he kill them?'

'Oh no. Victor would never be satisfied with something as mundane as murder. Although, I think their deaths were probably inevitable once he used Edmond's technology to send them back. I assume you've heard of the Spanish Inquisition.'

Somewhere at the back of Jared's mind details surfaced of forced religious conversion through torture. 'I have a vague idea.'

'That's probably for the best. After I found out that was where Durand sent them, I looked it up. I read details I wish I could forget.'

'Why do the people allow it?' Beth asked. 'They should stand up to him.'

'Durand does it all behind closed doors. Only the committee and key members of the Guardian Elite know what goes on inside the Grand Chamber during those trials.'

'People disappear and the citizens don't think that's strange?' Aaron said. 'They don't ever question where they've gone? I refuse to believe that. If they're letting it happen, then they're guilty, too.'

'How convenient to see everything in terms of black and white,' Millicent said. 'I wonder if you would be quite so self-righteous if you were in their position.

'The citizens are frightened. Durand's bigotry doesn't stop at religion. If you don't agree with his opinions on women's education, then you might earn yourself a one-way ticket to the Salem witch trials. Being an educated woman back then left you open to being accused of witchcraft.' Millicent reached for a glass of water on the coffee table and took a shaky sip. 'Then they were drowned, hanged or burned.' The sides of her mouth tugged down. 'It doesn't stop there. We are never sure what will set him off. I've lost count of the number of citizens he's...disposed of.' She fixed her stare on Jared. 'And all of this using your grandfather's technology.'

Guilt prickled Jared's skin. By saving him, his grandfather had provided the means to sentence all those people to death. Or worse.

'That's not Jared's fault,' Beth said.

'You're quite right, dear. It doesn't make them any less dead though, does it?'

A knocking at the door silenced them all. As if remembering it was her unit, Millicent sprung to her feet. 'Who is it?'

'Sienna.'

Millicent's shoulders slumped. 'One moment.'

Sienna barged through the door before it was even fully open. In her arms she carried a stack of blue clothing. 'Why are they here?'

'They've come to help,' Millicent said.

'Too little, too late,' Sienna said, looking directly at Jared.

Jared didn't know what to say. 'Okay.'

'Sienna, hush,' Millicent said. 'If we are going to free the people of the Sanctuary, we need to work together. Because believe me, the Durands won't go down without a fight.'

Sienna puffed out an exasperated breath. 'Fine. Put these on. You don't exactly blend in wearing ...whatever that is.'

Jared looked from his tunic to the blue uniform she'd dropped into his arms. 'No thanks.'

'Are you serious? You may as well hand yourself in now then.'

Beth squeezed his arm. 'It's just clothing. No different from the costumes we wear for the shows.'

Jared wanted to tell her it was very different. He'd feared the guardians for so long that his stomach flipped at the sight of Yale blue. But he couldn't explain, not with Sienna looking at him through narrowed eyes.

'Change in the bedrooms,' Millicent said.

Jared shrugged on the uniform, hoping the faster he did it, the easier it would be. And for a while it worked. It was seeing Beth and Aaron in the uniform that left him mute.

'Just clothes,' Beth repeated.

'At a distance, you might get away with it,' Millicent said. 'If anybody gets any closer than that, the game's over anyway.'

'What exactly is the game?' Sienna asked. 'I mean, you do have a plan, right?' Nobody spoke. 'Well, that's just great.'

'We're …we're going to stop him,' Jared said. 'Take him hostage, if we have to.'

'Hostage?' Aaron shook his head. 'No. We need to finish this.'

'You mean kill them?' Jared asked. 'This isn't you talking, Aaron. You're not a murderer.'

Aaron's Adam's apple bobbed as he swallowed. 'Maybe I am now. Maybe what they did changed me.'

'Well, whatever you plan to do, you're going to need these.' Millicent unlocked the door of the bureau Beth had so admired. She pulled out two of the laser guns used by the guardians. 'Here.'

'No.' Jared took a step away.

'Jared, will you see sense?' Aaron said. 'They aren't going to surrender because we ask them nicely.'

Jared took the weapon and tucked it into his belt, beneath his jacket.

'Give me your hand,' Millicent told him.

On instinct, Jared held it behind his back. 'Why?'

Millicent tugged at his sleeve, pulling his arm towards her. 'If you're really intending to try and reason with Durand, you'll need this, too.' She put the stamper, like the one that had pierced his skin all those years ago, to his flesh.

'Absolutely not,' Jared said. 'I draw the line there.'

'This machine has been modified,' Millicent said. 'It doesn't include the locator element that you received as a child. I must admit, it's not exactly legal. The committee don't know I have it.'

'No way.'

'But Jared, Durand doesn't have a chip either. I guess he didn't want anybody keeping tabs on where he was going.'

'I don't care. You're not putting that thing under my skin.'

'If neither you or Durand have a chip, you realise you won't be able to speak to him? Not alone, anyway. Unless, of course, you learnt French on your travels.'

'As long as somebody else there has a chip—'

'Believe me, you don't want to challenge him in front of an audience. He loves nothing more than playing to a crowd, shocking people with just how vicious he can be.'

Aaron peered at the machine in Millicent's hand. 'So it's just a translator, right? Like in the movies?'

'Yes,' Millicent said. 'I assume you don't speak Dutch. But with one of these chips, it doesn't matter. You can understand every word I'm saying.'

'In which case, give the chip to me. I won't be leaving Jared's side anyway.'

'Me either,' Beth said, offering Millicent her arm. She looked at Jared and shrugged. 'Anyway, it might be useful for the shows, once all of this is over.'

Jared knew it made sense. But looking at Beth and Aaron, dressed as guardians and offering up their hands to be chipped, a rumble of unease travelled through him. Already the Sanctuary was beginning to shape the people he cared for.

The Book of Durand

I loved my mother. But only when she was drunk. You probably think me harsh.

But when she was sober, she was a hard woman to love, all jagged edges and prickly words. When she drank, she softened.

I like to think she was made up of two people, that she also absorbed a twin. But whereas I obliterated mine, they shared one body. During the day, the hard one held an icy grip over the pair of them. But she melted away with a glass of wine and the other mother – the one who liked me – could take control.

The wrong mother opened the door the day of the fight.

'How can I help you, Captain Moss?' She spoke to him, but her eyes were trained on me.

'I'm afraid Martin has been causing a little trouble.' Caleb's hand rested on my shoulder and, as he talked, I felt his fingers tense and dig into my flesh. I don't think he did it on purpose; my mother just had that effect on people.

'And what has he been up to?'

'He started it—' Her glare silenced me, and I studied my shoes.

'He assaulted another student during a friendly sparring match,' Caleb said.

'Well, isn't fighting the point of sparring?' she asked.

'No, mam, especially not when the other boy has no helmet on and is looking the other way. Did your husband tell you he pushed a boy into the lake the other day? Luckily he wasn't hurt but...'

On the walk to our unit, I had practised my story. But as Caleb listed my misdemeanours, my words fell away.

'Thank you for bringing him home. Rest assured, I'll deal with it.'

'I think at the very least he should—'

She cut Caleb off with her sharpest tone. 'I said I would deal with it.'

'Okay.' He took a step back; I envied him his retreat. 'Well, have a nice evening then.'

I risked a glance at her. She was wearing her most saccharine smile, perhaps hoping to sweeten him up after snapping. 'You too, Caleb.'

She guided me through the door and closed it behind her. For a moment, she rested her forehead against it.

I took the opportunity to plead my case. 'Honestly, I—'

Her fist landed on my temple, jerking my head to the side. It astounds me, the logic of teaching a child not to hit by hitting them.

'Mamma, please!' I covered my head with my hands, but she continued to rain down blows upon me as I backed into a corner of the room. Sliding down the wall, I crouched with my face pushed against the stone.

I know how it must have looked. Even at fifteen, I was a head taller than her. A lot of people would have enjoyed seeing me cowering from somebody half my size. You probably would have been one of them. I can't say I blame you.

I stayed in that corner long after she stopped hitting me.

When I peered at her from underneath my arms, she was fixing her hair back into place. Her nose crinkled when she noticed me looking at her. 'You're an embarrassment. Get out of my sight.'

Susan

Susan saw Reed coming and veered in the opposite direction.

'Can I talk to you?' Reed struggled to match her stride.

'Sure,' Susan said, quickening her pace. 'How can I help you?'

'Well, you could slow down for a start.'

She fixed a smile to her face. 'Sorry. What was it you wanted?'

He pulled a handkerchief from his pocket and wiped it across his forehead. 'Maybe we should have this conversation somewhere—'

'Somewhere...more comfortable?' She clasped her good hand to her chest. 'Doctor Reed, are you propositioning me?'

'What? No! I would never...'

She'd always had a black sense of humour, covering some of the most difficult conversations of her life with thickly applied sarcasm. Making this odious man uncomfortable was just a pleasant side effect of that. 'I'm just teasing. Is this hospital business? My hand is still not usable. Didn't David tell you? I'm focusing on the education side of things for now.' She held her bandage aloft like an amulet that could ward him off.

Reed straightened up and jutted out his chin. 'If it were hospital business, you would be the last person I would go to.'

'Excuse me?' She held his eye, deciding silence was the safest course at this point. The trouble was, he appeared to have decided on the same tactic.

He cocked his head to the side and surveyed her for the longest time. Finally, he spoke. 'You aren't Susan Cole.'

'That's ridiculous. I don't have time for this.' She turned on her heel in a show of contempt. In reality, she wanted to hide her rising panic.

'I have proof,' he said to her back.

She considered asking him what he knew, but decided the details didn't matter. She just wanted to get back to her unit and warn Robert.

Reed shuffled his feet as he hesitated. The heavy slap of his shoes told her he had decided to follow.

'Aren't you going to ask me what I know?'

'Nope.' Susan stopped as the tunnel she had led them down branched in two. She was pretty sure the one to the right led towards the Michalowice chamber. Voices echoed from within. She had no desire to bump into anybody while she had Reed in tow, so she turned to the left.

'I've suspected it since you first arrived. I saw pictures of Susan Cole after she published her work on advances in endovascular surgery.'

'Yeah, not my catchiest title, I'll admit.' Susan's head spun and she willed herself to focus. 'What's your point?'

'They were grainy, but you look nothing like her.'

'I'm really not interested in your delusions. Now leave me—'

They had come to a dead end. The rock at the end of the tunnel stuck out in jagged grey peaks. Large chunks of them had been chiselled away and lay scattered around the floor.

The fight fell from both her words and her frame. There was nowhere left to run.

'You'll have to talk to me now,' Reed said. She could hear

the grin he sieved his words through. 'You offered yourself so willingly for the genetic tests. A mother's love, I guess. But that's the thing. Susan Cole wasn't Luca's mother. Not biologically, at least. He was adopted. It's clearly stated on his medical records.'

It felt as though the air were being sucked from the tunnel, and Susan dragged in deep unsatisfying breaths.

'So either you forgot that you adopted your son, or you are not Susan Cole,' Reed said. 'We can do a test if you like, but I think we both know what we'll find.'

She steadied herself, standing with her face so close to the end of the tunnel that she could feel the warmth of her breath reflected back at her. 'What is it you want from me?'

'The truth. Who are you?'

She turned. 'Just a mother trying to keep her child alive.'

The triumph disappeared from his face and was replaced by a scowl. 'Don't give me that. You aren't some heroine, facing adversity. You are a thief who stole another's hard-earned place and most likely condemned her to death. If you didn't kill her outright, of course.'

The accusation was like a gut punch. 'Of course not. I would never—'

'Don't bother denying it. I won't let you get away with this.'

As Susan tried to step around him, he grabbed her wrists.

'Get off me,' she said, twisting her arms within his grip.

'You won't be freeloading off this community any more.'

As he pulled her back towards him, she pushed him away, hard.

It was the way his eyes widened that she noticed first.

But it was only when a dreadful thud reverberated around the tunnel that she realised what had happened.

Reed fell to his knees, swiping at the back of his head as though he could somehow wipe away the wound that had formed there. When his hand came away coated with blood, he held it up to her in confusion, before he slumped forward.

Susan watched as the back of his white shirt turned crimson. She took a tentative step towards him. 'Doctor Reed?'

He didn't answer.

Susan grasped his shoulder and gave him a shake, before springing away from him. 'Can you hear me?'

Silence.

'God, what have I done?' she said, turning to run for help. Then she stopped.

Maybe if she got someone to him in time, they could save him. Maybe he'd make a full recovery and be free to tell the first person he saw exactly who she wasn't.

She slid down the side of the tunnel and looped her arms around her knees. 'If you're still here, Doctor Reed, please know I didn't want this. I'm truly sorry.' Then she sat and waited.

Chapter Six

The Book of Durand

I needed a friend. Since I'd beaten Seb, the other members of the Guardian Elite had kept their distance. Some of the younger ones had even begun to flinch if I moved too fast around them. Part of me enjoyed the power. But the rest of me was just lonely.

Luca hadn't returned to training since I'd pushed him into the lake. I must admit, I felt guilty about that. But not enough to seek him out and apologise again. I'd had enough rejection.

However, when I saw Luca and Evie standing there, I didn't think I had anything left to lose.

'Are you still mad?'

'Mad?' Luca asked. 'You have to care about someone to be mad at them. And I don't think about you at all, to be honest.'

His words cut deep. Not that I'd let him know that. 'Oh come on. It's not like you two are perfect. What about the way you abandoned me in the museum?'

'We didn't,' Evie said. 'We were hiding.'

'Yeah, we got to hear the whole thing.' Luca stuck out his lip and put on a whining voice. 'I'm sorry sir, please don't tell my parents.'

'Leave him alone,' Evie said, although the smirk she wore was just as much a betrayal as Luca's words.

'Well, it's your turn next,' I said. I wracked my brain, speaking my words slowly to give myself more time to think. 'I dare you to...'

'You didn't even ask me yet.'

I hadn't considered this. We had got so caught up with the adrenaline of the dares that I hadn't even thought of truth as an option.

Luca pretended to give this some thought before putting me out of my misery. 'Fine. Dare.'

I knew I had to make it good after my humiliation in the museum. It only took a moment for inspiration to strike. The parallel tracks of one of the salt mine carts ran either side of my feet. There was no cart to be seen, because nobody used them any more. That was something I planned to remedy.

'Ride one of the carts the length of a tunnel,' I said.

Luca studied the tracks and followed them with his eyes. 'Which tunnel? Some are a lot longer than others.'

I was surprised to realise that he had not just accepted my dare, he was entering into negotiations. 'The one by the Michalowice chamber. Nobody will be there at this time of day.'

It didn't take us long to get to the tunnel, and we soon surrounded a cart. I looked at Luca, who in turn was looking at Evie. There we were, a Mexican standoff, each willing the other to protest or back down. None of us did.

Luca took a step away from the cart.

'Second thoughts?' I asked.

'You don't have to do this,' Evie said. 'It's a stupid idea; you could get hurt.'

This annoyed me. It's not like she'd come up with any better ideas. Also, I wondered if she would be so concerned if it were my dare. 'If you're scared—'

'Oh, shut up, Martin,' Evie interrupted.

I glared at her. 'I was going to say, if you're scared, I could do it with you.' That hadn't been what I was going to say at all, but my mouth ran away from me.

'I'm not,' Luca said.

'But maybe you should do it, anyway,' Evie said. 'I don't think we should be allowed to dare something that we aren't willing to do ourselves.'

'Okay.' My stomach lurched.

We circled the cart like a breeder assessing a horse.

'It looks like it will still work,' Luca said.

'I think so,' I agreed, with absolutely no clue if that was true or not.

'How will you stop it once it's going?' Evie asked.

I ran my hand over the long pole at the front. 'I think this is the brake. If it doesn't work, we'll jump. It'll stop one way or another.'

'You mean by crashing?' Luca looked uncertain.

I shrugged. 'Nobody uses them any more anyway.'

And so, it was set. We removed the bricks securing the wheels.

I swung my leg over the top of the carriage.

'What are you doing? Luca asked. 'I'm not getting in. What if we don't get out in time?'

He put one foot on the chassis of the cart and planted the other on the floor. I followed suit. We wouldn't be able to reach the brake from there, but it didn't matter. We had no intention of using it, no matter what we claimed later.

'It's not too late to change your mind.' The giggle Evie gave contradicted her words; there was no way we could back out now.

Luca and I exchanged a final glance before each pushing a foot off the floor. The cart creaked forward.

'Well, that was an anti-climax,' Evie said.

We ignored her and pushed again. And again. The cart began to gain momentum, so that soon my foot was scuffing along the floor and I had to hold it aloft.

The air whipped my face as we barrelled down the tunnel. The rough wood of the cart bit my sweaty palm, but I held on tighter.

Luca whooped beside me. 'This is amazing,' he shouted over the rumbling of the cart.

And it was. For a few fleeting moments. Then the fear set in. How long had we been moving? How deep was the tunnel?

I turned to share my concerns with Luca just in time to see him disappear from the side of the cart.

I, too, let go. I wish I could say I landed gracefully, but I did not. My body decided to follow the cart down the tunnel, whereas my feet, relieved to be back on solid ground, planted firmly and refused to budge. This contradiction left me sprawled on the tunnel floor, chips of salt rock cutting into my skin.

'You two are crazy!' Evie jogged to where I lay.

Luca finished dusting off his knees before he joined us.

An echoing crash left us all speechless and staring down the dimly lit tunnel.

Evie cupped her hand over her mouth, suppressing a laugh. 'So much for the brakes.'

I don't know why we followed the cart down that tunnel. I told myself it was so we could put it back where it belonged. But now, I think it was to see the destruction we had caused. And if destruction was what we wanted, we weren't disappointed.

The cart looked pretty much unscathed. If it hadn't been for the way its front wheels appeared to be climbing the wall at the end of the tunnel, you might have thought the miners had abandoned it there. Luca and I walked around it, trying to assess whether it was safe to pull it from the mound of salt rock on which it sat.

But when we got to the other side of the cart, we saw that it wasn't salt rock on which it rested. An alabaster hand poked from under it. With a sickening jolt I realised we must have hit somebody and their body was now pinned beneath the cart.

A sound, somewhere between a squeal and a wretch, escaped Luca and he bent double.

'We need to go,' I said, trying to move Evie away.

'What's wrong?' She pushed past me. 'Is that a person under there? Oh my God, have you hit a person?'

'Shut up,' I snarled at her.

And she did. But she continued to stare at that motionless hand, its fingertips clawed towards the ground as though it planned to drag its owner out as soon as we turned away.

We looked at it for a long time.

Susan

Susan knew it was her fault. After Reed went missing, David convinced the committee that extending the chipping programme to all members of the Sanctuary immediately, not just the children and new arrivals, was the safest course to protect the community from another tragedy.

The citizens lined up along the various tunnels, each waiting for their turn at the desks in the no-man's land in between. The way the citizens stood there, docile and obliging, reminded Susan of the farm she was raised on. Not that it was much of a farm. Her parents had neither the patience nor the know how to raise anything impressive, be that crops or children.

Of course, they blamed the ground. Her father said their farm was built near the site of an abandoned Nazi extermination camp. They'd levelled it to cover the evidence. But still, he said their land must have been used by the camp in some way, because when you dug down, you'd find patches of earth mixed with sand and ashes and bones. 'Those mass graves,' he told her, 'are the reason our farm is cursed.' She was pretty sure the reason for that was vodka and stupidity.

But there were a few animals they'd managed to keep alive. She did what she could to help, the animals being their only source of income. Together she and Glen would tug the cattle by their harnesses so they could be branded. Susan hadn't thought about it until that moment, but with the sizzle of skin the animals went from free beings to property. A commodity. The cattle would balk and bawl as the metal was applied. It seemed the citizens of the Sanctuary had no such sense, each compliantly holding out their hands.

She got to the front of the queue.

'Which sector are you?' the clerk behind the desk asked.

'Sorry?'

'Sec-tor.' He broke the word in two. 'Did you attend the meeting?'

'Of course,' Susan lied. When all the citizens had been called to the Grand Chamber, she'd hidden in her unit, praying nobody would find her. That wouldn't be a possibility after today. But when she'd heard Durand would be leading the meeting, she'd seized the opportunity, feigning illness to Robert and Luca. 'I'm just...'

'She's STEM.' Father Durand placed a hand on her shoulder and Susan's body went rigid. 'This is Susan Cole. One of our most esteemed doctors.'

Was that sarcasm that tinged his words? Susan couldn't tell; insincerity seemed to be his natural tone of voice.

'Sorry, Doctor Cole,' the clerk said, and brought the stamp down on her hand.

Susan looked from the blemish it left and up to Durand. 'I...I wasn't well.'

He batted away her apology. 'I think we got off on the wrong foot. You and I could be very useful to each other, if we can put the past behind us.'

Useful. Whether that word came from David or Durand, it meant nothing good. That's when Susan realised she had been wrong. This process wasn't like branding day on the farm. It was much worse. She was being sized up for the slaughter.

~

Seb

Doctor Chorazycki's premonition came true with startling speed. As Seb moved between the lower camp and the extermination area, he watched as more and more prisoners were brought to their knees by the disease.

'Keep your eyes on your work,' Jacob warned him.

But it was impossible not to notice as the bouts of coughing and vomiting felled the men around him. And if he had noticed, he had no doubt that before long the guards would, too.

Galewski had spread the word. The camp was in decline and there was no way to hide it from their captors any more. Now it was about negotiating some level of mercy.

When Seb saw the Ukrainian officer Manchuk talking to Galewski, temptation got the better of him. He knew it would earn him a whipping if he was caught listening. He was only supposed to be in the lower camp to work. But when the fate of a large portion of the camp was at stake, he couldn't resist.

'Ten is not enough,' Galewski said. 'There are nearly eight hundred men living in this camp.'

'That is what Stangl has offered,' Manchuk said, stamping out his cigarette with his boot. 'This is not a negotiation. Take it or leave it.'

'Fifteen, that is all I am asking for. Fifteen beds.'

Manchuk fell silent, and Seb had images of him reaching for his weapon, ready to punish Galewski for his stubbornness.

'I'll pass on your request,' Manchuk said. 'But don't get your hopes up.'

But to Galewski this was as good as a triumph. As soon as the officer was out of view, he beamed at this assumed victory.

'What were you thinking?' See asked. 'Are you trying to get yourself killed?'

'I would imagine snooping around like that would get you a similar punishment.' Galewski walked towards the barracks.

Seb followed. 'Don't forget what he did to Silva.'

'As if I could. But as terrible as that was, it was the first step towards change.'

'What do you mean?'

'Fifteen beds to be used by sick prisoners, who will be officially exempt from work. After that, who knows. A prisoner infirmary, perhaps.'

Seb did not want to ruin his friend's mood by pointing out that they had only agreed to ten. 'What's that got to do with Silva?'

'This is down to his parting gift to us. Do you know what that was? Fear. They are scared of us, Seb, though they'd never admit it. They know we outnumber them and that we can access tools that can be used as weapons, just as Tomas did. What do you think all of these random searches have been about?'

It was true that security had become more stringent with security, but he'd put it down to the perverse whims of the likes of Kuttner. The thought that he could ever provoke any feeling but disdain in their captors had never occurred to Seb.

'Fear is power, as these monsters well know,' Galewski said. 'I have no plans to end my days here, but if that's God's will then I will use the little power I have to help the prisoners before I go.'

'You're a good man.'

Galewski ignored the compliment. 'Get back to the extermination area. Stangl wants everybody in line for his announcement at roll call.'

Seb gathered his things and hurried back. The men were already gathering by the time he got to the roll call area. Franz Stangl stood at the front. No matter how many times he saw him, Seb was always shocked by his appearance. His doll-like features didn't marry with the ruthless killer inside.

When the men were all assembled, Stangl paced up and down the line. 'We are aware that the typhus epidemic plaguing our camp is causing panic.'

The men kept tight lipped. They all knew the fate of the sick in Treblinka.

'We are doing all we can to stop the outbreak spreading any further. You will have noticed the buildings being sprayed regularly with disinfectant. We are also in the process of setting up a laundry, as we know that here in the extermination area you do not have the same access to clean clothes as in the lower camp.'

The availability of clean clothes, referred to like it was a privilege of the lower camp, was down to the prisoners stealing from the bundles left by the dead.

'But we can only stop this epidemic by working together,' Stangl continued. 'We are playing our part and you must play yours. You are highly trained, valued workers, and we do not wish to waste time or resources replacing good men. For that reason we are setting up an infirmary for you in the extermination area. If you are ill, you must remain in the barracks tomorrow morning. Our own physician Doctor Chorazycki will assess your condition and choose patients for the new infirmary. You will not be harmed; you have my word.'

The word of a murderer, Seb thought. It was worth so little. But what choice did they have?

Susan

Susan Cole, Luca Cole, Robert Cole, Edmond Pearse, Benjamin Reed. Five names, five lives ruined by the actions of her family. Susan repeated them over and over in an act of self-flagellation.

Any hope she had of putting it behind her, of burying her guilt deep within, was pointless. It had been over a month since Edmond's attack, and still it was all anybody wanted to talk about. Susan suspected that, for the majority, the hurried gasps and dramatic whispers weren't born of concern. Dinner table fodder, that's what they'd turned it into. People she'd barely spoken to since arriving beckoned to her, keen to see if Laura had passed on any new information. Their morbid fascination revolted Susan. Not that they'd know that; their enthusiasm blinkered them to her bowed head and vague answers. She wondered if the truth would dampen that enthusiasm. *Yes,* she could tell them, *I know all about it. In fact, my husband is the one who pummelled our noble founder into unconsciousness. Thank you for asking.* Although Susan liked to think they'd be horrified, she suspected it would just ignite their interest. She wondered if they'd be so keen to ask about Edmond if they knew about the body of Doctor Reed lying undiscovered in the nearby tunnel. In their macabre minds, surely a death would trump an assault.

The school was a respite from it all. The children seemed oblivious to everything that was going on. At least she hoped they were. If it weren't for the constant threat of bumping into Laura, she might even have been happy there.

Susan was heading home after finishing her classes for

the day when a guardian stepped into her path. 'All citizens are to report to the Grand Chamber.'

They liked to do this. Compulsory meetings were often called with a moment's notice. Susan assumed it was a control thing and most of the time tried to roll with it. But today, she'd had enough. 'I just want to go home,' she said, trying to push past him.

He grasped her shoulders and tried to turn her round. 'It's not a request.'

'Get off me.' Susan tried to wriggle away.

'I said—'

'What's going on?' Marney stood at the mouth to the STEM tunnel.

The guardian took a step backwards. 'Mr Malone wants everyone in the Grand Chamber.'

'Okay. Well, this isn't necessary. I'll walk in with her.' Marney hooked her arm into Susan's. 'Are you okay?'

'I'm tired and just want to get home. I don't see what's so urgent that it can't wait until tomorrow.'

'Me neither,' Marney said. 'But I heard it's something to do with Edmond Pearse.'

Susan let out a puff of irritation. 'Sorry.' She forced a smile. 'It's just, he's all anybody wants to talk about lately. As though, just because I've taken a few classes at the school, Laura would confide in me.'

'Well, don't worry, I have no desire to talk about him.'

Susan tilted her head. 'And why is that?'

'Don't get me wrong,' Marney said quickly. 'I really hope they get the scum that attacked him.'

Susan felt heat crawl from beneath her collar at Marney's description.

'And I wish him all the best,' Marney continued. 'But before I came to the Sanctuary, Edmond and I had some...professional differences. I think it would be a little insincere if I went throwing myself across his sick bed now.'

'That's refreshing. You're the first person I have heard say a bad word about him.'

'Now, now. Don't put words into my mouth. Anyway, we seem to be doing a great job at not talking about him by talking about him. I've been meaning to ask how things are going at the school.'

'Fine.'

Marney frowned. 'You don't sound too enthusiastic.'

'Sorry...It's just...I've got some things on my mind.'

'If there's anything—' Marney's eyes fixed on a point over Susan's shoulder. 'Laura!'

As Laura stopped in front of them, Marney faltered. 'How are you? And your father, of course?'

Tiny veins had turned Laura's eyes a watery pink. Paired with the dark shadows under her eyes, it was clear she hadn't been getting much sleep. 'We're all doing fine. Edmond is on the road to recovery.' The way she rubbed the top of her own arm, as though comforting herself, made Susan wonder who she was trying to convince.

'Of course he is,' Marney said with a little too much enthusiasm. 'The apocalypse barely slowed him down. He'll take this in his stride, too.'

Laura didn't say anything for a while, and Susan saw Marney glance at her in her peripheral vision. *If you're hoping for somebody to bail you out of this awkward little exchange,* Susan thought, *best not look to the wife of the man who nearly killed her father.*

Finally, Laura spoke. 'Jared's waiting for me. I'd better go.'

'If there's anything...' The words tumbled from Susan's mouth, cut off by a traitorous lump in her throat. She swallowed it down. 'Anything I can do for you, let me know.'

'Thank you.' Laura headed towards the chamber.

'That poor family,' Susan said. And she meant it. Laura's son was about Luca's age. What right did they have, she thought, to detonate his world just to safeguard their own son's future? 'Is she close to her father?'

'I don't think so.'

'I doubt it makes it any easier.' Susan knew this from experience. She envied those who grew up knowing they were loved. When she'd lost her own parents to addiction, it was the relationship they'd never have that she mourned.

'No,' Marney said. 'I don't imagine it does. We'd better get in there before David sets his glorified hall monitors on us.'

When they entered, many of the pews were already full. Susan saw Robert standing at the end of one, waving her over, ready to usher her into one of the last two seats on the row.

'Looks like I'm wanted over there,' Susan said.

'So I see. I meant what I said. If you want to talk...'

'Thank you.'

Susan slid past Robert into the pew.

'Why are we here?' Robert asked as she was seated.

Susan couldn't stop irritation tinging her words. 'How am I supposed to know? David and I aren't exactly buddies.'

'I thought maybe he'd mentioned it at one of those Citizens' Voice meetings you go to.'

'Don't be ridiculous. At best I'm window dressing. At worst his pawn. He doesn't tell me anything.'

The heavy wooden doors of the Grand Chamber opened. A familiar man walked through them. Susan had seen him many times, wandering the tunnels, ranting about the walls caving in. She knew she should have shown compassion, asked if he was okay. Instead, she'd told Luca to stay away from him.

'That's Julian Manning. He's an engineer here,' Robert said. 'Do they really need to cuff him like that?'

Susan hadn't even noticed the restraints looping his wrists. 'We don't know what he's done. Maybe he's dangerous.'

'It just seems excessive for one man.' Robert paled as David took the stage.

Clearing his throat, David began. 'Thank you all for coming tonight...'

'Look,' Robert hissed into her ear. 'Front row.'

Susan could just make out the back of Edmond Pearse's head, his stubborn tufts of hair unmistakable. 'Thank God.'

Susan was so overwhelmed with relief that she missed David's words as he addressed the crowd. Whatever he said left the Grand Chamber cloaked in an eerie stillness.

It was Julian who broke the silence. 'David, will this take long? The air ducts are overdue their checks.'

'No, my friend, this won't take long.' David turned back to the crowd. 'The committee have faced an impossible choice. We knew that whatever we decided, there would be those who disagreed. Banishment was one option we discussed. But how can we, in good conscience, send a vulnerable person to the surface when they are unable to care for themselves? That would not be mercy. And, on the off chance he was found by survivors, what would stop him giving away our location? Somebody so unstable cannot be expected to keep our secret, to keep us safe. I'm sure none of us want looters, or worse, at our door.'

Just the word looters made Susan's stomach lurch. She pushed away the memory of calloused hands against her skin, cigarette breath against her face, and tried to focus.

'Permanent imprisonment was another option,' David continued. 'But the resources and manpower necessary to sustain that scenario...It is the rest of you who would pay the price, and that just is not fair.'

A woman in the row behind whispered to her neighbour. 'He's right. But we can't have a lunatic like that running around. Have you seen what he did to Doctor Pearse?'

Robert's hand tightened over her own. He'd heard too. Mystery solved. It was Edmond's attack that Julian was on trial for.

'We must protect the weakest members of our society.' David looked directly at Edmond. 'We made a promise to provide you all with a sanctuary. I swore to protect you from dangers both on and below the surface of the Earth. I intend to keep that promise.'

David nodded and a guardian walked onto the stage. He pulled a weapon from the holster on his belt.

Bile rose in Susan's chest. 'I can't watch this. Let me out.' She got to her feet, intending to slide from the pew.

Robert tugged her back. 'Sit down.'

David drew in a steadying breath. 'Laws were broken, and justice must be swift – for the safety of us all. Julian

Manning, the committee finds you guilty of attempted murder, and we sentence you to death.'

The world flared in a flash of light and Julian disappeared in a blizzard of particles. Susan stared at the empty space that remained where he'd been only moments before.

The scream brought her back to her senses. Somewhere in the crowd a child wailed. She watched as Laura Pearse cupped her son's face in her hands, willing him to calm down. People tried to shuffle past them so that mother and son were jostled in every direction, adding to his anguish.

'What have we done?' Susan said to herself. Then she repeated the names: Susan Cole, Luca Cole, Robert Cole, Benjamin Reed, Edmond Pearse, Laura Pearse, Jared Morgan, Julian Manning.

The Book of Durand

They say there are three versions of every story: yours, theirs and the truth. But I'll try and be as honest as I can about the events after we crashed the car. I think that's the least I owe Evie.

'We need to tell somebody,' she said, clutching the railing of the lake.

I gawped at her. 'Don't be stupid. Do you want to be banished?'

'No, but...whoever that is, they must have a family. Somebody who will miss them.'

'She's right,' Luca said. 'We do have to tell somebody.'

I wanted to shake him, to shake both of them. Murder was very different from putting a little lipstick on a statue. Above all, I was terrified that this would confirm it; I really was the monster everyone, including me, suspected I was. 'You're insane, both of you.'

Luca held up his fist to me, and for a second, I thought he was going to hit me. 'They will know we were there.'

He was right. Although my father had it removed later so that he could go where he pleased and do whatever he wanted in the Sanctuary, at that point Luca was chipped. Evie, too.

'Then, let's think this through first. We can't just blurt it out to the first guardian we see.'

'Caleb,' Luca said. 'He's nice. And he knows us. He knows we'd never have done this on purpose.'

They were right; he was the best choice. But still, I couldn't bear the thought of him knowing what we'd done. However, somehow, I knew David would understand it all.

The dates, the lake, everything: it was all about power. Dominance. And those were terms he dealt in.

'No. I'm going to speak to David. Please,' I said. 'Trust me. Just give me until the morning. Come on, you saw that guy. He's dead. Twelve hours won't make any difference.'

Luca and Evie glanced at each other.

'Just until morning,' Luca said. 'That's all the time you get.'

It irritated me, the way he spoke like he was in charge. But more than that I feared lines were being drawn, with me as the culprit on one side and them on the other.

I'm guilty of many things, but not of lying about the body. I did exactly as I'd promised and went to David that night.

'I killed somebody,' I said as he opened the door to his unit.

David's eyes widened for a millisecond before he said, 'And good evening to you, too.'

'I'm not joking. I really did kill somebody.'

'Then I guess you'd better come in and tell me about it.'

So I told him everything. When I finished, he was silent for so long that I began to squirm.

'Leave this with me,' he said finally.

'When will the guardians come for me?'

'I think we can forego the handcuffs for now. I'll come and talk to you tomorrow.' He stood up and I realised that he wanted me to leave. 'And Martin? Let's keep this between us for the time being.'

Days passed, but I heard nothing from him. Still, I waited, sure that he'd come through for me.

I knew what Evie and Luca must have been thinking.

The deadline had passed and, as far as they knew, I'd done nothing. On the third day, they cornered me in the dining room.

Luca stepped into my path before I could reach the queue. 'So?'

I reached around him for a tray. 'So what?'

'Don't be obtuse, Martin.' Evie's eyes were bright, lit with a mix of adrenaline and irritation. 'What did David say?'

I shrugged. 'He said he'd handle it.'

'You told him we killed somebody and that's all he had to say? You're lying,' she said.

'I'm not. But thanks for the show of confidence.'

She studied me for the longest time. Then she growled with frustration and turned on her heel.

Luca dithered.

'Aren't you going to follow her?' I asked.

'I think I'll let her calm down first. Did you really tell him?'

'Yes.'

He chewed at his lip. 'Was he angry?'

'It's hard to tell with David.'

'Yeah. Not knowing what will happen is the worst part of all this.'

'Well, don't worry. I was honest. He knows it was my idea. If there is a punishment coming our way, I'll take it.'

'Why would you do that?'

I gave it some thought. In all honesty, I hadn't even considered throwing the two of them under the bus, but I think that was mainly because I knew everyone would just assume it was my fault anyway. I didn't say that, though. 'I don't know. I figured I owed you one after the lake.'

That seemed to please him, so much so that we ate together, each of us careful not to mention Evie or the dares.

It was when we walked back to our sector that we noticed a group of people trailing towards the Michalowice chamber. Of course, we followed.

Only they weren't going to the chamber, but the tunnel that diverged from it.

'Oh no...You don't think...' Luca paled.

A crowd was gathering at the mouth of the tunnel where, only days ago, we'd crashed the car.

Evie stood in the middle, next to Caleb. 'I swear, it was here.'

'Maybe you dreamt it,' Caleb said.

'It was real.'

He put a soothing hand to her shoulder. 'Sometimes nightmares seem real to me, too. But you know you're safe here, Evie.'

She backed away from him. Then she caught me looking. 'Martin, tell him there was a body.'

David stepped from the crowd before I could speak. 'Don't try and get your friends to back up your little charade, young lady. We've told you already; there is no body.'

'I...Luca? Tell them. Please.'

Luca stared at the floor. 'I don't know what you mean.'

Evie fled, the echo of the soles of her sandals hitting the salt rock lingering long after she disappeared.

As the crowd dispersed, David walked over to us. 'Quite the display she put on there.'

'What...What did you do with the body?'

David sighed. 'Not you, too. You boys listen. This isn't a game. Stories like that scare people. And when people get scared, they do silly things.'

Luca gasped. 'I swear we—'

'Enough! I don't want to know.' David tutted. 'I expected better from you boys.'

As he walked away, I felt Luca's eyes boring into me.

'I did tell him. I swear.'

But Luca didn't believe me. How he explained away the disappearing body, I don't know. He shut me down every time I raised the topic. I guess, now that he's gone, I will never get the chance to persuade him of my innocence.

Jared

'Jared, will you please sit down,' Millicent said.

'I'm nervous. Can't we just go and get this over with?'

'He'll still be asleep in his unit,' Sienna said. 'The man simultaneously manages to believe everybody loves him and that everyone wants to kill him. There will be guardians at his door. You'd never get past.'

'She's right,' Millicent said. 'Better to take him by surprise. He's supposed to be presiding over a trial today. There's no way he'll miss that. Sienna will sneak you into the Grand Chamber before it starts.'

Sienna's head snapped up.

Millicent ignored her glare. 'You should all rest for now. Try to eat something.'

'What did they do?' Jared asked. 'The one he's putting on trial.'

Millicent's brow knitted. 'Absolutely nothing.'

'Then why—'

Sienna sniffed. 'It's a bit late to start concerning yourself with the welfare of the citizens now.'

Jared noticed the way Aaron and Beth glanced at one another, confirming to him that the hostility he felt radiating from Sienna wasn't just in his head. He considered ignoring it, but he really wanted to understand why she was so angry with him. So when she cleared the breakfast dishes from the table, Jared followed her into the kitchen. 'Have I done something to offend you?'

'Why would you think that?' she asked.

'I don't know. You just don't seem to like me.'

'And there we have it,' she said, as though what he'd said

had won her a bet.

'I don't understand.'

'You think it's all about you. I don't dislike you, Jared. You haven't featured in my life at all since you and your grandfather flitted off into the sunset. Beyond trying to piece back together the fragments of the society that you fractured, of course.'

'Oh. Sorry,' he said, because he didn't know what else she expected of him.

'Ugh. There we are again. That little boy lost act. You got to become a martyr round here; the boy who sacrificed his place in the Sanctuary to break free. The people hoped that you'd come back for them. Or that they might get the same opportunity you did. It almost tore this place apart.' She dumped the dishes into the sink. 'People like my parents were left to vouch for you, argue that you weren't some dangerous enemy of the state we needed to hunt down.'

'I...I didn't realise.' Jared hadn't considered that he'd had any impact at all on the Sanctuary since the day he left.

'Why would you? Still, I'm sure you'll get a hero's welcome when the citizens see you're still alive.'

'I didn't realise others were so unhappy here.'

'Did you think to ask?' Sienna held him in a steely gaze. 'While you've been off on your adventures, the likes of me had to stay behind and try and influence this place from the inside. Freedom wasn't an option for me. And my parents...When they tried to loosen the shackles of this place, when they suggested there might be other options, Durand made them pay.'

'What—'

'I don't want to talk about it.' Her tone softened. 'You

realise that now you're back, the citizens will try to turn you into a leader. The prodigal son returns. You'll give them hope. Are you sure you're up to the respons—'

The nasal tone of Victor Durand's voice filled the air.

Good morning, citizens of the Sanctuary.

'Where's that coming from?' Jared asked, plugging his ears against the boom as he walked back to the dining room.

Sienna groaned. 'The tannoy system. It was meant for security. Now they use it to inflict this drivel on us, every half hour from the moment we open our eyes. All day, every day.'

Our society is built upon the principles of justice and judgement.

'Can't you just turn it off?' Beth asked.

'Well, I had thought of that, dear,' Millicent said. 'But no. There is no off switch.'

'Yeah,' Sienna added, 'and tampering with the speakers is a criminal offence.'

Colossians 3:25 tells us that the wrongdoer will pay for what he has done. Punishment will be swift.

'That's...intense,' Jared said, wondering what it must be like to be assaulted with such relentless poison.

Follow the rules. Be a good citizen. And be certain of this: if you do not, his will shall be done. I am but his loyal servant.

'I'd like to say it becomes like white noise eventually,' Sienna said, 'but I've never managed to block it out.'

'How did Durand get so powerful?' Beth asked.

'When David disappeared, people were frightened,' Millicent said. 'And there Durand was, selling himself as the father figure of the Sanctuary. He promised to guide and protect them, and that's exactly what they needed to hear. We didn't realise it was him we needed protecting from.'

'Besides,' Sienna said, 'with his sons at his side, he made quite a formidable force.'

'Sons?' Jared asked. 'I thought he had just one child.'

'A lot of things changed after you left.' Sienna punctuated her words with a chuckle, although Jared didn't understand what was so funny. 'Well, before you left really. But I don't think any of us saw it coming back then.'

'Saw what coming?' Aaron asked.

Sienna shrugged. 'None of us know what happened to Serena Durand. But after she disappeared, Durand chang—'

'He didn't change,' Millicent said, her words sharp. 'His mask just began to slip. Victor Durand has always been a nasty piece of work. I just never suspected he'd be evil enough to use the most vulnerable amongst us to do his bidding.'

'Who?' asked Beth.

'The orphans,' Millicent said. 'The unfortunate children of the banished. They are puppets now, and Durand is pulling the strings.'

～

Seb

The next morning, the men sat debating whether those who were ill should confess and hope Stangl's offer was genuine.

'Well, I'm not staying,' one man said. He swayed as he got to his feet, his sallow skin betraying the infection pulsing through his veins. 'I'll take my chances out there.'

'But Stangl wasn't wrong,' another said. 'The number of transports is shrinking all the time. They can't replace us as easily as they once could, even if they want to.'

The door swung open, banging against the wall behind and cutting short the debate. Stangl and his men entered, Galewski just behind.

'Those of you who are sick will have the day to rest. The doctor will come and assess your condition shortly,' Stangl said. 'The rest of you, line up for roll call.'

A flurry of men exited the barracks, Seb among them. He hung by the door, waiting for Jacob to catch up.

'Now,' Stangl told Galewski, 'choose your fifteen.'

'Please,' Galweski said. 'Not again.'

All colour had drained from Jacob's face by the time he reached Seb.

'What's going on in there?' Seb asked. 'I thought the doctor was coming.'

'Nothing good,' Jacob said. 'Come on.'

As they walked towards the half-finished barracks, Jacob waved away all further attempts to discuss what might have happened. So when Seb saw Sadovitz in the vegetable garden as they passed, he walked close to the plot, hoping to catch his eye.

Sadovitz scanned the area before walking towards him.

'Have you heard? Stangl killed the prisoners who admitted to having typhus.'

'All of them?'

'No. A handful were selected to go to the new infirmary. Apparently, that makes him a man of his word. The scum made Galewski choose.'

'What about Marcus?' Beyond his concern for the boy, Seb knew Marcus was integral to any plan for rebellion.

Sadovitz nodded. 'He made the cut. Just. Stangl said that Galewski could pick ten men. When Galewski pleaded for fifteen, Stangl made him get on his knees and beg. Marcus was the eleventh prisoner chosen.'

The Book of Durand

You've never mentioned what Luca and I did to you that day in the tunnel, not long after you arrived. Aren't you curious about whether I regret it? The truth is, I don't. That probably wasn't what you wanted to hear, but I promised to tell the truth and I've decided that, for however much time I have left, I'm going to be a man of my word.

It wasn't personal, if that helps. I was just so angry. At my mother. At Seb. At the world. And there you were, looking every bit the victim.

Besides, I don't know if you remember, but it was Luca who started it. 'If your mother and grandfather are called Pearse, why is your last name Morgan?'

If you'd just shut up things might have been different. But you had to run your smart mouth, telling us it was none of our business. Maybe it wasn't. But who were you to say that? It might have looked like I lost control. Although I saw it as the opposite. I was finally taking some control back.

And if Evie hadn't got involved, that might have been the end of it. But she charged in, leaping to your defence. I didn't even see her coming. That's what it was like with her. She was insidious. I hadn't seen my love for her growing any more than I'd noticed her distaste for me bloom. Can you imagine what that's like, falling in love for the first time only to suspect she despises you? The punch she delivered was almost as much of a shock. When I licked my lips, I tasted the coppery tang of my own blood.

'Leave him alone.' She'd looked directly at me when she said it.

I stared at Luca, waiting for him to back me up or to admit his guilt.

Instead, he held up his hands. 'Don't look at me. I'm not hitting a girl.' As though that had been my suggestion.

She turned to him, her face twisted into a snarl. 'Go on. I'll let you have the first swing for free.'

I honestly think she'd have fought us both to protect you. And if she was prepared to go to those lengths to protect a virtual stranger, I don't know why I was shocked by the rumours that spread around the camp soon after. Only we both know that they weren't just rumours. Evie was willing to kill to protect herself. Not that there's anything wrong with that. To me, that seems the most natural instinct in the world.

Did I tell you that on the day Evie was arrested, she came to me for help? I used to daydream about Evie turning up on my doorstep. But when I found her standing there, my words betrayed me.

'Luca isn't here,' I said.

She frowned. 'Why would he be?'

'I don't know. I just assumed you were looking for him.'

'No. It was you I came to talk to.'

My father's voice boomed from behind me. 'Hurry up and close that door, Martin. Your mother isn't well. She doesn't need a draught.'

'I'm sorry,' Evie said. 'I should go.'

'No, please, come in.' My mind raced with the possibilities as to what she could want to talk to me about.

She slid past me so close that her hair brushed my arm. 'Are you sure this is okay? I can leave.'

'Of course...' But I realised she wasn't speaking to me.

My father's smile did nothing to banish the shadows around his eyes. 'You'd better come in and sit down. Martin, get her a towel.'

I'd been so shocked to see her that I hadn't noticed the map of pink water marks covering her dress. 'What happened? Why are you wet?'

She stared down at her clothes, as though she too had only just noticed. 'I had to wash it off,' she said, wrapping her arms around her to guard herself from the cold.

'Wash what off?' I asked.

My father interrupted before she could reply. 'I told you to get her a towel.'

I went to the bathroom and rummaged in the linen closet. But I didn't go straight back to them. Instead, I lingered at the door.

'Where did you get the knife?' my father asked.

'The old museum.'

I thought back to the day we'd broken in. I could still hear the distinct clang the knife made as I dropped it to the floor. *Please*, I prayed, *don't tell him I was with you.*

'Where is it now?' My father was using what I'd come to think of as his 'institution' voice. He'd used it with my mother when she'd been ill, during those endless days stretched out within the pastel green walls of the psychiatric ward. It sounded like he'd been coaxing her down off a ledge. In some ways, I suppose, he had been.

'I threw it in the lake when I cleaned off the...' She crumpled. I couldn't bear to hear her sobs.

As I stalked into the room, I had no idea what I was going to say, how I was going to make it better, but I had to try. She looked up at me, her face streaked with tears.

'Here's your towel,' I said. Her life was disintegrating around her and that was all I, the person she'd chosen to turn to for help, could think to say. Here's. Your. Towel.

'I'm going to make our young friend some tea,' my father said, and busied himself in the kitchen.

I sat next to her. 'Are you okay?'

'No.'

'Can I do anything to help?'

'No.'

Resentment bubbled inside me. After all, she had come to me. I'd had no time to prepare, no opportunity to learn the lines of the soap opera she'd thrust me into. So don't judge me too harshly for what I said next. 'Then why are you here?'

'You're right,' she said, getting to her feet. 'I should go.'

'Nonsense,' my father said, as he returned with her drink. 'Sit down.'

She plonked down on the sofa without missing a beat, the teaspoon rattling on the edge of her saucer. What can I say? When my father gave an order, people obeyed.

'Drink up,' he said.

Evie put the cup to her lips and took a tiny sip.

'Does your mother know you're here?' Father asked.

She took another gulp. 'No.'

'Well, we will have to tell her.'

'Please,' Evie begged, 'don't.'

'I promise you're safe here,' my father said, taking her empty teacup. 'Try to rest for a while. You must be exhausted.'

'I am,' she said, her lip trembling.

I don't know when my father called them. Perhaps when

he excused himself to check on my mother. But when the guardians knocked, Evie's head was lulled to one side. She didn't wake at first.

'Miss. You need to come with me,' the guardian said.

She looked at him through heavy lashes, only responding when he encircled his fingers around her bicep and pulled her to her feet. 'Get up.'

As they led her away, she shot me a look over her shoulder loaded with disappointment.

'It wasn't me,' I called after her. But my father closed my words inside when he slammed the door behind her.

He wagged a finger at me. 'Corinthians 15:33. 'Bad company ruins good morals.' Choose your friends more wisely, Martin. Our family has a reputation to uphold.'

That was it. The girl who had dominated my every waking thought had come to me for help, and I'd failed her. She deserved better.

'That little girl is a murderer,' my father told me after she was marched away.

I stuttered my response. 'But she's my friend.'

'Well, one day such a friend might prove useful.' He chuckled at that last comment like he'd told a joke. I didn't laugh. 'But still,' he continued, 'I want you to stay away from her. At least until we know where the chips have fallen.'

My sadness must have shown, because he huffed. 'You'll make new friends. And believe me, you have too much work to do to waste your time on girls. You're going to be a leader, Martin. Act like one.'

The fact I didn't want to be a leader was irrelevant to his plans. But since then I've learnt that with leadership comes power, and that can be very useful. If I'd had any then, I could have stopped them banishing her.

'Are you happy now? You got what you wanted. That must make you happy.' Those were Evie's words the day she left. I am not self-centred enough to think she was talking to me. I doubt I was even an afterthought during her last moments in the Sanctuary. But still, they stung more than any punch she ever threw. Because we'd let her down, every one of us.

Susan

When Susan got back to the unit, she found Robert sitting on the sofa, his fists to his temples. 'What's wrong?'

He didn't meet her eye. 'David wants to see us. He said he needs another favour.'

'But you told him we were done with all of that. What you did...that was it. We're quits.'

'Well, I guess he doesn't see it that way.'

'Did he say what he wanted?'

Robert shrugged. 'Just that he needed both of us.'

'No. I am not having this. We had a deal.' The door slammed shut behind her, cutting off Robert's protests.

As she neared the end of the tunnel, her anger was clouded with doubt and her pace slowed. She needed to give this some thought. David was too clever for her to try and take him on without a semblance of a plan.

Susan lingered at the end of the tunnel in the the no man's land in between sectors. She was about to turn on her heel, to go back to Robert and map out their next steps. But she faltered outside a familiar unit. Marney had pointed it out to her on the day she'd walked Susan to the school.

Susan knocked.

Pulling the door closed against the sound of squealing girls, Marney flashed her an apologetic smile. 'This is a nice surprise. I'd invite you in, but as you can hear, it's feeding time at the zoo.'

Susan hesitated. 'You're a mother.'

'I don't get it. What's the game? Things we know about each other?'

'I need to ask a favour.'

'Sure.'

'Listen first. And don't say yes if you can't keep your word.'

'Now I'm intrigued,' Marney said.

'If something happened to me, could I trust you to look after Luca?'

'That is a very strange question. But I would never let anything happen to a child.'

'I need more than that. Not that you wouldn't let anything happen to him, but that you would care for him. Like a guardian. I know it's a lot to ask and that we barely know each other, but I don't know who else to go to for help.'

'Susan, that's a huge commitment. Surely there's someone more—'

'I know. I never should have... I'm sorry I disturbed you.'

'Wait. Please, tell me what's wrong.'

'I can't,' Susan said. 'I really wish I could, but I can't.'

Marney sighed. 'Are you in danger?'

'I think so. At the very least, I don't think we will be able to stay here. But Luca...He's too fragile right now to take back up to the surface. He needs time for the medication you prescribed to kick in.'

Marney rubbed her brow. 'How long are we talking?'

'In all honesty, I don't know. As little time as possible. I love my son, Marney. I will come back for him.'

'I just...why me?'

'Because you're strong. You'll protect him.'

Marney reached for her hand. 'Against whom?'

Susan pulled away. 'It's better I don't say. Please trust

that I wouldn't be asking this if I wasn't desperate. I don't know who else to turn to.'

'Okay,' Marney said. 'If he needs me, I'll be here for him. And when you come back, we'll be waiting.'

Jared

'I want to come with you,' Beth said. 'We shouldn't split up. Not again. Let me help.'

Jared knew any reassurances that he would be back, that they wouldn't lose anybody else in their group, would sound as empty as they felt. He could promise no such thing and it sent dread running through his system.

'You will be helping,' Jared said. 'We lost so much in the fire. Collecting supplies with Millicent is the most useful thing you can do right now.'

Beth lowered her voice. 'Let Aaron do that. I can handle myself. He's just a kid.'

'I know you can,' Jared said. 'But I don't think I could stop him coming with me, even if I tried.'

'We've got to get moving,' Sienna said, waving them towards the door.

'What's the rush?' Aaron asked. 'It's still early.'

'This is the best time to go. The guardians will be at shift change. The citizens will have just got up. But it doesn't mean we're safe. There will still be a few guardians patrolling.'

'Won't you be able to pick them up on that?' Jared said, pointing at her locator.

'As you well know, not everyone in the Sanctuary has a chip,' Sienna said. 'The Durands, for instance. Let's go.'

They followed close behind her, waiting while she checked around each corner. Too close, in fact, because when Durand's voice blared through the tannoy again, and she froze, Jared stomped on her heel.

'Sorry,' he said.

She shot him a withering look, but Durand's booming voice interrupted her before she could say anything.

Citizens of the Sanctuary,
An insidious cancer has nestled its way into the bosom of our society. A rot that threatens to spoil all that we have worked so hard to build.

Aaron covered his ears. 'Has it been half an hour already?'

'I guess so,' Sienna said. 'Although on special occasions he'll have his minions play the recordings on a loop.'

Jared glanced at her uniform, wondering just how this strong-willed woman became counted amongst that number.

She caught him looking. 'We should keep moving.'

There are citizens amongst us who think themselves above our laws. Perhaps above even the judgement of God himself.

'He likes the sound of his own voice, doesn't he?' Jared said.

Sienna sniggered. 'You don't know the half of it.'

Revelations 21:8. 'As for the cowardly, the faithless, the detestable, as for murderers, the sexually immoral, sorcerers, idolaters, and all liars, their portion will be in the lake that burns with fire and sulphur.' We will root them out and make them pay...

'Wait.' Sienna put a hand on Jared's chest. His heart fluttered below her palm. 'I'm sure I...' She craned her neck to look around the corner. 'I thought I heard someone. Maybe it was my imagination. It's hard to tell with that idiot blithering on.'

I am God's instrument, and he acts throu—

A high-pitched whirring sound came from the speaker, and the recording screeched to a halt. In its place, music drifted from the speakers.

Sienna gasped. 'What on Earth...'

Its notes, light and sweet, drifted on the currents of the air.

'It's beautiful,' Aaron said.

Sienna stretched out a hand as though she could feel the rhythm weaving between her fingers. 'I haven't heard music since before I came to the Sanctuary.'

The music played for only a few seconds more before it was truncated by silence.

Sienna ducked her head and drew her sleeve across her cheek. 'Somebody will pay for that.'

Aaron frowned. 'Why? It was just a bit of music. If the scientists here can replicate the technology for time travel, surely they can rig an old record player or something. It can't take that much power.'

'It's nothing to do with wasting resources,' Jared said. 'It's about control. Music is inspiring. Freeing.'

Sienna nodded. 'And those are the last things Durand wants us to feel.'

'Well, apparently someone is looking to change things,'

Aaron said. 'Somebody wanted the people to remember what they're missing.'

'I think you're right,' Sienna said. 'It's not the first time something like this has happened. Durand's election posters were defaced. Although, if you ask me, the devil horns suited him.'

'Well, whoever it is,' Aaron said, 'they might be the closest thing we have to an ally in this place.'

~

The Book of Durand

'Shouldn't we wake Mamma?' I asked. In the days since she'd hit me, I had been trying to win her approval. The trouble was, I seemed to see less and less of her. I worried she was falling into old habits. I worried more that it was my fault.

'No. Let her rest.' Father cursed as he again failed to fasten his tie.

'She'll be annoyed if she misses the party.'

He shot me a glare that told me the matter was not up for debate. 'She's tired. Let her be.' He pulled the red tie from around his neck, threw it onto the couch. Then he picked up a blue one instead, as though it were the fault of the colour that he couldn't tie it. 'David needs our support if he is going to get elected again.'

'But he's a sure thing. Nobody would dare run against him.'

'Don't be naïve, Martin. There are people in here who would rather blame the system than their own shortcomings for not having everything they want. Laziness, that's their problem. They want everything handed to them.'

'Who does?'

'Never mind. The important thing is, we need David on that committee.'

Mamma opened the bedroom door, interrupting him.

'My love, there you are,' he said. 'We were just wondering when you would join us.'

She rubbed the heel of her hand into her eye sockets. 'I could sleep for a week. I don't know what's wrong with me.'

'Let me get you some tea. It'll perk you up. Then you can get ready.'

Mamma sat on the sofa. She blinked heavily, trying to clear the sleep from her eyes.

She noticed me watching her and gave a weary smile. 'Tell me what you've been up to, Martin. It feels like forever since I've seen you.'

I wanted to tell her everything. About the body in the tunnel. About Evie. But that wasn't how things worked between us. I was the one who cared for her. So instead I said, 'Not much. Captain Moss says we might get to go to the surface soon, if the weather holds out.'

'Really?'

'Don't pester your mother; she's just woken up.' The teacup rattled on the saucer as he passed it to her.

'He's not bothering me. I never get to see him lately.'

'That's because you're always asleep,' I said.

Father scowled at me. 'Go and get ready, Martin.'

He was annoyed with me for saying that, but it was true. I remembered only too well what happened the last time she slept so much, and that scared me. Still, I followed his instructions and went to change my clothes.

When I came back out Father was alone. 'Your mother isn't feeling well. She's decided to stay at home.'

My heart sank, but I wasn't surprised.

The party was being held in the Michalowice Chamber. The sweeping beams reminded me of one of the churches Father had worked in; I forget which one.

As the only teenager there, I felt out of place as soon as we arrived. I hung by my father's side without being introduced to any of the people that he spoke too.

That's why I was so pleased when I saw David. He noticed me looking and headed over to us. 'Well, if it isn't the Durands. Although, I see you are a woman down tonight.'

'Yes. Serena is unwell, I'm afraid.'

'That's a shame. But I appreciate the two of you making the effort. You'll have to excuse me. I have guests to keep happy.' David winked at me. 'But Victor, let's schedule a meeting soon. I have a proposition for you.'

'Now I'm intrigued,' he said.

'We'll talk soon.'

My father beamed. 'You see, Martin. Pretty soon I'll be indispe— Wait here.'

I followed his gaze over to Millicent.

'I'll just be a minute,' he said as he made a beeline for her. My conscience prickled at the feeling I was betraying Mamma, but I didn't want to be left alone, so I followed him.

Millicent didn't look happy to see him. 'You're out unguarded tonight, I see.'

'Don't be like that—'

'How lovely!' My mother's voice cut across the babble of the room. 'Don't mind if I do.' She snatched a champagne flute from a passing tray. Then she wobbled towards us, grasping the hem of her crimson dress so it didn't catch on her heels. It made me think of the night of the powercut, how happy she'd looked as she'd twirled in our sitting room. She wasn't smiling now. Still, she looked as beautiful as ever.

'Serena, what are you doing here?' Father grasped her elbow in an attempt to guide her away, but she shook him off.

'The same as the rest of you, I imagine. I've come to talk politics. That was what you two were talking about, wasn't it? Politics. Because I don't see what other business you would have with my husband, Millicent.'

'Not this again.'

Mamma looked Millicent up and down. 'Once upon a time they'd tar and feather whores. Now we elect them.'

Two perfectly round splotches of pink rose on Millicent's cheek bones. 'Get her out of here.'

Father held his hands out, pleading. 'I'm so sorry.'

'Enough.' Millicent silenced him, and everyone around them, with that one word. 'I've heard it all before. 'She's not well. She doesn't mean it.' Her lip curled as she mocked my father with a sing song voice. 'Well, I'm done. Either you keep her under control or she'll have to face the consequences.'

Mamma took an unsteady step forward. 'Are you threatening me?'

Millicent strode to meet her. They stood almost nose to nose. 'I don't make threats. I make promises.'

'Please, there's no need for this.' Father slid himself between the two women. Then he turned Mamma by the shoulders and tried to march her towards the door.

She whirled around. 'Let go of me. I'm perfectly capable of walking myself.'

'You're drunk,' Millicent said.

Mamma's mouth formed a little 'o'. 'I haven't touched a drop. Martin, tell her.'

'I...I haven't seen her drink anything.'

'Of course you haven't,' Millicent said. 'That's when you know it's bad, when they start hiding it.'

'How dare you?' Mamma shoved Father away and fled from the room.

'Go after her,' Father said, like I wasn't already following.

I caught up with her in the tunnel to the main entrance.

'Where are you going?' I asked.

'I'm leaving.' Tears streaked her face, but they were angry, resolute. 'Are you coming with me?'

'Where?'

'Anywhere she isn't. They're welcome to one another.' We reached the door and she beat on the reinforced metal. 'Let me out!'

I'm not sure who she was screaming at. Except for us, the chamber was empty.

'Mamma, please,' I said. 'This isn't doing any good.'

She stopped and looked at me. 'You're right. This won't solve the problem. If I leave, then she's won.'

'Yes. So let's go home and we'll talk to Father in the morning and get it all sorted out.'

She wasn't listening to me. 'The only way we can stay here is if we get rid of her. Then the three of us can be happy again.' She pulled me into her arms. 'You would do that for me, wouldn't you Martin?'

I breathed in the apricot smell of her shampoo, one of the few luxuries she bought from the outside. 'I don't know what you mean.'

She tipped my chin upward, so she was looking straight into my eyes. 'Kill her for me. Kill Millicent.'

'What?' I stepped away from her. 'I'm not killing anybody.'

'Then she's got to you, too. The perfect ready-made family.' She went to the barrier encircling the platform. 'I thought I could at least rely on you.'

'Mamma, come away.' In our first week or so in the Sanctuary, Pearse arranged for us to have a proper tour. I assume it was to help us settle into our new home. My stomach still turned when I thought about what the guide had said; there was a drop of around two hundred metres below the platform on which we stood.

'You can, but what you're suggesting is insane.'

She kicked off her shoes and stepped up onto the first plank of wood making up the barrier. 'That's what everyone is saying, isn't it? I'm insane or a drunk. Nobody wants to consider the possibility that I might actually be right.' She climbed onto the next piece of wood. 'Not even you.'

'Just come down.'

'There's no point. Nothing will change.' She teetered on the top of the barrier, her hands held out at her sides for balance. 'Maybe you are all right. I am crazy.'

'Please.' My voice felt tiny, constrained.

She began to turn, pirouetting in tiny steps on the balls of her feet as she clutched the hem of her dress. 'You'll be better off without me.'

I don't know whether it was her that wobbled or the barrier. The effect was the same either way. Her arms began to pinwheel and her eyes became so wide that I could see the whites all around her irises.

We never know what we're capable of until we're put in a situation like that. The first surprise was my reflexes. I'm not sure my heart even finished a whole beat before I'd grabbed her hand.

We stared at each other, stunned. Only her toes were still on the platform. She curled them like the claws of an owl, as though she hoped to hold on using them alone.

Our arms were stretched taught between us, our hands clammy but firm. She looked at them, locked together, and gave a laugh of relief that bounced around the cavern. The echo hadn't even stopped when I let go.

I'm sure it was a trick of my mind, but she seemed to hang in the air for a moment, her crimson dress ballooned around her. Certainly long enough for her to realise what I had done. The look of resignation on her face will stay with me forever. She didn't even scream.

Don't judge me. Like I said, until you're in such a situation, you never know what you're capable of.

Chapter Seven

The Book of Durand

I've made some poor choices. I know that. It would be easy for me to lay the blame for how my life has turned out at the feet of my parents. Or at David Malone's. Or even yours. Especially yours. But I take responsibility for my actions and, in truth, I have only one real regret. But I'll come to that.

The morning after I let her fall, I sat cradling my mother's empty teacup. It was the only one in the unit. I don't know where my father found it, but she'd looked at him like he was a hero when he'd presented her with it. She'd always insisted tea tasted better drunk from porcelain. I traced my finger over the hint of pink lip gloss still lingering on its edge.

My father hadn't been home that night, and when he finally walked in, his grin was wide. That is, until he saw me cradling the teacup. 'Don't drink that!'

'I hadn't planned to,' I said, turning it upside down to show it was empty.

'Good. Cold tea is disgusting.' He took the cup from me and walked to the sink. 'Where's your mother?'

I'd thought a lot about how to answer that, sitting there alone, but had reached no conclusion.

Father frowned. 'Is she still asleep?'

'I guess.'

He grunted. 'Tired herself out, humiliating us like that.'

'Where have you been?' I asked, not that I was interested. I just wanted to change the subject away from Mamma.

Father beamed. 'Making plans with David. Martin, it's beyond what I'd even hoped for. I thought David had seen me as a useful ally, hoped he would come to see me as indispensable. But this...Martin, the whole of the Sanctuary will not just follow me. They'll love me.'

'That's great.'

Perhaps it was the lack of enthusiasm behind my words or the absence of any follow up questions, but his enthusiasm dulled. 'Yes, it is. Anyway, I will need my rest. I'm going to sleep in your room.' He paused. 'Wake me when she shows her face. I'll deliver her morning tea along with a stern talking to. She could have blown this for us.'

When the door clicked behind him, I went to the sink and stared at that innocent-looking cup. Something about the way he had balked at seeing me with it in my hand made me uneasy.

Then I took down the canister of tea. My father always insisted on making it, his way of taking care of her. Even if she had decided to make it herself, she was too short to see the bottle of pills hidden behind the cannister. I turned the bottle over and it rattled. Most of the label had been peeled away so that only the name of the medication was left. Triazolam. I'm not sure who the medication had originally been prescribed for. But I was certain of one thing: my father had been drugging my mother.

I thought back to her tears and protests, how she'd insisted that she wasn't drunk. I don't think anybody believed her, not even me. So, you might have already guessed, but my one regret? I killed the wrong parent.

Susan

'Luca, we need to talk to you,' Susan said.

Luca perched on the seat next to her, staring from under a fringe grown too long. 'Are you mad at me? What did I do?'

'You haven't done anything.'

'That we know of,' Robert added, looking at his son through playfully narrowed eyes.

'Just listen to me, okay?' Susan cupped his face so he couldn't turn away. 'No matter what happens, you need to know that you have done nothing wrong. Can you promise me that?'

'You're scaring me,' Luca said.

You should be scared, Susan thought. Every eventuality had played through her head in minute detail. What if they couldn't find somewhere? What if they were killed up there and he was left alone? Fear was the appropriate emotion. Personally, she was terrified.

'There's no need to be afraid,' Robert said. 'But we do need you to listen carefully.'

Luca's eyes flickered towards the door. Susan could relate, thinking that she'd like to escape the conversation, too.

Robert's words tumbled out, as though he were trying to get it over and done with. 'We can't stay here any more. Your mother and I need to find somewhere safe for you.'

'What do you mean?' Luca asked. 'You said this was our home. Why do we need to leave?'

'Because this place can never be our home,' Susan said. 'I tried to convince myself it could be. But we are not the Coles.' She forced a smile. 'Georgie Porgey pudding and pie—'

'I hate that song,' Luca said.

'Sorry. It was your favourite once.'

'A lifetime ago.'

'Don't be in such a rush to grow up. You will always be my baby.' Susan kissed him on the temple. 'You are very loved. Never forget that, George.'

'I prefer the name Luca.'

He squirmed away from her, his rejection leaving a stinging emptiness.

'Where are we supposed to go, anyway?' he asked. 'We can't go back to the surface. It's not safe. Besides, I don't want to. I've got friends here.'

Susan and Robert glanced at each other.

'There is another option.' Susan had gone back to speak to Marney the previous evening to ensure she'd been sincere, that she understood the magnitude of what she'd agreed to.

The heat of Robert's gaze warmed her cheek. He'd already unleashed the full weight of his judgement before grudgingly agreeing. It was a convenient scenario for him; by arguing to take Luca with them he got handed a solution with none of the guilt.

And so it was agreed, by everybody but Luca.

Susan hesitated. 'You could stay in the Sanctuary... without us.'

'But...but where would you be?'

Susan brushed the hair from his face. 'On the surface, looking for somewhere safe for us to live.'

'No,' Luca said. 'I'll come, too. I changed my mind. I don't mind going back up there.'

'No, Luca, you were right,' Susan said. 'It's not safe.'

'But we'd be together.'

Susan felt tears threaten. 'We will come back for you.'

'So what, I'm just supposed to stay here by myself?'

'No, Marney has promised to look after you. She's a good woman. You will be safe here with her.'

'For how long?'

'There's no way for us to know that. But do you remember what Doctor Pearse said when we arrived? Refuges like this place were being built all over the world. There must be somewhere. We'll be back as soon as we can.'

Luca was too quiet. 'When will you go?'

Robert squeezed his shoulder. 'Your mum and I are going to speak to Mr Malone and iron out the details.'

Luca almost bounced off his chair. 'Yes! Speak to him. He's nice. I know he will help us.'

Susan grasped his hand. 'Listen to me. Mr Malone isn't your friend.'

Luca twisted his fingers away. 'You don't know anything. He said I could be a guardian.'

'Of course you could,' Robert said. 'You'd be the best. But we aren't meant to be here.'

'Then why did you bring me?' Luca stormed off and slammed his door with such force that Susan's eardrums pinged.

They sat in silence, listening to the sound of Luca's sobs coming from the next room.

Finally, Robert spoke. 'I'm going to talk to David now.'

'No,' Susan said a little too quickly. 'Let me go.'

Susan knew exactly where David would be. It was his habit to circulate in the dining room at mealtimes.

When he saw her, he ushered her to one side. 'How can I help you?'

She had rehearsed her speech the whole way there. But when she opened her mouth only two words came out. 'We're leaving.'

'Well, I am truly devastated. Now, if you'll excuse me...'

'I haven't finished. We want to leave Luca here. Just until we can find somewhere safe.'

David pursed his lips, somewhere between confusion and amusement. 'You want to leave your son here unsupervised?'

'No, Marney has promised to look after him until we come back. Come on, David. Admit it. You don't want us here any more than we want to stay. Not with all that has happened.'

'I must admit, it'll be a relief not to have to worry about that smart mouth of yours running away with itself. But the Sanctuary is pretty unique, you know. Do you think you'll actually find anything like it up there?'

'We have to try. I can't live this lie any more.'

'Each to their own, I suppose. Personally, I find such honesty overrated.'

'So you will support us?'

David shrugged. 'Who am I to stand in your way?'

∾

The Book of Durand

I killed my mother. There, I said it. I killed her, and then I waited. To be found out. For justice. For punishment. I think I'm still waiting. But the consequences haven't arrived yet. Maybe that's where you come in.

When my father realised she was missing, I was pretending to nap on my bed. 'Martin, get up. Your mother's gone.' He was right in more ways than he knew.

I trailed after him as he stopped the citizens, asking if they'd seen her. But there was no desperate wringing of hands. He was playing the part of the dutiful husband burdened by the weight of an unstable wife. I'd seen the act a million times. Only I knew the truth. Many of her problems were of his making. I'd never hated him more.

Eventually a tremor of fear did accompany his words. After all, there were only so many places she could hide in the Sanctuary. Then he became frantic. I don't even think that was an act.

They didn't find her. How could they when the Sanctuary was surrounded at every angle by a maze of tunnels?

I thought about following her, you know. After she fell, I looked over the barrier for the longest time. But when it came down to it, I guess I was just too much of a coward.

Seb

They started dragging men from the barracks as soon as the workday was over.

'Why them?' Seb asked.

'I'm not sure, but I have my suspicions,' Freidman said.

When the door opened again, every face snapped towards it. Two guards stomped towards a bunk. The man on it scooted backwards, the blanket rucking up under his feet. 'I...I don't know anything.'

They yanked him off the bed all the same.

'They're taking the gold team,' Freidman said.

Seb slumped with relief. 'So we're safe.'

'Far from it. I need to talk to Bloch.'

Seb trailed after him.

'Bloch, have you realised—'

'Yes, the gold team. And Korland isn't back yet.'

Seb knew what that meant: the lazarett was doing overtime. The gold team would likely end the day in the pits.

'God help us,' Freidman said.

'I don't get it,' Seb said. 'I mean, it's awful. But rather them than us.'

'You're right,' Bloch said. 'You don't get it. There is a reason the gold team are being selected. My best guess would be the SS have discovered that they've been smuggling cash to the resistance.'

'For what?'

Freidman frowned. 'Weapons.'

'You...you don't think they'd give them our names, do you?'

'I don't think you ever know what you'll do until you stand over those pits.'

They sat in silence after that, the entire barracks falling into a lull. Still, every creaking board or heavy footstep left them rigid with tension.

Finally, the door to the barracks swung open, and Korland stepped inside.

Be ready early tomorrow,' the guard said. 'It's going to be a busy day for you.'

Korland sat on his bunk and let out a long sigh like a pressure valve releasing.

Bloch stood, ready to speak to him, but Freidman grabbed his arm. 'Not now. Give him some time.'

Bloch hesitated. 'All right. But we need to know what happened. And soon.'

'Yes, but if the SS are coming for us, I don't think a few minutes are going to make any difference.'

'It would give me time to find a weapon,' Bloch said. 'If I'm going down, I'm going down fighting.'

They didn't need to wait long. Korland tried to steady a tremor in his voice. 'They're still alive, you know. The gold team, they didn't go to the pits.'

'What happened?' Seb asked.

Korland shrugged. 'They were always going to make somebody pay for what happened with Doctor Chorazycki.' He must've noticed the exchanging of confused glances, because he added, 'You haven't heard, have you? Doctor Chorazycki is dead.'

'How?' Freidman's question was a whisper.

'He was ready to hand over the money to the guards when Franz came into the infirmary.

Doctor Chorazycki heard him coming and stuffed the money into the pockets of his coat. One treacherous note, sticking out, betrayed him.'

'Did he...Did he talk?' Bloch asked.

Korland smiled, an expression that seemed absurd to Seb considering the circumstances. 'He didn't give them the chance to ask. That vial of poison he'd been carrying around finally came in handy.'

'Who would carry something like that?' Seb asked.

'I'd say any man in here if he could get his hands on it. It's not so strange when you consider there are fates a lot worse than death.' Freidman studied him. 'For some people, the choice to die is the only bit of power they have left.'

Seb wanted to ask his friend if he included himself in 'some people'.

'Doctor Chorazycki knew they would try and bring him back,' Korland continued. 'But he wasn't going to give them that chance. Who knew heroes came in the form of bespectacled doctors?' Korland scanned the room to make sure everybody was listening. 'When Franz came in, Doctor Chorazycki downed his poison and grabbed a scalpel. Of course, that coward Franz backed off.

'That was all the time the doctor needed. He jumped from the first floor of the infirmary for good measure. By the time they got to him, he was dead. They wouldn't get a word from him.'

The barracks ignited in a flurry of chatter.

'Quiet,' Bloch said. 'What did the SS do?'

'I wasn't there. But one of my team saw them leading over Doctor Levkovski. They were insisting the poor woman worked some kind of miracle, saying they needed information from him. Personally, I think they were just annoyed that they didn't get to torture him before he died.'

'I wouldn't put it past them,' Freidman said. 'I guess that's why they wanted to speak to the gold team, to find out what Doctor Chorazycki kept from them.'

Korland nodded. 'The SS made them strip naked and walked them to the pits. Then they put a gun to their heads and threatened to shoot them if they didn't tell everything that they knew.'

'And did they?' Seb asked.

'I don't know. When I left, they hadn't said a word. If anything saves them, past giving us up, of course, it will be their skills. Not every prisoner could do the job they do.'

'Finding valuables in the bundles?' Seb asked.

'Yes. But they also take it from far more unsavoury places,' Korland said. 'For instance, would you know how to extract a gold tooth from a corpse?'

Seb's skin felt clammy. 'I hope I never have to learn.'

'Exactly. And the SS don't have time to train up more prisoners even if you wanted to.'

'What now?' Freidman asked.

'I guess we wait,' Bloch said.

An eerie stillness replaced the sleep that should have blanketed them.

When the door opened, Seb squeezed his eyes tighter. It was only when he heard the patter of bare feet on boards that he risked looking.

A trail of naked men entered.

After the thud of boots faded away, a lone voice said, 'We didn't talk.'

A barrage of questions was launched at the man, but Seb stayed on his bunk, letting the realisation that he would live to see another day in Treblinka sink in.

The Book of Durand

My mother haunts me. I mean that in a very literal sense. Each night she visits, still dressed in her crimson gown. She stands at the foot of my bed. And she waits. And she watches. And she judges.

Maybe she just wants to be found. It must be lonely down there in those unmapped tunnels. I begged the guardians to continue the search, even though I knew exactly where she was. I couldn't tell them that though, because if I did then I would have to confess to my role in her death. My father told me that they'd already done all they could, that it was impossible to search every nook of the salt mine. I think, after the shock subsided, he was afraid they'd find her alive.

So she haunts me. She comes to me in that split second between sleeping and waking. Then the memory of her stalks me through the day. It could be worse, I suppose. Isn't it a horror movie cliché that spirits become twisted over time? Perhaps one night I'll wake to find her squatting on my chest like a demon, her perfect face ravaged by trauma and time. But for now, she just watches, and she waits, and she judges.

Perhaps she still wants me to join her, the question she asked me that night still fresh on her lips: 'Are you coming with me?'

I think that would be the honourable thing to do. But not just yet. First, I have some wrongs to right.

⌇

Jared

Wait here,' Sienna said, before heading to the door of the Grand Chamber. She cracked it open and peered inside. 'It looks cl—'

Chuckles echoed down the corridor. Sienna shot Jared a warning look that told him, in no uncertain terms, to stay out of the way. Jared slunk back into the shadows just as two guardians turned into the tunnel.

'If it isn't the boss lady,' one of them said, spitting the word 'boss' at her.

'I'm not in charge, as you well know, Devon.'

'Yeah,' his companion added. 'We know that. It's a shame you don't.'

'Will you just get over it. I didn't think it was worth our time following up. It was probably some poor sap breaking curfew to see his girlfriend.'

'You're going soft,' Devon said. 'The rules are there for a reason.'

'Speaking of rule breaking,' the other guardian said, 'you aren't on shift; you should be in your unit or on the way to the dining hall.'

'I...' Sienna left her sentence hanging.

Jared's heart beat in his ears, filling the silence she left.

'It's none of your business,' she finally said, but her words lacked their usual spark.

'Feeling a little defensive, Sienna? Why is that?' Suspicion laced Devon's words.

His companion sidestepped so that Sienna, with her back against the door, had nowhere to go.

'Get out of my way,' she said, her voice small.

Devon took a step closer. 'Not until we get a proper explanation.'

As if mirroring him, Jared stepped towards them. He had no idea what he would actually do if he was forced to defend her. Rush them and hope that Aaron followed suit, he supposed.

It turned out not to be an issue. Sienna swung her fist up and under Devon's chin. His teeth snapped together as she made contact.

As Devon nursed his jaw, his comrade shoved her against the door frame.

'Get off me, Felix, or you're going to regret it.' Sienna pushed him away, but he sent her reeling back again.

When Jared took another step towards them, Aaron grabbed his arm. A finger to his lips, he nodded to the opening door.

'What's going on?'

It was more than the man's uniform that Jared found familiar. Perhaps it was the wide blue of his eye, a tad too large for his face. It was only when he turned that Jared saw it wasn't mirrored on the other side. A patch, the same colour as his uniform, covered his other eye, the skin around it shiny with a landscape of old scars.

'She was hanging around the chamber,' Felix said. 'She's not on duty.'

'And? Neither am I.'

'But...Don't you find that a little suspicious?' Devon said, still clutching his jaw. 'The audio system is back there in your father's office. Maybe she's the one who—'

'I asked Sienna to meet me here. If you have a problem with that...'

'No,' Felix said. 'We just...Sorry.'

'Get back to your patrol.'

Felix and Devon scarpered off.

'Are you okay?' He put a hand on Sienna's shoulder.

She flinched away. 'I'm fine.'

He spread his hands wide. 'Okay. Just checking.'

'I'm sorry. Why did you lie for me? You didn't ask me to meet you here.'

He shrugged. 'I imagine you have your reasons.'

Jared could hear the hesitation in her voice. 'Well, I appreciate your help. Ollie, don't you ever get sick of this place? Don't you wish for...I don't know...more?'

'Every day. But our choices are pretty limited, Sienna. I don't really fancy a one-way trip to the surface. And that isn't even the worst option my father might suggest.'

'But we'd be free.'

'You're just tired. It was a long shift last night.'

'Yeah, you're right. I'm going to head back to my unit.'

'Good idea.' He turned.

Sienna's words stopped him before he could walk away. 'You do know it wasn't me.'

'What wasn't?'

'The audio system. I didn't play the music. I was here to—'

'I know. You don't have to explain anything to me. It was probably one of my brothers playing a prank. They do love a game of truth or dare.'

'So...so you don't think it's the beginning of an uprising?'

'No. I think it's some idiot who doesn't realise he's playing with fire.'

Sienna smirked. 'Definitely one of your brothers, then.'

'Now, Miss Hiatt, I won't have such disrespect towards the Durand name,' he said, although he couldn't stop his smile shaping his words. 'Go home and get some rest.'

He was already halfway down the corridor when Sienna called to him, 'Do you ever think about your real parents?'

He stopped midstep. 'Not really. But I've been a Durand for so long, I barely remember who Oliver Sawyer even was.'

Seb

Seb had scoured every corner, every team in the extermination area since he'd arrived. The carpentry work sent them to every part of the camp, often unsupervised, and he'd seized the opportunity to ask anybody he met if they'd seen Isaac. The ones who tried to be kind were the worst. They'd listen to Seb's description and confirm that yes, they were almost certain they'd seen someone who looked like that and they'd been shipped off to the Treblinka penal colony. Or they'd heard of a prisoner who'd escaped into the forest who could have been his friend. It was the enthusiasm that gave them away, as though they were determined to put a bandage on his grief, whether what they said was the truth or not.

As the days wore on, Seb had to assume that if Isaac had been there, he was dead already. But he couldn't let himself dwell on the idea, not if he was to keep any fragment of his sanity. Not if he wanted a chance to get back to the Sanctuary and make the Durands pay for what they'd done.

On his fifth day there, Seb woke with a start as Freidman shook his shoulder.

'We need to talk,' he said.

Seb slipped from his bunk and followed Freidman to his own bed at the far end of the barracks. Zialo and Jacob were already sitting on top of it, so Seb crouched on the floor.

Jacob eyed him with suspicion. 'Why is the boy here?'

'He's part of the resistance,' Zialo said.

'You're a fool. There is no resistance.'

'Well, we need to change that,' Freidman said. 'The time to act is now.'

'We don't have the numbers. Without the lower camp, they'll crush us within minutes.' Jacob crossed his arms over his chest, as though delivering the final word on the subject.

'Together we do,' Seb said. 'There must be nearly eight hundred men if we add in the lower camp. If we can somehow coordinate the resistance, then surely we can over-power them.'

'Exactly,' Zialo said. 'That's why Galewski put us here, after all. But we need to move soon, whether the lower camp is ready or not.'

'It would be suicide,' Jacob warned. 'We could never hope to seize control with so few men on this side.'

Zialo rubbed his hands over his face, tugging down his skin so Seb could see the pinks of his inner lids. 'Jacob, they've had us dig up almost every mass grave in this place and...dispose of the evidence. The prisoner transports are getting fewer every day. The job of the burning group is nearly done.' He paused. 'And we all know that, in Treblinka, you do not outlive your usefulness.'

Jacob puffed out a slow breath. 'Okay. Well, let's not let the last graves they make us dig be our own.'

'You're in then?' Freidman asked.

Jacob nodded.

'We need to get a message to Galewski so he can rally the lower camp,' said Freidman.

'We can do that,' Seb said. 'They let us move pretty freely around the camp.'

'The guard rooms on that side aren't finished yet,' Jacob said. 'Nobody will question us being there.'

As they made their way to the lower camp the next morning, Seb couldn't resist asking, 'Is that why you didn't want me working with you? You didn't realise I was part of the resistance, too.'

'Sure, if that's the answer you'd prefer,' Jacob said.

'I'd prefer the truth.' But even as he said it, Seb wasn't sure that was the case.

'You heard what Zialo said. Nobody here outlives their usefulness.' Jacob swallowed hard. 'I didn't fancy training my replacement.'

'Oh. I hadn't thought about it like that.'

'Good. You're young. You shouldn't have to dwell on such things.'

They found Galewski on the platform.

'Zialo and Freidman say it's time to act. Things are winding down in the extermination area. We don't know how long we've got.'

'I know,' Galewski said. 'It's no better this side. They are shooting prisoners for the pettiest things. Our numbers have fallen to around five hundred men.'

Seb gasped. 'Will there even be enough of us left to resist?'

'I don't know,' Galewski said. 'But I don't see what choice we have.'

A train rattled past them without stopping at the station.

'Could they help?' Seb asked.

Jacob frowned. 'The Malkinia transport? Sure, we'll have them hop off and...' He stumbled over his words. 'I don't know. Pick up a rock to hit the guards with.'

'No, I think he might be onto something,' Galewski said. 'There are nearly five hundred prisoners on that train. It goes past at 4:45 every day. We just need to find a way to stop it.'

'If they thought there was damage to the track ahead,

they'd have to stop,' Seb said. 'But how can we signal a moving train?'

'A flag. Or at least something that could pass for one,' Jacob said. 'The tailor shop keeps red material for the armbands.'

'Okay.' Galewski's voice wavered. 'I guess we're doing this. It's Sunday tomorrow and they will lock us in the barracks early. We need time to spread the word anyway.' He turned in a circle, running his fingers through his hair. 'Two days. Monday August 2nd will be when the uprising begins.'

~

The Book of Durand

There should have been a period of mourning. It doesn't seem right that only weeks after my mother's death, the hole in our family was filled. Not by another woman; my father has never shown any interest in filling that particular void. No, the gap was filled by a boy. He wasn't left in the cabbage patch or delivered by the stork. In fact, he was not a baby at all. At least not while he was part of my family.

Oliver joined us as a boy of about ten, and on the day he arrived he was locked in a cupboard, trying to smash his way out.

My eyes widened as I entered the unit. 'Who is that?'

'Just ignore him,' my father said, without answering my question.

So we continued with our day, neither of us mentioning the desperate pounding from the other side of the door.

Eventually, I couldn't take it any more. 'You can't just leave him in there.'

'I have no intention of doing so,' Father said. 'He just needs to calm down.'

I wasn't convinced that would ever happen. Oliver's rage gave him endless energy. He beat his fists against the wood. He screamed for his father. He cried.

But it turned out that by calm, my father just meant quiet. When Oliver's howls were finally replaced with hiccupping sobs, my father opened the door.

'That's better,' he said, his voice saccharine. 'There was no need for all that fuss. Now if you're ready to come out, you can eat with the rest of the family.'

And that was how it began. Father led Oliver from the cupboard and sat him next to me at the dinner table.

'I've been entrusted with a very important role,' Father said, although nobody had asked. 'There will be more young people like Oliver who, through no fault of their own, have been abandoned.'

Oliver frowned but made no comment on the word choice. It wasn't until later that I learnt that he hadn't been abandoned at all. He'd been forced to give evidence against his father, Jackson, with the whole of the Sanctuary watching. I don't think he's ever escaped the citizens' judgement for what happened that day.

'David has entrusted me...us...with the role of guiding them, spiritually and practically. This will take a lot of sacrifice from us all.' Father beamed. 'You are going to have to learn to share, Martin, because soon I will be father to a generation of lost children.'

That sounds nice, doesn't it? Only I quickly realised he wasn't expanding our family. No, my father was building an army.

Susan

Twenty-four hours. That was all the time David had given them to prepare to leave.

Susan imagined he thought this was a final act of control. In truth, it was far more time than they needed. Even if they had any friends to say goodbye to, which they didn't, David had forbidden them from telling anybody that they were leaving. It was better that way, he'd told them. Otherwise the citizens might think they could come and go as they pleased. Twenty-four hours felt like an eternity when they had nothing to do but pack and unpack one small bag, all they'd be able to carry on the unpredictable wasteland above.

Luca had barely left his room. When Susan tried to talk to him, he pulled the covers over his head.

'Please, we're doing this for you. We need to find somewhere our family can be safe.'

He pulled the blanket from off his head. 'Then take me with you. If we are a family, we should stay together.'

'I can't...'

'Why?'

'Because no child should have to face what's up there without even knowing there's a safe home at the end of it.'

'This is because of my fits.'

Susan sighed. 'Yes, partly. You don't need the added stress. I need to know you are happy and being looked after until I get back.'

Luca's lip trembled. 'But I want to stay with you.'

'I know.' Susan didn't know what else to say.

He said very little after that, just watched teary-eyed as they pretended to busy themselves with preparations.

Considering it would be the last time she would see her son for a while, Susan was ashamed of the relief that swelled when the guardians finally knocked. Luca's accusing gaze had become suffocating.

'Where's David?' she asked.

The guardian shrugged. 'Off being busy and important, I imagine. Strangely, he doesn't check in with me. Are you ready?'

'One minute.' Susan pulled Robert aside.

'This isn't right. He said he would be here.'

'Why do you care? Did you think the two of you would share an emotional goodbye?'

'No...It's just...I don't know. I thought he'd want his smug face to be the last we see before we leave.'

'Well, I for one will be happy if I never see his face again.'

'Yeah.' She turned to Luca. 'It's time to go.'

'Please, no. Take me with you. I'll be good. And besides, I'm better now. I won't get sick again.'

'Luca...' Susan's face crumpled, and she turned so he couldn't see.

'We need to get going,' the guardian said.

Susan swiped away a tear. Then she held out her hand and felt a rush of relief when Luca took it. Kissing the top of his head, she said, 'It's just for a little while.'

Together, they walked towards Marney's unit. Robert knocked on the door.

'She does know I'm coming?' Luca asked.

'Of course.' Susan forced a smile. 'She will just have been called to an emergency at the hospital.'

Luca looked as unconvinced as she felt.

'Yes,' Robert said. 'We'll meet her there.'

'I was supposed to take you straight to the exit,' the guardian said.

Susan spoke through clenched teeth. 'Well, it looks like we're going to have to take a little detour.'

She looked pointedly at her son, praying the guardian would take pity.

'Whatever,' he said, his version of empathy sounding a lot like boredom.

Susan willed herself not to run as they headed towards the hospital. 'She'll be there,' she said, as much for her own benefit as Luca's.

She caught Robert's terrified stare.

'She will be there,' she repeated.

They heard the commotion from outside the dining room a whole tunnel away. 'What is that?' Robert asked the guardian.

The man ignored him and headed towards the source of the noise. The three of them followed.

Susan stared in horror. Marney was being marched from the dining room. David trailed behind her.

As Marney passed, Susan tried to get her attention. 'Where are they taking you? Will you still be able to look after Luca?'

Marney looked at her blankly. 'I'm sorry... I don't...'

'Marney, please, I'm leaving today. You have to look after my son.'

'I'll do my—' Her sentence was truncated when the guardians dragged her forward. She strained to look at Susan, panic creasing her brow.

'Get back.' The guardian who had been leading Susan

towards the exit tugged at her arm.

David stopped at their side, two guardians with him. *Never without backup*, Susan thought.

'What happened?' Susan asked.

'That's none of your business.'

Susan spluttered. 'None of my business? She was supposed to care for my son while I am gone.'

'Another poor choice on your part. But don't you worry about Luca.' David smiled at Luca and the boy took a small step backwards. 'I've made arrangements for him. He will be well cared for.'

'No...Not by you.'

David laughed. 'God, no. As much as I am a fan of this young man, I wouldn't know where to start with caring for a child. Father Durand has kindly offered to care for him while you're away.'

'No, I don't want that evil man poisoning my child's mind.'

'Well, how does the saying go? Beggars can't be choosers.'

Susan turned to Luca. 'It's okay. We will postpone the trip until we know what's going on with Marney.'

'Yeah,' said Robert. 'Or we'll find somebody just as good.'

'Nonsense,' David said. 'Durand is the perfect choice. Besides, Luca will have Martin for company. You'll like that, won't you Luca? It will be like having a brother.'

'Thank you,' Susan said, trying to keep the strain from her voice. 'We really appreciate your concern. But this is a decision we need to make as a family.'

David clicked his fingers, and a guardian moved towards Luca. 'Well, I am sorry, but things have already been put into motion.'

'Please, David!'

'Knock off the tears. Luca will be much better off without you.' David leant close to her ear. 'I know what you did. Do you know Luca and his friends found Reed's body?'

'What?'

'They thought they'd killed him. You let a bunch of kids think they were murderers.'

'How did—'

He stepped away from her. 'It wasn't hard to put together. You were seen with him right before he disappeared.'

Robert frowned. 'Who? What's he talking about?'

'Nothing.' The tunnel around her began to spin. 'He's delusional.'

'Don't worry,' David said. 'I took care of it for you. And I'll take care of Luca, too.'

'Mom?' Luca stared at her, wide-eyed, as the guardian placed a hand on his back and guided him away.

'No, we are staying,' Robert said. 'Get off him.'

The remaining guardians looked at David.

'You heard me,' he said. 'Escort the Coles to the exit.'

Robert lunged at David. 'You can't just take our child from us.' A guardian hooked an arm round his throat and pulled him away.

'I think you'll find I just did.'

'Luca!' Susan called. 'We will come back for you!'

Luca tried to twist to look at his mother but was propelled forward by the guardian behind him.

'We love you, Luca!' Susan shouted as the guardians dragged her away.

The Book of Durand

Nobody is irreplaceable. I know that. But I thought my position as the Durand heir was secure, whether I wanted it or not. How wrong I was.

When the Coles abandoned Luca (and we were later told in no uncertain terms that was what had happened) my father was only too happy to step in. That afternoon, David turned up at our door, Luca beside him clutching a plastic bag of clothes. 'I think Luca needs a friend right now, Martin.' David gave him a little push, and Luca stepped over the threshold, into our home and family.

Whilst Father merely tolerated Oliver and me, he saw Luca through a different lens. He polished his ego until it gleamed. Where once Father had assured me leadership was in my future, it seemed it was Luca who was now destined for greatness. From that very first day, Father dripped poison into his ear. It spread through his system, burning away any semblance of the boy who entered the Sanctuary.

'We won't leave you,' Father told him. 'Not like they did. You're one of us now.'

And eventually it was true. My father always treated me like I was the wrong son. I think with Luca, he thought he'd found the right one.

The difference in Luca made me think of that day in the hospital, when Mamma told me that once she'd found a changeling in my place.

After that visit, when I'd told my father about it, he'd laughed. 'There were a lot of stories like that in the small town she was from. She's just confused, Martin. At the moment, it is difficult for her to tell fiction from reality. Pay her no mind.'

But now there's something about that story that rings a little too true for comfort. Only my father isn't the hero of the story, he's the one swapping babies for changelings. Maybe not in a literal sense, but he had a way of turning a soul dark.

I'm not making excuses for what Luca did to you. Nothing can make up for what you've lost. But if I was in any doubt about how my own faults were shaped, I saw the process in action with Luca. Monsters are made, not born. Luca Durand is all the evidence I need of that.

Not that my bitterness lasted long; he wasn't exactly breaking up a happy home. Sure, we danced around one another for a while, neither wanting to be the first to bring up the tunnel or the lake. Or Evie. Still, I was hopeful that we could fix what we'd broken and go back to what we were. But in the end, it wasn't friendship or love that brought us together, it was irritation.

Oliver didn't slide into our family with as much ease. His whining was incessant. Clenched jaws and eye rolls soon gave way to swift punches and barbed insults. I admit, I'm not proud of that. But you have to remember, we were teenagers shadowed by a small boy. We were under orders from my father to include him in everything, and so he was tethered to us like an anchor, dragging us down. Is it any wonder we wanted to break free?

But with Luca, I don't think it was just about irritation. Violence wasn't unusual for him; he often hurt those who crossed his path. Cruelty had become a habit for him since his parents' departure. Although with Oliver it turned into something...more. Luca had a vendetta against him, that much was clear. His reprimands were a little fiercer than mine, his slaps landed a little harder. Perhaps he saw something reflected in Oliver, a quality he disliked in himself. Vulnerable, weak, Oliver was everything Luca was determined not to be.

When I suggested that maybe he should ease off, he tutted at me. 'I'm doing it for his own good. Don't you want him to be strong like us?'

One day, Father called for Luca and me. 'Lay off Oliver,' he said. Then he looked at Luca, the son who could do no wrong. 'I mean it. Enough is enough.'

Luca's jaw ticced, but he didn't argue. We both knew Oliver had ratted us out. I just didn't know the lengths Luca would go to in order to make him pay.

After that, the atmosphere in our unit was as foul as the plumbing. Which is saying something. The air was so thick with the stench that it forced its way into your mouth and clawed at your throat. Of course, my father took it personally. A man of his stature shouldn't be living in such conditions. I think the sympathy he received from the committee was...limited. After all, our unit wasn't the only one affected, and the other citizens were expected to just get on with it. You have to remember, my father's influence wasn't what it is now. He came home clutching a bottle of drain cleaner, mumbling about lack of respect.

Eventually, enough citizens complained that something had to be done. That or they'd have a mutiny on their hands.

It turns out that it was the body of Doctor Reed causing the stench. It had become lodged in a tunnel feeding one of the air ducts. As soon as I heard, I knew he was the man we'd killed when we crashed the car. None of us knew for sure how he got there. But still I had nightmares about it: Reed dragging his corpse through the tunnels using that cold white hand, searching for me. However, that isn't the point of me telling you this.

One morning, I was heading into the bathroom, when Luca blocked my way. 'Let Oliver go in first. Come and eat with me.'

I thought nothing of it. But as we returned to our unit after breakfast, I heard guttural howls of pain.

When we burst through the door, I saw my father using the showerhead to flush water over Oliver's face. 'Help me,' Father said as he tried to hold the writhing boy still. When Oliver's sobs waned to pathetic hiccups, Father turned the water off.

'What happened?' I asked.

Father left Oliver curled tight on the bathroom floor. 'Somebody put this, without a lid, on top of the cabinet. It spilled over him when he opened the door' He held out the bottle of drain cleaner, pointing it at me like an accusation. 'Why?'

'I...I didn't. It wasn't me.'

If he believed me, he didn't say. 'What are people going to think? He's been with us only weeks and he's...' Father dropped his voice to a whisper, '...probably blinded. I'd better get him to the hospital.' Oliver gave a little mew as Father hauled him from the floor. 'Let's get you fixed up.'

Later that night, Father bought him home. The side of Oliver's face was a mesh of red welts, and gauze covered one eye.

All Father had to say on the matter was, 'Accidents will happen.'

Luca and I never discussed how the drain cleaner ended up open and balanced on the edge of the bathroom cabinet. There didn't seem much point. A small mercy was that Luca left Oliver alone after that. In fact, he would happily deliver a whipping to anybody who spoke out of turn to our brother, especially about his cloudy eye. So maybe he felt guilty.

I learnt something that day, too. I'm sure you'd like me to say it was a lesson on empathy and tolerance. Sorry to disappoint. It was more valuable than that. I learnt never to cross Luca.

Chapter Eight

The Book of Durand

I'm not exactly the team type. But with the Guardian Elite, it wasn't a choice. After Luca and Oliver joined our family in quick succession my father needed a more practical solution. He couldn't take in every 'abandoned' child, not at the rate they were banishing any citizen who stepped out of line. He needed to be able to control and mould them without worrying about the pesky details of their care. Although I can assure you that the three of us living under his roof got none of that either.

His solution? He turned the Michalowice chamber into a dormitory, with rows of beds filled with little boys crying for their parents. And the odd girl, too.

I know what you're thinking: why did the other citizens not step in? A few tried. It didn't end well. But the majority told themselves that the treatment my father was doling out was somehow deserved, and if they just did what was right, they'd be fine. The trouble was that Father's definition of what was right was pretty warped. Even I could see that.

Speaking of which, did Sienna tell you what happened with her family? Beyond the official charges of inciting civil unrest, I mean. All of that came later. In my father's eyes their initial crime was speaking up for your grandfather; that's what put them on his radar. Autonomous thought has never been a quality he valued. After that, it was just a matter of when he'd get rid of them, not if.

Of course, that was back when things were done out in the open. When the Sanctuary at least presented the facade of being a democracy. The rumbles of unrest and questioning of his decisions didn't sit well with him. So now justice is delivered behind closed doors, although I'm using justice in the loosest definition of the word.

Seb

'Who's this?' Seb asked as Freidman entered the room with a stranger, a stocky man with a crack across one of the round lenses in his glasses.

'This is Sereni,' Freidman said. 'Go on.'

Seb hesitated.

'Sereni's a good man, Seb. We have to involve as many capos as we can, or they won't have a clue what's happening and may try and keep their men out of it. Besides, we need them to collect together anything we can use from their areas.'

'He's right,' Jacob said. 'Galewski already has Korland on board.'

'I can't imagine he took much persuading,' Zialo said. 'Leading the lazarett team must have been pretty awful.'

Seb tried to block out the memory of gunshots piercing the wooden building.

'Okay,' Zialo said. 'I see why stopping the train would help us. But what then?'

'Seb is going to work with Marcus and the other putzer boys to get as many weapons as they can from the store and give them to the different teams,' Jacob said. 'Everyone needs to be able to fight when the time comes.'

'And they're just going to walk them out of the store?' Sereni asked. 'It's attached to the SS living quarters. Don't you think that will make them a little suspicious?'

'Hopefully at that time they'll all be out at their posts,' Freidman said.

'Besides, they don't need to walk them out of the front,' said Jacob. 'One of the bars on the back window is only secured with putty. If one of the smaller boys can get in between the fence and the back of the barracks, then Marcus could pass them through.' He shrugged. 'I guess the guy who built it didn't know what he was doing.'

'No,' Zialo said. 'I think he knew exactly what he was doing.'

'I still don't know how I feel about getting the boys involved,' Seb said. 'They're all so young.'

'That's true,' Jacob said. 'But you couldn't ask for a braver bunch. Besides, they've smuggled things from the store before.'

'Really?'

'Sure. The SS have the putzer boys doing errands all over the camp,' Freidman said. 'So when the lock broke and we managed to get a copy of the new key, nobody questioned why they were hanging around the storeroom. They stole a box of grenades.'

'No detonators though,' Zialo added.

'They weren't to know they were kept separately. And they returned them before the guards were any the wiser.'

'Still,' Jacob said. 'I think it would be good for Seb and me to work with them.'

'What then?' Sereni asked.

'Well, each area will...dispatch their own guards.'

Sereni went a shade paler. 'A necessary evil.'

'So, that's it,' Freidman said. 'This is really happening.'

'Yes,' Seb said. 'Tomorrow we get the weapons, kill the guards, stop the train and escape into the forest. What could possibly go wrong?'

None of them answered.

Seb spent the morning collecting together anything that

could be used as a weapon. Screwdrivers, chisels, he sharpened anything that he could to a point. His breath caught in his chest every time a guard passed, or the tools clattered as he dropped them into the bucket. A mixture of the August heat and his nerves left his shirt stuck to his skin.

Jacob had gone to pass out the ones they'd already prepared. He was also going to leave two trollies by the storeroom, ready for them to hide the weapons inside. Considering all he had to do, Jacob hadn't been that long. Still, every muscle in Seb's body felt rigid until the moment his friend walked through the door.

Seb was surprised to see he was grinning. 'What are you looking so pleased about?'

'I've just been talking to Lichtblau and Lubrenitski over in the garage. They've gathered together any tools that could be useful and said the storeroom team have filled canisters with fuel.'

'That's great,' Seb said, still not quite sure why Jacob looked so happy. 'It's all going as planned then.'

'Yes, and they gave me this as a souvenir.' Jacob held up a black wire. 'They tore it out of the armoured car. Do you think it's important?'

'Put it away,' Seb said, trying not to laugh. 'The guards will see.' They both scanned the door outside the workroom but didn't see anybody. 'It's too quiet.'

In the distance, Seb heard chattering voices. 'You spoke too soon.'

They ducked back behind the door frame as the two guards passed. Three more followed just after.

'Where are they all going?' Jacob asked.

Seb frowned as he struggled to hear what they were

saying. 'The Bug River. It's so hot that Franz is allowing a whole group of them to go with him for a swim.'

Jacob gawped. 'You speak Ukrainian?'

'No...I mean, a little.' Seb ran his thumb over the bump of his chip.

'That would have been useful information to share from the start. You know what this means, though? If they're too precious to work in this heat, our odds just got a little better.'

The Book of Durand

Moulding a personality is easier than you think. It just takes pressure and time. I witnessed first hand my father accomplish this with many types of boys.

The quiet ones were an obvious target. Easy prey. But there was no sport in that for him. He liked a challenge.

The cocky boys were his favourite, the ones who thought they could charm him with playful nudges and banter. But their attempts at manipulation were futile; when it came to that they'd met the master. He'd deflect their smiles and jokes with a deadpan expression that would stop them cold. I think he enjoyed unpicking the stitches of their carefully curated arrogance.

It wasn't any of them I remembered most though; that honour fell to Harry. He was angry even before he became one of my father's conscripts, ready to snap at the smallest of perceived slights. While the other boys fulfilled their duties without the slightest complaint, he sat belligerent and fuming on his bed.

Hardly public enemy number one, I know. But he frightened my father. Not because he might hurt him; by that point Father had more than enough guardians under his control to quash one argumentative teenage boy. It was because my father couldn't break him, couldn't find that vulnerable fracture that he could prize his fingers into to tear Harry apart.

One day, Harry interrupted my father's daily sermon. 'Just let me go to the surface. I'll be fine alone.'

It was the first time he'd spoken to my father beyond the

odd grunt, so I guess he saw this as progress. 'But don't you want to be Elite?'

I think Harry's shrug annoyed him more than a no.

'You have to answer me,' Father said.

Harry sat up straight, the first bit of interest I had seen from him since he had arrived. 'Why?'

'Because...because I said so.'

We all knew how pathetic that answer was. Although the rest of us had the sense not to show it. Not Harry. My father's beat of weakness split Harry's face into a grin. That was a mistake.

The next time my father saw him, he didn't look for Harry's weakness. Instead, he looked to the other boys. 'Harry doesn't think the rules apply to him. So, if he needs to be punished, so will all of you. Perhaps this will make you more likely to lead by example, give him the encouragement to conform that he needs.'

There were no dramatic gasps or clutching of chests. But there were glares. Lots of glares.

Father was true to his word. Every time Harry refused a request, the entire dormitory was punished. Free time was cancelled. They were put on basic rations. And just as he'd planned, the boys made Harry pay.

The list was impressive. Harry was blindfolded and abandoned in a tunnel to find his own way back.

They made him eat dog food. Although there were no pets in the Sanctuary, we kept what was found on the surface, just in case the rations ran low.

While working in the kitchen, his hand was plunged into boiling water. Accidentally, of course.

They soiled his bed.

Naturally, Luca, Oliver and I didn't sleep in the dormitory. A line was drawn between us and the new recruits from the beginning. Although my father may have wanted every child under his care to view him as a parent, to him he had only three real sons.

So how do I know all of this? Luca told me. 'They needed a little push to do what was needed,' he'd said. Apparently, Father wasn't the only one shaping little boys into little monsters.

Still, none of it had the desired effect. Harry still refused to fall into line. Then one day he disappeared. The guardians found his ruptured body deep below the part of the salt mine that we inhabited. Did his suicide mean my father had won, that he'd finally broken him? Father would say so, but I don't agree. Even at the end, Harry defied him. That's something I'd never managed. I wish I'd had the chance to know him better.

Jared

Jared followed Sienna into the Grand Chamber.

Aaron trailed behind, his mouth hanging open. 'This place is amazing,' he said, heading towards one of the stone staircases and disappearing up onto the balcony.

'Was that Oliver Sawyer?' Jared asked.

'Not any more. Now he's Oliver Durand.'

Jared shook his head.

'What?' Sienna asked.

'I knew his father. Well, I met him once anyway.'

'Most people knew Jackson,' Sienna said. 'He was pretty popular in the Sanctuary. Until David banished him.'

'David wasn't acting alone, though,' Jared said. 'I don't understand how Oliver could stay with Durand. Jackson was fighting against everything he stands for.'

'Of course you don't understand,' Sienna said. 'Because you had options. Your grandfather literally bent time and space to make sure you had a way to escape.'

'That's not really how it...' When he saw the glare she gave him, Jared's sentence trailed off. 'I guess I was lucky.'

'Yeah, you were. Oliver's mother died before he arrived here. Then they took his father from him. To make it worse, David made him testify against him. After David made everybody think it was Oliver's fault, who else did he have to turn to but the Durands?'

'I didn't think about it like that.'

'I know. We can't all afford your moral compass, Jared.'

Jared sagged with relief when Aaron bounded back down the stairs and stopped in front of them.

'What do we do now?' he asked.

'It's still early,' Sienna said. 'They won't be here for a while.'

Jared nodded towards the committee chamber. 'Then we wait.'

'There's a storeroom at the back. We can hide in there, maybe try to get some rest.'

Jared almost laughed. 'That doesn't seem likely.'

'Suit yourself, but Durand tends to make up his schedule as he goes. We could be here a while.'

As Sienna led them into the storeroom, a light buzzed into life. It revealed not the tiny cupboard he'd expected but a vast room lined high with shelves filled with every delicacy Jared could imagine.

'Wow,' Aaron said. 'Quite the haul they have here.'

'Well, they have to cater for their soirées,' Sienna said. 'No matter that they have the rest of the citizens on basic rations.' She made her way to the end of the aisle and sat with her back to the shelves. 'If anybody comes in, they won't see us here.'

'Can I ask you something?' Jared said.

'That depends on what it is.'

'How did you end up as a guardian?'

'You ask that like I had a choice.'

'Well, didn't you?'

'No, I didn't.' She tugged her shirt from her waistband. 'All of the children that Durand laid claim to officially have his family name. Everyone knows there are only three sons who he actually cares about, but by law he is father to us all. Did you know that?'

'No.'

'Now you do. So according to the Sanctuary records, my

name is Sienna Durand.' She pulled her shirt up, revealing her torso.

Jared looked away.

'You're not embarrassed by a little flesh, are you? Look.'

Jared did as he was told. On her belly, a scar in the shape of the letter D marred her flesh.

'I refused to answer to Sienna Durand at roll call. Wherever I could, I signed my real name. So I was punished. They cut his initial into my skin so there was no escaping who they said I was.'

'Who did it?'

'Durand was behind it, even if it was his sons who actually did the deed.'

'Oliver?'

'No. Ollie's not like them. Anyway, I don't want to talk about this any more.'

Crossing her arms, she closed her eyes. 'Get some rest. We'll hear them when they arrive.'

Jared sat against the wall opposite. Of all the places he'd visited in the world, all the disasters he'd seen, the Sanctuary was still the place he felt most vulnerable. There was no way he wanted to let down his guard for a second. But he hadn't slept since Beth had hammered on his door back in Rome, and he soon found his head jerking forwards as his exhausted body betrayed him. He fought it, willing his senses to stay alert.

So it surprised him when Aaron shook him awake in what felt like seconds later. 'Shhh. There's someone out there.'

Jared listened. There was no denying that there was a

voice, an angry voice, coming from inside the committee chamber.

Jared turned to Sienna. 'Wake up.'

She startled and sat bolt upright. 'He's here already.' She tugged back the sleeve of her uniform to look at her watch. 'This isn't right. They've changed their plans.'

The three of them crept towards the door.

'Find out who did this,' Durand said.

Aaron turned to Jared and spoke in hushed tones. 'He's fuming bout something. Maybe the music—'

'Jared can understand him as well as we can,' Sienna said. 'The chip will work for anybody in its vicinity. As long as Jared doesn't try to talk to him alone, there will be no problem.'

'No chance of that.' Jared put a finger to his lips and pushed the door ajar, releasing the rumble of Durand's voice into the storeroom. It had been years since he'd been forced to listen to the Sanctuary sermons, but still Durand's words left his skin cold and clammy.

'I mean it, Martin,' Durand continued. 'We need to put a stop to this before it escalates. Although, of course, if you can't handle it, I could ask one of your brothers...'

'I've told you already, I will sort it. Why can't you have faith in me?'

Durand left Martin's question hanging. 'Let's get today over with. The Sanctuary doesn't need any more martyrs. Seb needs to disappear.'

Jared gasped. When he'd left, Seb had been a key member of the Guardian Elite. It was impossible not to remember the day when, together with Martin, he'd held him below the surface of the lake. They'd thought themselves so powerful as they told him it was best he stayed away. How the mighty had fallen.

More voices flooded the room.

'It's time,' Durand said. 'Stand up straight and remember you're a leader, Martin. What's left of the world is watching.'

'We've missed our chance.' Sienna massaged her brow. 'We'll wait until it's over—'

'No,' Aaron said, a little too loudly.

Sienna cupped his mouth with her hand.

He shook her off but lowered his voice. 'No. They aren't getting away again.'

'Let's just hold off long enough to see what we're up against.' Jared eased the crack open a little further and peered outside.

A blazing red light forced him to squint. Somebody had opened a portal, and one lonely figure was silhouetted in front of it.

'Please, he's just a child.' Jared was shocked to hear Millicent's voice. It wasn't long since they'd left her and Beth in her unit. Jared prayed his friend was safe. 'Can't we think of some more suit—'

A dark figure strode towards her. Durand. 'Leviticus 20:13: 'If a man lies with a male as with a woman, both of them have committed an abomination; they shall surely be put to death.' If anything, I am being merciful.'

'Please, Victor.'

'He knew the law and still chose to break it. I'm doing my best here, Millicent. If we let this disorder continue then we'll end up like David. Besides, he's no child. He's a grown man who must now face up to the consequences of his actions.'

'But—'

'Enough!

His tone was vicious, and Jared saw Oliver and Martin inch away. But Millicent didn't even flinch.

'All right,' Durand said. 'I'm not a monster.'

'So you'll reconsider?'

'No. The sentence stands. But I will make sure he has company for his journey. It would be wrong to split up such a winning team.'

Durand smiled at his sons as though he'd made some hilarious in-joke. They stared back, deadpan.

Durand signalled towards the door.

Isaac was led into the room by a guardian. Luca.

'It's him,' Jared said. Just the sight of Luca brought back the pain of Nell's loss.

'Who?' Aaron asked.

'Luca. The one who started the fire. The one who killed Nell.'

'Then let's go.' Aaron tried to jostle Jared out of the way.

Sienna pushed him back. 'Engage your brain first. We've got to be smart about this.'

Aaron turned in a frustrated circle. 'I won't let him get away again.'

Pressing his eye back to the crack, Jared struggled to make out who else was in the room.

'You've got it all wrong.' Despite the waver in Seb's voice, Jared recognised it immediately. Seb was the figure standing in front of the portal. 'He's nothing to me.'

'Oh, really?' Durand asked. 'Well, I guess you'd better tell him that.'

'You...you mean nothing to me.' His vocal cords seemed

to hold back the words, strangling them. Despite all that had passed between them, Jared couldn't help but feel pity. 'Happy?' Seb asked Durand. 'You can let him go.'

Durand sieved his words through that same malicious grin. 'I'm not stupid. Now move yourself, or I'll think up somewhere far worse to send him. Only it will be without you.'

'It's okay,' Isaac said. 'At least we'll be together.'

'I've got to do something,' Jared said. 'He's sending them...I don't know where, but somewhere terrible.'

Jared put his eye back to the door, just in time to see Durand shove Seb through the portal. 'No!' He sprinted from the storeroom, already pulling the weapon from beneath his blazer. 'Stop!'

Durand stared at him, his mouth hanging so low that Jared could see the plump pink tongue within. He clutched a weapon at his side, the shock of seeing Jared apparently making him forget he held it.

Jared grasped the opportunity and looked around him for a suitable hostage. It wasn't what he wanted, but with no other bargaining chips, he had no choice. Jared grabbed Martin before he could run.

'Oh hey, Jared,' Martin said, as though they'd just bumped into one another in the dining hall.

Jared stared at the men encircling him. 'Put down your guns or I'll shoot him. I mean it.'

'I'm sure you do,' Durand said. 'But then what? Are you going to fight your way out of here alone?'

Jared frowned, wondering why he would say such a thing when Sienna and Aaron were in the storeroom right behind him. 'No, I'm not...' He bit his tongue. Of course,

Durand didn't know he had allies with him. '...not afraid of you.'

Durand pursed his lips, making Jared wonder if he was questioning the clumsy end to his sentence.

'Okay,' Durand said. 'Where do we go from here?'

Jared had no idea. 'We...we open the portal and let Seb back through.'

Durand shook his head. 'I can't do that.'

'I'm not bluffing.' Jared pushed the gun harder against Martin's temple. 'I'll shoot him, if you make me.'

'So you say,' Durand said. 'But do you think killing him will weaken our cause? The people of the Sanctuary will hear what you've done, how you've taken one of the guiding lights of our community, and they'll hate you for it.'

'They'll see you for the twisted sociopath that you are.'

Jared's doubts must have shone through, because Durand said, 'You don't seem that sure. Nor should you be. The Sanctuary will be united with me in mourning. Martin will be the saviour of the human race. You want to save us, don't you Martin?'

For a moment, Jared thought his own heartbeat had drowned out Martin's reply. Then Martin gave the faintest, 'Yes.'

'You'll be a martyr,' Durand said. 'For generations to come, they'll praise you.'

'Victor, have you lost your mind?' Millicent asked 'He's your son. Just put the gun down.'

'Shut up. You're weak, Millicent. You always have been. But Martin is like me; he sees the bigger picture. His death will help us secure a better world.'

Jared felt bile burn his throat. There was no way he

could go through with this even if he'd wanted to. Of all the outcomes he'd anticipated – shootout, standoff, surrender – the prospect that Durand would so willingly sacrifice his son had never entered his head.

Durand raised his weapon. 'Just as God so loved the world that he gave his only son, I must be prepared to sacrifice the ones closest to me to save what is left of mankind.'

Jared ducked as far behind Martin as he could, whilst continuing to hold onto him. Still, had Martin put up the slightest resistance he could have slipped from Jared's grasp. Instead, the fight appeared to leave him.

'But he's your child,' Millicent said, incredulous.

'Well, it wouldn't be much of a sacrifice if he wasn't somebody precious. Now, Jared, make your move.'

'No. Let him go,' Luca said. Adrenaline had stapled Jared's attention to Durand, so he hadn't noticed Luca creeping closer.

'Don't get involved in this, Luca,' Durand said.

'You hurt him, and I swear to God I'm going to make you pay,' Luca said.

'Why?' Jared asked. 'Because he's like family? Well, that's how I felt about Nell. And you took her from us.'

'You brought that on yourse—'

He had no chance to finish his sentence. Aaron pounced from the storeroom and barrelled straight into him. He ploughed his fists into Luca's face again and again.

'Stop!' Durand said, following their movements with his weapon. 'Get off him.'

The two men rolled over and over on the floor.

'No,' Jared cried, as Luca flipped Aaron over. Clutching

the sides of his head, he smashed Aaron's skull against the floor of the chamber.

'Good,' Durand said. 'Hold him there.'

But Aaron reached a hand up, snagging a handful of Luca's hair and tugging him down again. Now on top, Aaron pressed his forearm across Luca's neck. 'Why couldn't you just leave us be?'

Luca smashed his knee into Aaron's groin, sending a yelp echoing around the chamber.

Durand aimed the weapon at Aaron's head.

Jared let go of Martin and stepped towards him. 'Don't. Please.'

Aaron collapsed onto Luca, who pushed him onto the floor and clambered from under him. Just as Durand fired. He quickly realised his mistake, but it was too late to take it back.

'No. God no,' Durand wailed.

Luca's eyes widened as his skin began to glow. Then his particles separated and bounced around the chamber.

'No. My boy,' Durand said, dropping to his knees and scraping at the floor as the matter that had been Luca blinked out of existence.

Durand knelt in silence, staring at the spot where Luca had been. Aaron staggered to his feet and took the weapon from his hand.

Jared looked over at Martin. He made no move to resist. Instead he watched as his father wept silent tears. The same father who'd been so willing to let him die.

When Jared fixed the weapon on him, Martin simply shrugged. Then he took his gun from his belt and put it on the floor.

The Book of Durand

If you had asked Luca his version of events, I'm sure it would be very different from mine. After all, nobody is the villain of their own story. But he wasn't always the twisted caricature of a human that you came to know. When we first met, he was exactly what I'd been waiting for – a friend. My father would say, 'Ask and you shall receive.' I think it's more like be careful what you wish for.

When he joined our family, I smiled and gave lip service to the brotherhood that had been inflicted on me. In truth, early on I saw what he was. My replacement. The new improved Durand heir. I think part of me always held that against him.

Not any more, because in the end, when my life was on the line, Luca was the only one who spoke up for me. He was a true brother.

Besides, maybe that means there is hope for you and me yet. Because if my best friend can become my biggest threat and then my only advocate, then perhaps the boy who was once my nemesis could become my ally.

Jared

Jared held a hand out to Aaron, helping him to his feet. 'Are you okay?'

'Not really,' Aaron said, pressing his hand to his scalp and then examining the blood left on his palm.

'You will be. We'll find a medilaser; that's an easy fix.'

'I'm glad something is,' Sienna said. He hadn't noticed her follow Aaron from the storeroom, hadn't questioned why Oliver Durand hadn't jumped in to save his brother. She held her weapon aimed at him. 'What now? There may only be three...two guardians in here. But there are plenty out there. When they realise what's happened, they'll storm in, all guns blazing.'

'They don't have to,' Oliver said.

Jared's eyes narrowed. 'If you're suggesting we surrender...'

'Not at all. I'm suggesting you're smart about this. There are plenty of citizens who like things here exactly how they are. They aren't going to let you breeze in and change a system that serves them very well. You have to expect some resistance and come up with a plan on how to deal with it.'

For the first time since Luca's death, Durand looked up. 'Traitor.' Then he spat at Oliver's feet. 'I raised you as my own.'

Oliver knelt next to him. 'I know you did. But that doesn't mean you were kind.' He looked up at Martin. 'What do you say? Is it time to end this? We'll face what comes next together, as brothers.'

'Martin won't fall for your tricks,' Durand said. 'My

blood runs through his veins and there is just no substitute for that.'

'Martin,' Jared said. 'I promise you'll get a fair trial. No more bloodshed. No more death.'

Martin nodded.

Durand tipped his head back and howled. 'You disgust me, the both of you. I have no sons. Not any more. Luca was the only one of you worthy of my name.'

'You're right,' Oliver said. 'I never deserved to be a Durand. No child did.' He turned to Jared. 'You'll get no resistance from me.'

'Where did he send Seb?' Isaac asked.

'I don't know,' Oliver said.

'Liar!'

'I swear, he didn't—'

'The war,' Martin said. 'He sent him back to World War Two.'

'You're going to have to be a little more specific than that,' Jared said.

Martin's eyes flickered towards his father before he quickly looked away. 'Warsaw train station, during the deportations.'

'Deportations?' Isaac asked.

Martin hesitated. 'To the death camps.'

'No.' Isaac's legs gave way and he sat down hard on the floor. 'He...he can't be. I'd know.'

'Does it matter anyway?' Sienna asked. 'Can't we just open the portal to at the time and place Seb was sent to and bring him back.'

Isaac's face lit up. 'Yes, let's do that.'

'I'm sorry,' Jared said, 'but it doesn't work like that. Life in that specific timeline will have moved on.'

Durand sniggered. 'You brought this on yourselves.'

'Shut up,' Aaron said. 'Jared, is there any way to know where he was sent?'

'Maybe. If there is some historical record of him in the timeline, then I'll do my best to find it. Where's the computer he used to program the orb?'

'I'll get it,' Oliver said.

'No you won't.' Sienna jabbed her gun towards him. 'Tell Aaron where it is, and he'll fetch it.'

'You don't trust me?' Oliver asked.

'I trust nobody but myself and God.'

'I thought we were friends.'

'Yes,' Sienna said, nodding her head towards Durand. 'But I don't think anybody can be certain of your loyalty right now, Ollie.'

'Okay. Well, I hope that's something I can resolve.' He pointed towards the chamber at the back. 'I'll show you.' Aaron and Sienna trailed behind him.

Millicent reached a hand out to Isaac.

He waved it away and pushed himself up. 'It's a little late to play the Good Samaritan.'

'I...I tried to stop it. You heard me, Jared, didn't you?'

'She's telling the truth,' Jared said.

Isaac's lip trembled and he put a hand to his mouth to cover it. 'This has been going on for months. Years, even. She could have stepped in at any time. But her life here was a little too comfortable to risk.'

'I'm sorry you feel that way,' Millicent said, and headed towards the chamber.

'She did try, you know,' Jared said.

'You haven't had to live here for the last four years. Some things are unforgivable. I, of all people, should know that.' He stared at Jared for the longest time.

Jared began to squirm under his gaze, wondering what it was Isaac wanted him to say. 'Okay,' he said, turning away.

'Wait,' Isaac said. 'Why are you helping us?'

'Why wouldn't I?'

'We don't deserve your help. Not after what we did to you at the lake.'

Jared frowned. 'I don't see what one has to do with the other.'

Isaac's eyes brimmed. 'And there's the difference between us.'

Jared fidgeted, not sure what he would do if Isaac broke down and cried. 'Give me some time and I'll see what I can find.'

'Thank you.'

Jared spent the next few hours sieving through endless historical records. When he blinked, the negatives of images he wished he could unsee were burned onto the back of his eyelids. Emaciated prisoners, gas chambers with claw marks on the walls, pits for burning bodies: he saw them all. He'd almost given up hope when he came across a witness report.

The interviewer noted that, although the man was elderly, he spoke with such clarity that he could have been recalling an event from the day before.

Interviewer: Tell us how you escaped from Treblinka, Marcus.

Marcus: Courage and friendship. Those were really all that I had left in that place.

Interviewer: Go on.

Marcus: I was part of the resistance at only 14 years old. Can you believe that?

Interviewer: You must have been an amazing young man.

Marcus: I don't know. Maybe. I had to grow up fast. They robbed me of my childhood. On the day I arrived at Treblinka, it was as part of a group of four. My mother, sister and baby brother were all sent to the gas chamber.

Interviewer: I'm so sorry to hear that. So you were alone in Treblinka.

Marcus: I didn't say that. I had friends. They kept me alive, quite literally. Typhus nearly got me.

Interviewer: And the day of the uprising?

Marcus: Between them, they ensured I made it. They were brave men. Galewski, Freidman, Zialo and...

Interviewer: It's okay if you don't remember.

Marcus: Do I look like I've lost my mind? I could never forget any of them. It's just, the one I was thinking of went by two names. At roll call they called him Reuben. But I knew the man who saved my life as Seb.

They all turned and stared as Jared entered the chamber. 'It looks like Seb was deported to Treblinka.'

'Okay,' Isaac said. 'At least it wasn't Auschwitz.'

'That's not good news.' Jared spoke quickly, as though getting it over with might lesson the pain. 'I wouldn't wish any of those places on my worst enemy, but Treblinka was one of the most terrible.'

'Why have we not heard of it?' Millicent asked.

'The Nazis destroyed it to hide their crimes.' Jared's throat felt constricted, as though his own body were willing him to spare Isaac the pain his words would cause. 'It was an extermination camp. It operated for just over a year, but it's estimated that around 900,000 people were murdered there.'

Isaac sat down at the committee table. 'Then it's hopeless.'

'I found only one mention of Seb. At least I think it was him. He was part of the resistance. Because of them, nearly one hundred people survived.'

Isaac smiled. 'That sounds right.'

'Can we go back and save him?' Aaron asked.

'Honestly? I have no idea. All of the experiments I carried out with my grandfather on changing historical events suggest not.' Jared nodded towards Durand. 'But without him, Seb never would have been in that timeline. So maybe we can change his fate.'

'Then let me try,' Isaac said. 'Open the portal now and I'll go back and find him. Then I'll bring him home.'

Durand snorted. 'Let him go. It will save me getting rid of him too, once I free myself from these.' He jangled the cuffs that Sienna had snapped over his wrists.

'You're sure?' Jared asked. 'If you wait until we've decided what to—'

'No,' Isaac said. 'Please. Send me now.'

Jared knew he would do the same if it were somebody he loved. 'Okay. Let's do this.'

The Book of Durand

I saw you watching me after Luca died. You're a hard man to read. Was it pity I saw in your eye? Suspicion, perhaps. Or maybe you were wondering if I believed your promises of a fair trial.

I'll tell you. I was considering Oliver's question: 'Is it time to end this?'

My answer is yes.

Luca is dead, and Oliver never wanted to be part of our family to start with. So I think, once my father is gone, the Durand name should die with me. That's what I was thinking.

Seb

'There were supposed to be two of you,' Seb said.

'Leon is already behind the storeroom. We thought it might be better if we go separately.'

'Good thinking. Are you nervous?' Seb asked.

'No,' Marcus said, a little too quickly. 'Maybe a little.'

'That means you're smart.' Seb handed him a screwdriver. 'Take this to dig out the putty. You have the key?'

Marcus nodded. 'Okay. I'm going to keep watch.'

Seb hung between the guard house he was supposed to be extending and the vegetable plot. Sadovitz stood in a nearby field, turning over the hard August earth. Other than that, they were alone.

Still, Seb tried to look busy, should one of the Ukrainian guards have chosen to stay behind and man the nearby watch tower.

After no more than a minute, Marcus came back towards him at a trot. Seb wanted to yell for him to slow down, to tell him that he'd draw attention to them. Only when Marcus reached him without gunfire raining down on them did he let out a puff of relief.

'It's no good,' Marcus said. 'There's still an officer in the barracks. There's no way we can get the weapons past him.'

A burning nausea turned Seb's stomach. 'I guess I could—'

'Let me.' Sadovitz dropped his spade. 'Galewski asked me to keep an eye out in case you needed help. It's probably the night guard. He won't be happy about being disturbed, but I'll get him out somehow.'

A rush of relief flooded over Seb. 'What will you say to him?'

'I don't know. I'll make something up.' Sadovitz pointed to the watch tower. 'There's no guard up there. I saw him leave. The one on the other side shouldn't be able to see you if you keep close to the building.' Sadovitz headed towards the living quarters.

Seb turned to Marcus. 'Hide behind the bins until they're gone.'

By the time Sadovitz led the SS officer from the barracks, Seb was rummaging in his tool bag, his back to them.

'They're over in the potato field,' Sadovitz said. 'We've split them up for now, but I think we'd better allocate them to different teams.'

The officer grunted in return.

Marcus darted from behind the bins as soon as they were out of view.

'Walk,' Seb said under his breath.

Marcus fumbled with the lock and slipped into the storeroom, pulling the door closed behind him.

At first Seb thought it was nerves that sent a shiver through him. A familiar crackle raised the hairs of his arm. Tiny sparks of lightning fizzed in the air. Seb touched one, and it branched off like a crack in a window pane.

He'd seen energy like this before. Only this time the portal that tore a hole in the air wasn't red, it was blue. It widened like a disapproving eye peering sideways into the world of Treblinka.

Isaac bounded through it straight into his arms. 'Thank God. I thought I'd lost you.'

'Are you real?'

'Of course I am.' Isaac grabbed his hand. 'Come on, we've got to go back through. The gate won't be open for long.'

Seb took a step back. 'No, I can't leave. Not yet. I promised I would help.'

'Are you mad? You know what happens here today, don't you?'

'Yes,' Seb said. 'Which is exactly why I can't go.'

'Listen to me.' Isaac took his hand and tried to pull him towards the portal. 'Out of all of the men who are going to resist, less than a hundred will actually survive. Please. We need to go. This is history. It's already happened. We have a future.'

Seb dropped his hand. 'Not to them it hasn't. Not to me.' He took a step away. 'I don't think you have any real idea where we are.'

'I do. We're in Treblinka.'

'Hell. That's where we are. My part might be small, but I won't let them down.'

Isaac looked at the portal and then back at Seb. 'Well, I'm not leaving without you. So tell me how I can help.'

'I can't let you do that.'

With a crackle, the portal snapped shut behind them.

'I guess that decides it,' Isaac said.

Chapter Nine

The Book of Durand

I've been reading your book. I don't know why that surprises you; there's not much else to do in prison. That's a catchy title by the way. 'The Book of Jared'; it must have taken ages to come up with.

Did I like it? I wouldn't go that far. But it seemed honest. I think that's a value all of us down here have been lacking for a while now.

When you first suggested I tell my own story, I didn't see the point. No matter what my motives, who would side with the son of Victor Durand? But then I got thinking about the rules of the old world. There were laws that protected good Samaritans. Otherwise you might save somebody from drowning only to be sued when you break their ribs trying to pump the water from their chest.

But people who refused to put their own lives in danger to help others were also protected. And, had I stepped in and stood up against my father, my life would have been. Son or not, my father wouldn't have thought twice about sacrificing me to his cause. I think he proved that much. Perhaps there are those amongst us who would understand the predicament that put me in. Some of them might empathise with my situation.

Although now I realise it's not about the reader at all. Whether anybody ever chooses to flick through these pages and stamp their judgement on my life is irrelevant. It's about me, putting my side across, and for the first time feeling heard.

Seb

Jacob was true to his word. They found the two trollies just where he'd said they'd be at the other end of the vegetable garden.

'You grab that one,' he told Isaac.

Seb cursed the squeaky wheel as they headed to the other end of the barracks to meet Marcus and Leon. When Seb rounded the corner, Leon slid behind the barracks and grabbed the first bundle. Despite the boy's tiny frame, he still had to inch forward, pressing his cheek to the wood.

'Who's that?' Marcus asked, nodding at Isaac.

'My friend, Isaac, from the extermination area. Galewski sent him to help us.' The fact that Marcus didn't question him made Seb feel worse about lying, but there was no time to dwell.

'There wasn't as much as we hoped,' Leon said as he wriggled out. 'We got some boxes of grenades—'

'And detonators,' Marcus added.

'Other than that, we only found a few pistols and about a dozen rifles.' They passed them over, wrapped within bundles of sacking. Soon the two trollies were nearly full.

Seb covered them with some offcuts of wood. 'We need to get these out as soon as we can. Do you remember where you are taking them?'

The boys nodded. 'We're to meet Jacob by the latrines, and he is going to take the trolley to the extermination area.'

If all had gone to plan, Jacob would have already given out the tools they'd gathered and would be back to meet the boys. Then he'd pass the guns to Freidman's burning team at the pits.

'Good. Don't forget to pick up any scraps of wood as you go. That's what Jacob told the guards the trollies are for, and we don't want them to get suspicious.'

They watched the boys until the barracks hid them from view.

'They're so young,' Isaac said.

'Yeah. And if what you said is true about less than one hundred people surviving today, then they probably aren't going to make it.'

'I'm sorry. I know I was being selfish. It's just—'

'Believe me. I get it. But I intend to do anything I can to help them.'

'Then let's go.'

They headed for the potato plot. A woman stared at them as they approached. Without a word, she dropped the bundles they passed her into a bucket beneath her workbench.

There next stop was the blue team. With no transport that morning, they'd been put to work in the storehouse, sorting any valuables from the bundles of previous passengers.

'I need you to stay here,' Seb told Isaac. 'We don't know if there is a guard on the other side of the store, so you need to stay out of view. Have you got it?'

Isaac nodded, but Seb could see he wasn't happy. Since they were children, Isaac had always been the protective one. Waiting on the side lines wasn't in his nature.

'I mean it, Isaac. They'll shoot you without a second thought.'

'I know.'

Seb shoved the trolley over the threshold to the storehouse. Korland was untying bundles of clothes, searching them for anything valuable, and dropping anything else into a pile to be burnt. Documents, photographs, children's toys – fragments of lives, now categorised as rubbish.

As he approached, Seb saw a piece of blood-red cloth sticking out of Korland's pocket. 'If the guards see that, they're going to have questions.'

Korland grabbed his chest. 'Don't scare me like that. I thought you were Kuttner.'

'Well, I'll take that as an insult. Where do you want these?'

Korland took the weapons and buried them amongst the discarded clothes.

'I take it that's our flag,' Seb said, pointing to the cloth. 'How are you planning to get to the platform to signal the train?'

'I'm not sure. I'll find some excuse to go to the other storeroom, I guess.' He shoved the red cloth deeper into his pocket.

'Good luck,' Seb said.

'You too.'

Isaac had waited around the corner, pressing himself as close to the wood as possible.

'Okay. Korland's working over at the well. You need to wait—'

Seb noticed the grimace on Isaac's face. 'Are you okay?'

'Don't you smell that?'

Seb sniffed. Yes, he could smell something. Fuel. But they were nowhere near the refilling station.

He looked around and saw a man with a tank strapped to his back. This had become a common sight in the short time

Seb had spent in Treblinka. With the many typhus outbreaks, the SS had ordered bleach to be sprayed around the barracks regularly. But it wasn't bleach that Seb could smell. It was gasoline.

When the man turned, Seb saw that it was Sereni. He raised a hand to Seb, before continuing to spray the wall of the SS barracks. That's when Seb realised that the resistance wasn't just planning to escape. They were going to burn the whole place to the ground.

The Book of Durand

Although he never would have let anybody know it, jealousy was really what drove my father to pursue you through time. His sense of entitlement has always been overwhelming; why should you get an option for escape that he didn't?

That wasn't the only reason, though. The fact is nothing brings people together like a common enemy. When you killed David and our community began to fracture, you were the obvious choice.

'Dogs and sorcerers,' he'd say, spitting on the ground, whenever we mentioned your family. It was his favourite Revelations quote and summed up his opinion of you, the boy who murdered our leader and ran. He was never going to let the people forget that.

Replicating Pearse's invention and bringing you to justice became an obsession to him. Although perhaps your grandfather wasn't quite the genius everyone assumed, because he didn't wipe his work from his computer history. Or maybe he was complacent, assuming nobody would understand it. He might have been right, if it hadn't been for the hive mind of the STEM sector.

History is littered with cases of prisoners used in experiments. So when the scientists of the Sanctuary finally reproduced Pearse's work, Father declared our criminals the perfect test subjects. The problem is, much like the Nazis of World War Two, he had a warped idea of who the criminals were.

The first...victim, that's what I'll call him. Because I knew even then that's what they were. I just wasn't brave enough to help. The first victim was unmemorable.

Confused but docile, he was blindfolded and shoved through the portal. I think the lack of resistance disappointed my father.

But I'll never forget the next one. Thoughts of her ambush me when I least expect them. They led her in unshackled and with no blindfold. I wasn't surprised. Demure, manicured, she hardly seemed a threat.

As the portal tore a hole in the air, she bristled with fear. Before she could even know what was in store for her.

'Please,' she said, backing away. 'I'll keep quiet.'

'Too late,' my father said, drawing out the words. 'Boys, grab her.'

Luca and Oliver grasped an arm each.

'Don't make this more difficult,' Oliver said. Although I think he meant more difficult for him, not her.

'I'll tell the people I was wrong, that no election is needed. Please.'

At first Father revelled in the begging. He made a show of considering her plan. Then he shook his head. 'That won't cut it. But...'

'What? I'll do anything. Just let me go back to my husband and daughter.'

'Names. That's what I want. I know you aren't the only one spreading this poison. Tell me who else is involved, and I'll let you stay.'

She stood up straighter. 'My opinions belong to me alone.'

Father shrugged. 'Then you'll face your punishment alone, too.'

I felt the heat in her glare even from where I stood by the orb.

It was probably the dignity she showed that annoyed him most, the way she held her head high.

Father added, 'Although that girl of yours has a smart mouth. Maybe I should save myself some time and send her with you now.'

She was half through the portal when she turned and raked her nails down my father's face.

'Push her through,' he yelled at my brothers, whilst trying to pry her from him. 'Close the damn portal, Martin.'

I stood there, numb. Until she was through entirely, there was nothing I could do.

'Martin!' Father screamed at me from behind her flailing arms.

Then Luca was beside me, swiping his hand across the orb.

And she was gone. I won't go into details. She deserves more than your last thoughts of her to be of blood splatter and entrails. All you need to know is that's how Sienna's mother died, half in this world, half in another, fighting for her daughter.

I don't think Sienna knows. The rumours, started by us, said her parents were banished together. I think it would be cruel to tell her now. Although maybe the closure would be a release. What do you think? Would you want to know?

Seb

When Seb reached the well in the sorting square, Salzberg was standing motionless beside it.

Seb followed his line of sight towards the prisoner barracks. 'Is everything okay?'

'I don't think so. Some of my team went into the barracks. Kuba followed them in, and none of them have come out yet.'

'Shall I try and get closer to take a look?'

'No...Yes.' Salzberg let out a frustrated groan. 'I told them to wait for the signal. They might have ruined everything. And for what? To collect some—'

Kuba stalked from the building.

'Kuttner's on duty,' Salzberg said. 'Kuba will be going to tell him what he's found.' Salzberg waved to his team, and they flocked to him.

Salzberg rummaged in the trolley and began passing weapons out to his men.

'What are we going to do?' Seb asked. 'There's no way we can begin the rebellion early. The train won't be here for another hour.'

'We'll have to manage without them,' Salzberg said. 'Unless...'

'What?'

'If we kill Kuttner quietly before he can raise the alarm, maybe we can get the plan back on track.'

Seb's heart sank as he looked over Salzberg's head. 'I don't think he's going to go down quietly.'

Kuttner stalked towards them, dragging Leon by the hair

behind him. Leon tried to get to his feet but fell to his knees, again and again, begging Kuttner to let him go.

Finally, Kuttner yanked him up. 'On my way here, I came across this streak of filth. What did he have inside his coat?' Kuttner threw a handful of notes onto the floor.

Seb looked over at Isaac, who now peered around the corner of the barracks, and shook his head. Isaac disappeared from view.

'And I hear he is not the only one stealing in this camp,' Kuttner said, glancing at Kuba, who stood just behind him, staring at the floor.

'We've fed you, housed you, given you work, and this is how you repay us.' Kuttner grabbed Leon by the tops of his arms and lifted him, so they were facing one another. 'So, are you going to tell me what you are planning? Why do you need all that money?'

The only response Leon gave was heaving sobs.

'Fine,' Kuttner said. 'We will see how long your silence lasts in the lazarett.'

Seb reached for the trolley, hoping that Salzberg had left a weapon inside.

There was no need. Salzberg put his thumb and finger to his mouth and gave the faintest whistle. Every prisoner looked at him, but he nodded to only one, who stood a few metres behind Kuttner.

The prisoner drew his gun and fired.

The shot tore through the air, bringing a shocked stillness to the camp. Kuttner froze and stared down at his shoulder. It was only when a maroon patch bloomed on his jacket that panic twisted his features.

He dropped Leon, who seemed to bounce to his feet, blood freckling his pale face.

Meanwhile, Kuttner ran for the SS headquarters. He tripped several times, but still the shots the prisoner continued to fire fell short. The door opened, and Kuttner launched himself over the threshold.

'Okay,' Salzberg said. 'Those of you with grenades, aim them at the headquarters.'

The air was sucked from Seb's eardrums, pinging them back with an angry snap as the grenades exploded.

He looked back towards the side of the prisoner barracks to see Isaac in the same crouched position, arms wrapped around his head.

Considering the noise, Seb was disappointed to see that the far end of the SS headquarters was splintered and blackened, but still stood.

Another explosion rattled the camp. 'Was that the fuelling station?' Salzberg asked.

'I think so,' Seb said, wondering if Lichtblau and Lubrenitski had made it out alive. 'We need to get out of here.'

'Bring whatever tools you can and get to the fence,' Salzberg called to the prisoners.

Seb turned over the trolley, scattering the last few items within. He picked up a pair of pliers and, beckoning to Isaac, ran for the fence.

Salzberg was already hacking at it with a saw. 'Here, let me try,' Isaac said. 'You get the men organised.'

Salzberg didn't question Isaac's presence. With a high turnover of workers separated into the different camps, strangers were a way of life.

Seb worked at a different link in the fence, twisting at the metal with the pliers. He was about to throw them to the floor in frustration when he heard Salzberg say, 'Move, you idiot.'

Seb turned to find Kuba, arms spread, trying to block the path of three prisoners. 'If you leave, they'll hunt you down and kill you.'

'They'll kill us anyway, Kuba,' Salzberg said.

'No, they promised. If we play our part, after the war there will be a place for us. Our own city.'

Seb wished he hadn't seen what happened next. One of the men pulled out a hammer and smashed it down on the back of Kuba's head. His eyes widened, and he patted at his scalp. Then he slumped forward into the dirt.

The man pulled the hammer from Kuba's skull with a sickening crunch.

'Why did you do that?' Salzberg asked. 'He might have listened. I might have persuaded him.'

The man stared down at Kuba's body. 'Because no man escapes his sins.'

Before Salzberg could respond, rifle fire from the watchtower sent men hurrying past him and up the fence.

'We've got no choice,' Isaac said. 'We're going to have to climb.'

Seb knew he was right. If they made a break towards the extermination area, they'd be faced with three more towers. Seb couldn't risk the possibility of them being manned.

'Okay.' He dropped the pliers to the floor and started to climb.

Seb was quick, so much so that Isaac was soon lagging behind. The bullets pitting the earth below and whizzing past his head gave added incentive.

It wasn't until he neared the top that he faltered. A man lay tangled in the barbed wire. Seb didn't have to question whether he was alive or not. Dead eyes peered back at him through the chain-link fence.

'Hurry up,' Isaac yelled.

'I can't.' But as he watched Isaac flinch away from a bullet, he knew he had no choice. Heaving himself up, he used the body as protection from the barbed wire, repeating to himself over and over that the man was gone and could no longer feel the metal biting into his flesh. And then he was over, Isaac landing with a thud close behind him.

Through the links in the fence, Seb saw a familiar figure begin to climb. He had lost his glasses, but the thin wavy hair, swept back from his scalp, was the same. Before he got even halfway up, he was hit. 'Sereni!' Seb called. He landed with a thud.

'You can't help him,' Isaac said, pushing him on.

They ran only a few metres before a second fence blocked their way. As they reached the top, Seb was relieved to see that someone had thrown a blanket over the barbed wire. Still, it sliced his palms and ripped at the skin on his calves. Adrenaline alone got him to the other side, and he ran towards the forest, Isaac at his side.

Jared

Jared paced the length of the Grand Chamber. 'I never should've let him go alone.'

'And what were you supposed to do?' Aaron asked. 'Leave us here to deal with Durand and his cronies?'

Martin sat on the floor of the chamber, his arms looped around his legs. Oliver leant against the edge of the raised platform, the one his adopted father had delivered so many sermons from. Neither looked up at the mention of their family name.

Only Durand seemed to be listening to the conversation. His black eyes flitted from Jared to Aaron and back again.

'Our priority has to be getting back to Beth and planning our next move,' Aaron said.

'She's fine,' Millicent said. 'I've left her with...a friend.'

Jared didn't need to ask who. He wondered if Millicent had told his mother how Beth arrived in the Sanctuary, and whether she was hoping, expecting, to see him. Reconciling had always been a matter of when, not if, to him. He wanted to see her, and not just because he wanted answers about her part in his grandfather's fate. Now it occurred to him that it might be a conversation he would never have. The last time he saw her might actually have been the last.

He walked over to the orb. 'I need to go back and find them.'

'Why do you do this?' Aaron asked, his fists balled at his side. 'Not everything and everyone is your responsibility, Jared.'

'You don't understand. If my grandfather knew how his

invention is being used, it would destroy him. If I can save just one life, then that would be…I don't know, something.'

Aaron sighed. 'Okay. Millicent, can you cover for us long enough for him to try?'

'I think so.' She looked at Sienna, who still held her gun aimed at the Durands. 'With such important business to attend to, I imagine the Durand family would prefer not to be disturbed today. Leave it with me.' The doors clunked shut behind her.

'You agree then,' Jared asked. 'Saving them is the right thing to do.' He didn't know why he craved Aaron's approval so much, but he did.

'No,' Aaron said. 'I think you're crazy. But if it will bring you some peace, who am I to stand in your way? Just make sure you come back. I've lost enough family.'

Family. The weight of the word, laden with warmth and responsibility, pressed down on Jared. 'I promise I'll do my best.'

Jared took the orb from the stand and replaced it with his own. He had to admit, they'd done a fantastic job at reproducing his grandfather's technology. The orbs were almost identical. With the computer already programmed, it really made no difference which he used. Still, it didn't feel right to use the Durands' orb, not when it had been created for nothing but evil.

The orb began to pulse and glow.

'You'll never find them,' Martin said.

Jared was surprised to hear his voice, and not just because it was the first thing he'd said since that whispered 'yes'. Also because there was no glee in his words. They were flat, wrung of hope.

Aaron shot him a withering look. 'We don't need your opinion.'

'I've been studying the map of Treblinka,' Jared said. 'The fence by the sorting square was the nearest reported escape route to where Isaac arrived. That's where I'll start.'

'Why?' Durand had sat so quietly until that point that Jared had almost forgotten he was there. 'Because you want to play the hero?'

'I want to save my friends,' Jared said.

'Friends?' Durand stood up. 'Hardly. David and I knew, you know, what they did at the lake. We thought it might do you some good. Knock you back into line. But we didn't order it done. No, it was all the idea of your friends.'

The fear and rejection flooded back to Jared. 'I...It doesn't...'

Oliver groaned. 'Just sit down, Victor. Nobody wants to hear your bile.'

'You will call me Father! Your lack of respect sickens me. After all I've done for you.'

'That's true. I'm sure neither Martin or I would be the men we are today without you. And Luca would have been a little less twisted and a lot less dead.'

Durand slapped him, hard. 'Don't you say his name.'

'Sit down.' Sienna jabbed her gun towards him.

'Oh, you're giving me orders now, little girl? Tell me, have you ever even fired a gun?'

Sienna didn't answer.

'I didn't think so. Your hand's shaking. I should have banished you with your parents.'

Sienna grasped her wrist with her other hand to steady it. 'I can still aim well enough.'

'Then shoot.' Durand spread his arms wide.

Sienna didn't move. The only sound was the crackling of the portal as it began to open.

'Yeah, I didn't think so.' He turned to Jared. 'I've been a father, not just to those boys, but to this whole place. Can't you see? Everything I've done has been because I love the Sanctuary and want it to survive.'

'No... I...'

Durand's tone was so reasonable, so calm, yet his words managed to churn Jared's thoughts.

'Don't listen to him,' Aaron said. 'Remember what they did to Nell. They're monsters, the lot of them.'

A ripping sound filled the air as the portal opened.

'I won't,' Jared said. 'Let him say what he wants; he won't change my mind.'

Durand pounced, looping his fingers around Jared's throat. 'Then you can die with them.'

'Sienna, shoot him,' Aaron called.

'What if I hit Jared?'

Durand tightened his grip, making Jared wheeze as he fought to drag air into his lungs. At first, he put the sparks that filled his vision down to a lack of oxygen. Then he remembered that the portal was opening.

He met Aaron's eye, hoping that somehow he would understand that he had no choice. The Sanctuary would never survive with Durand still there, ready to seize power at any opportunity. Durand had to face justice, and it was only right it was by his own design.

Jared threw himself backwards through the portal, Durand still clinging to him.

The Book of Durand

As I watched my father choke the breath from you, I could sympathise; it felt as though he'd been doing the same thing to me my entire life.

When you launched yourself through the portal, him still clutching at your throat, do you know what my first thought was? Not outrage or grief. It was that now I'd be free. Not literally, of course. I've done far too many shameful things for that. But free of him.

Then why did I follow the two of you through? It's a fair question. Not for love or loyalty. The truth is, I panicked. I didn't know who I was without him, how to exist. Oliver was once a Sawyer. Luca was once a Cole. I've never been anybody but Martin Durand. I guess, just in that moment, living anywhere but in his shadow seemed too terrifying a future to contemplate.

Seb

Seb dropped to his knees and scrambled through the underbrush. The sun was still high. After years of living in the fake light of the Sanctuary, it was strange to find himself wishing it away. But with it blazing through the canopy, the guards were certain to see him.

He'd lost Isaac somewhere between the perimeter fence and the dash into the forest. Gunshots had pitted the ground around them, dictating their paths. Although he wanted to stick his head above the bushes and look for him, he didn't dare. Not yet. Not while gunfire still echoed between the trees.

The crunching of leaves gave Seb the hope that Isaac was nearby and looking for him. It was dashed when the boots of two Ukrainian guards stopped in front of the bush he hid within.

Seb clasped his hand over his own mouth and tried to take shallow breaths. The guards continued on, but Seb remained still and under cover.

The gunfire seemed to last forever, punctuated by the occasional scream. The forest was cloaked by smoke. Seb would have liked to congratulate Sereni on a job well done. His only regret was that, from where he hid, he couldn't see it burn.

It must have been close to an hour before Seb decided the area had quietened enough for him to look for Isaac. He got to his feet but stooped as low as possible. Scanning the area, he saw no sign of him.

The smoke at ground level had been bearable. Now it invaded his nostrils and stung his eyes. From his trips out of the camp to collect wood, he knew there was a glade nearby and headed for it.

As he got closer, the air began to clear. Seb was relieved to be able to breathe more easily, but he was very aware that as the smoke disappeared, so did his cover. The snap of a twig sent him hurtling behind a tree.

Once he dared peek around the trunk, he was relieved to see Marcus, turning in circles.

'Marcus, what are you doing? Get over here.'

'You made it,' Marcus said, running towards him.

Seb grabbed his arm as soon as he was in reach and yanked him low. 'It's so good to see you,' he said, patting him down for signs of injuries. 'Well, you seem to be in one piece.'

'I'm fine. But I can't find Galewski.'

'He got out, too?'

Marcus nodded. 'Yeah. He did.'

Seb wasn't sure he wanted to know but had to ask. 'And the rest of the organising committee?'

'When Kuttner grabbed Leon, I ran for the extermination area. Freidman and Zialo stayed to fire at the watchtowers so the rest of us could escape. I...I didn't see them after that.'

Seb wasn't surprised to hear that his friends had risked their own lives to save the others. He prayed they had had time to get out themselves.

'Jacob ran in a different direction from us. For a while we were with a group of survivors, but the guards found us, and we lost them too. I guess we went in a circle and ended up back here. Then Galewski disappeared, too.'

'Well, we have each other now. We'll head for the glen where the smoke is clearer, but keep to the tree line.'

'We can't. I know Galewski's around here somewhere. A guard shot him in the leg, so he can't have got far.'

'There will be hunting parties out looking for us. We've got to move.'

Marcus took a step away. 'Galewski wouldn't leave us. Not if he had a choice.'

'I know. Okay. We'll do a quick sweep and then we have to go.'

They scanned the area around then, Seb flinching at every snapped twig. 'I don't think—'

'There he is!' Marcus ran towards a pair of boots sticking out from behind a tree.

They were worn away, with grey socks visible through the holes, so Seb was sure it wasn't a guard. Still, he didn't want to risk it. 'Marcus, wait for me.'

The boy slowed as he neared the tree. 'Why didn't you wait for me? Galewski?'

Seb knew he was dead as soon as he saw him. Galewski's eyes were glazed, and his mouth had fallen open into a round o.

'What's wrong?' Marcus shook his shoulder and Galewski slumped onto the floor, his cheek against the root of the tree.

'I don't understand.' Marcus's voice was a whisper. 'He said it was just his leg, that he'd be fine.'

Seb noticed that Galewski's hand was curled around something. He pulled back his fingers and found a vial.

'What is that?' Marcus asked.

Seb didn't need to read the label to know it was poison.

He knew from the stories of Doctor Chorazycki's death that some men in the camp kept a stash of it, just in case. But he couldn't tell Marcus that, not when the boy had been so sure that Galewski wouldn't leave him. Then Seb thought of the second part of Marcus's sentence. Not if Galewski had a choice. Looking down at the bloated flesh of Galewski's leg, Seb knew he hadn't. With that injury, it would only have been a matter of time before the SS tracked him down, and Marcus along with him.

'It's nothing. Just a bullet shell,' Seb said, as he tossed the vial into the bushes. 'Galewski was probably trying not to worry you.' Seb took a last look at the man who'd been both his saviour and his friend, before he tried to guide Marcus away. 'Come on. He wouldn't want us to risk getting caught.'

'Stay where you are.' They'd been so distracted that they hadn't noticed the Ukrainian guard approaching. He must have been around Seb's age, perhaps younger.

Seb raised his hands. 'Please. Just pretend you didn't see us.'

'I can't do that,' the guard said.

'Of course you can. Just keep on walking.'

'I don't *want* to do that. You savages killed a lot of good men back there.'

'What's he saying?' Marcus asked, the conversation lost on him without a chip.

Seb ignored him. 'How about just the boy? I won't resist if you let him go.'

The guard smirked. 'No.' Then he pulled the trigger.

The Book of Durand

My father loved to quote the bible. But, like I said, I don't think that was anything to do with faith or religion. Underneath all the pomp and ceremony, I'm pretty sure the only thing he believed in was himself.

I imagine he just thought it gave weight to his words. But the lines he selected were as inconsistent as his moods. One moment, the God of Exodus, forged of war, fierce and angry, might suit his purpose. The next, the God described in Romans, embodying love and peace.

That scenario makes me uneasy. I don't like the idea of others snipping parts of my history and deciding they represent me. None of us exist without context. But who gets to choose the deeds that represent us? Which of our words, half remembered and regurgitated by others, summarise our lives?

Which is why I'm grateful for the opportunity to give my side, warts and all. I've done my best to be honest. I know you'd see right through it if I was anything less than authentic. Besides, if I'm going to be judged anyway, it's better it's done based on my own words. And the truth is, I'd really like to live.

Seb

Nothing happened. Just an empty metallic click.

The guard's eyes widened, and he shifted the gun from his shoulder to reload.

Seb knew there was no chance of reaching him in time, but what choice did he have? He crouched, ready to pounce at him.

However, before he even had a chance to move, a figure launched itself through the bushes into the guard. Although Seb could only see the back of his head as he wrestled for the gun, that was all he needed. 'Isaac!'

The gunshot sent birds up into the air, shrieking. Seb wanted to follow their lead and howl out his despair as Isaac fell to his knees.

The guard looked rattled, a sheen of sweat covering his face. He pointed the gun first at Isaac, then at Seb, swinging it between the two of them. 'Both of you just stay—'

The axe sliced into the crook of the guard's neck. He looked at it, puzzled.

Only when Jacob pulled it from his flesh did the blood begin to flow. It trickled to the ground, and the guard knelt in it as the strength left his legs. He slumped face forward into the rotting vegetation of the forest floor.

Seb ran to Isaac's side. 'I need to put pressure on the wound,' he said, taking the shirt Marcus offered and balling it into place.

'There's so much blood,' Isaac said.

'You're fine. It's mostly his. Come on.' Seb tried to pull him to his feet.

Isaac groaned. 'No, please, I can't.'

'You have to. We need to get you—'

'Where?' Isaac's skin was grey. 'There's nowhere for you to take me.'

'I...' Seb suppressed a sob. 'Then I'll get you help. I'll find someone.'

'I'd rather you just sat with me,' Isaac said.

Seb watched the spasms of Isaac's chest pumping blood from his wound. 'Okay. You rest now.'

'Shall I go and find somebody?' Marcus asked.

'Not now.' Seb kissed Isaac's temple. 'We're going to sit for a while.' Seb lifted Isaac so his head was in his lap. Then he stroked Isaac's hair until his eyes closed and his body stilled.

~

Jared

Jared prised at Durand's fingers, but his grip was firm. He bucked and twisted below him, but Durand just squeezed harder.

At first, Jared was desperate to get away, determined to keep his promise to Aaron and to save Seb and Isaac. But then, as he began to swim in and out of consciousness, it didn't seem to matter as much. Finding Seb and Isaac was likely a hopeless task. And his mother and Millicent would take care of his friends. Maybe it was time to rest.

'Lâche-le!'

The words, incomprehensible to Jared, penetrated the fog, dragging him from the gloom. And there he was, Martin Durand, his arm hooked around his father, trying to pry him off.

'Traître!' Durand beat at Martin's wrist, letting go of Jared in the process. Durand ducked under Martin's arm and squared up to him.

Jared scrambled away from the two men and sat trying to catch his breath.

'Was ist los?' None of them had noticed the SS officer approach. He took another step towards them and repeated his question. 'Was ist los?'

Even if Jared had been able to answer, his swollen throat wouldn't allow him. But as Durand opened and closed his mouth wordlessly, Jared realised that, with no chip either, he was just as helpless.

Not Martin, though. He stooped, picking up a piece of crimson cloth from the floor and rubbing the fabric between his fingertips. Then he stood tall and answered the soldier in fluent German.

The Nazi's eyes narrowed, and he took a step towards Durand. Reaching out a hand, he tore off his clerical collar. 'Verhaften Sie ihn!' Durand stared at his son through confused eyes. 'Martin.' His feet left twin trails as the guards dragged him away. 'Martin!'

So they were left alone, Jared and his bully.

Jared forced words through his constricted throat. 'What...did you say to them?'

'It doesn't matter,' Martin said.

'You saved me.'

Martin said nothing.

'Thank you. You did the right thing.'

'I think my father might disagree.' He twisted the blood red material in his hands. 'But—'

'Murderer!' Seb charged towards them, fists flying.

One landed square on Martin's cheek, and he collapsed to the floor.

Jared looped an arm around Seb's waste. 'No, please. Calm down.'

'Calm down? Isaac's dead.'

'I'm sorry, but—'

'But nothing. He's going to die for what he's done.'

Jared grasped his shoulders. 'Maybe, but not like this. He'll stand trial.'

'Why should he get justice when Isaac and I didn't?'

'Because you're a good man.'

Seb stopped. 'You really believe that? Even after what we did to you?'

'Yes. At least I hope so. Though, I guess we don't really

know each other any more. But I don't like to think that one bad deed can undo a lifetime of good.'

'Thank you. It was Isaac's biggest regret, you know. Both of ours. If we could undo it...'

'I know. Seb, why did you come back here?'

'I didn't know where else to go. I thought perhaps I could help my friends.' His face crumpled. 'And maybe I'd get lucky and one of these monsters would kill me along the way.'

Jared kicked at the dirt, wishing he knew how to comfort him. 'Please don't talk like that. Isaac wanted to get you home. Let me do that. For him.'

Seb nodded.

Holding out a hand, Jared hauled Martin to his feet. The three of them stood, shoulder to shoulder, as Jared pulled the orb from his pocket and opened the portal.

The Book of Durand

My mother haunts me. I know I've told you that before. But now I know for sure that it's true. Don't worry, I'm not angling for a plea of insanity. Or even your sympathy.

But when I saw that red cloth, the same colour as her favourite dress, just lying there, I knew she was sending me a sign. She was saving me.

When that soldier looked at me, I knew exactly what to say to him. 'That man isn't my father.' Because he wasn't, not in any real way. He did nothing to earn the title.

The rest of what I said was lies. It's amazing how easily they came to me. We were visiting nephews of one of the officers. The man had attacked us. And, of course, all of this was delivered in Mamma's mother tongue. A language Victor never bothered to learn.

I haven't seen her since. Maybe I won't again. She saved me, and perhaps that was her way of saying she forgives me. It probably helped that she got what she wanted: just her and Victor, together, forever.

But where does that leave me? I'm responsible for the deaths of both of my parents. And if Seb is to be believed, I killed Isaac, too. If I've learnt one thing from being the son of Victor Durand, it's that people don't forgive easily.

Given you've played a part in felling two dictators, some people in the Sanctuary will look to you as their leader now. Whether you want that responsibility or not.

Not all of them, though. The likes of David Malone and my father cannot exist in a vacuum. They need allies to keep them on their pedestals. My father may be gone, but they're still here. Just because they choose to lurk in the shadows, don't think they're any less dangerous. If anything, those are the ones to watch, the false friends who would smile at your face and then plunge a knife in your back.

Whoever curses his father or his mother shall be put to death. That's what my father would have said about what I did.

I did far more than curse them, so I suppose by that reasoning, your decision is pretty clear.

Do I agree with what he did to those he deemed criminals? No. That is my honest answer. And you must admit, I'm nothing if not honest. The truth is, I care very little who the citizens choose to worship, what politics they choose to embrace, who they choose to love.

However, it takes courage to stand against one's father. Especially one as manipulative as mine. I know it took me too long but, in the end, I did stand up to him. Doesn't that count for something?

So let's get back to the matter at hand. You've heard my story. I don't pretend to be innocent. Although I don't think it's totally my fault. After all, when you are raised to be a monster, how do you escape your fate?

I want to change. Given the opportunity, I'd like to at least try to make my life about more than power and control. But whether I'm given that chance isn't my call. I know my destiny is down to you.

A Note From Cher

Around nine hundred thousand people were murdered in Treblinka between July 1942 and October 1943, before the Nazis levelled it in an effort to conceal their crimes.

When I visited the site in 2015, had I not been accompanied by a guide, I wouldn't have understood the significance of the concrete blocks, symbolic of the train tracks that so many travelled along on their last torturous journey. I might have walked past the rectangles of black basalt without realising they marked the former crematorium where so many bodies were burnt. The significance of the two hundred and sixteen stone markers, each bearing the name of a city or town where Jewish people were transported from, might have been lost on me. The central memorial, representing a tombstone, looms over the site. In front of it are inscribed the words 'Never Again'.

The research I needed to do to write Seb's timeline often felt overwhelming both in volume and its emotional impact. But many of the characters described during Seb's imprisonment in Treblinka were based on real human beings that suffered barbaric treatment. Marceli Galewski, Adolf Freidman, Zialo Bloch, and Jacob Wiernick are just a few of the courageous men that I had the honour to learn about. Their stories shouldn't be lost to the passing of time.

I hope you enjoyed reading The Book of Durand as much as I enjoyed writing it. Leaving a review is a great way to help other readers find my books. I don't have the advertising budget of some of the bigger name authors, so a review on Amazon, Goodreads or any other online platforms that you use would be really helpful. I would be very grateful for your support.

Please review The Book of Evelyn by scanning the QR code at the top of the page or by following this link:

The Book of Durand - Amazon Review Link

The Book of Evelyn

What do you see when you look at me? I am a killer; there'd be no point denying it. And in all honesty, I'd do it again. Help was never coming so, to protect myself, I learnt to sting.

Liar, troublemaker, victim: Evie has been labelled all these things. Nobody expected her to add 'murderer' to the list. Branded a criminal and exiled from the Sanctuary, the Colony offer her refuge and Evie begins her training as a beekeeper. But she soon learns that there is an unimaginable evil lurking just outside.

The Pack are bloodthirsty and organised, and they've picked up Evie's scent. With the Colony under attack, Evie accepts that the answer to their problems lies in her past. The Sanctuary's technology could save them. But even if she can persuade her old friend Jared to help, can she bear to return to the people who tried to destroy her? With her life on the line, Evie must decide who to trust...and who she is willing to sacrifice to survive.

For more information, check out cherjones.co.uk, visit The Book of Evelyn on Amazon or scan the QR code above the blurb.

<u>Chapter One</u>

What do you see when you look at me? I am a killer; there'd be no point denying it. And in all honesty, if I had to, I'd do it again.

Of course, I had my reasons, both when we were children and more recently. Not that the citizens of the Sanctuary ever cared about my motives. I overheard their whispers and caught their stares. They studied and feared me. But then, maybe they were sensible to be cautious. Because the truth is, when cornered, I have no idea of what I'm capable.

Bug says I'm a leader. I'm not. He's confused that with being a fighter. The difference is that one is a choice, and the other is born of necessity. I've been fighting for so long it's become part of the fabric of who I am. I'm not sure I even know how to stop.

I bet you are wondering why I'm asking you this. It's because I lost myself somewhere along the way. I wish I could see myself the way you seem to, Jared. To you, I'm still the little girl who waded into that lake to retrieve your coin. I hate to shatter that illusion, but she's long gone. I did what I had to do. Help was never coming so, in order to protect myself, I learnt to sting.

Not that it made any difference. Despite all the promises I made myself, here I am, asking for their help. I've come full circle, back to the citizens who abandoned me to put my own pieces back together. But it wasn't that easy. Somehow I got them muddled, and the person I've forged is a stranger to me. My edges have become jagged and there are gaps where there were none. Unfortunately for my enemies, the missing pieces are the parts that would have allowed me to show them mercy.